DEMON'S DOOR

DEMON'S DOOR

Graham Masterton

This first world edition published 2010
in Great Britain and in the USA by
SEVERN HOUSE PUBLISHERS LTD of
9–15 High Street, Sutton, Surrey, England, SM1 1DF.
Trade paperback edition first published
in Great Britain and the USA 2011 by
SEVERN HOUSE PUBLISHERS LTD.

British Library Cataloguing in Publication Data

Masterton, Graham.
  Demon's door. – (Jim Rook series)
  1. Rook, Jim (Fictitious character)–Fiction. 2. English
  teachers–Fiction. 3. Psychics–Fiction. 4. Suicide
  victims–Fiction. 5. Korean students–Fiction.
  6. Supernatural–Fiction. 7. Horror tales.
  I. Title II. Series
  823.9'14-dc22

ISBN-13: 978-0-7278-6477-2 (cased)
ISBN-13: 978-1-84751-275-8 (trade paper)

Except where actual historical events and characters are being
described for the storyline of this novel, all situations in this
publication are fictitious and any resemblance to living persons
is purely coincidental.

All Severn House titles are printed on acid-free paper.

Severn House Publishers support The Forest Stewardship Council [FSC],
the leading international forest certification organisation. All our titles that
are printed on Greenpeace-approved FSC-certified paper carry the FSC logo.

ONE

He tried to shut the front door really quickly so that Tibbles wouldn't escape, but as usual Tibbles was much too nimble for him and fled through the gap like a shadow.

Jim stood at one end of the landing, holding out both hands as if he were appealing to some bolshy teenage son not to leave home. Tibbles sat at the opposite end, amongst the geranium pots, watching him with slitted eyes.

'OK, you feline retard, what are you going to do now?' Jim demanded. 'What day is it, durr-brain? Didn't I tell you fifty-eight times already that fall semester starts today, so what does that mean? That's right, I'll be teaching, won't I, so I won't be here to let you back inside, will I? And after about fifteen minutes you're suddenly going to start feeling hungry and thirsty, aren't you, and you're going to start licking your lips and thinking about that juicy Instinctive Choice shrimp dinner that you only half-finished, and that saucer of delicious creamy milk that you only had two laps of, and you're going to jump up on the window sill and go *miaow, miaow, purr-lease let me in, o great and worshipful master*, and guess what?'

Tibbles haughtily turned his head away, as if he was above all this kind of cheap sarcasm. A yellow butterfly flickered past him, close enough for him to have swiped it, if he had wanted to, and usually he would have, but this morning he remained aloof.

Jim said, 'Tibbles, you bozo, I'll give you one last chance. Look – watch – I'm unlocking the door. I'm opening it up for you. If you're really, really quick on your feet, you'll be able to get back inside before I close it again.'

He opened the door. He waited. Tibbles stayed where he was, at the far end of the landing, and yawned.

'I'll give you till a count of three. One . . . two . . . three. Three and a half. Three and three quarters. Three and eighty-seven eighty-eighths.'

Tibbles sat down now, and tucked in his paws.

'OK, have it your way,' said Jim. 'If you want to spend the whole day wandering around outside, licking out other people's empty tuna cans and drinking water from lawn sprinklers, that's entirely up to you. You'll regret it.'

He closed the door and ostentatiously double-locked it, as if Tibbles could have managed to unlock it, even if he had been given a key.

'There! I'll see you at seven, or maybe later, if there's a faculty meeting, or if I feel like going to the Cat'n'Fiddle for a drink or three.'

He picked up his worn-out brown canvas bag and went down the steps. Halfway down he turned around and raised his eyebrows at Tibbles one last time, but Tibbles ignored him. *Jesus*, he thought. *If cats could only get their paws into the holes in scissor handles, they would cut their little pink noses off, just to spite their goddamned faces.*

As he walked along the next landing, the door to Apartment 2 opened up, and Summer came out. Summer was a shiny young blonde, stunningly pretty, with huge blue eyes and a little snub nose and naturally pouting lips. This morning she was wearing a tiny strapless top in strawberry pink and very tight white shorts and a pair of pink wedge-shaped sandals to match her top. She had a diamond stud in her left nostril and she always wore at least half-a-dozen jangly bracelets on each wrist. She smelled strongly of some flowery, musky perfume, like J Lo Glow.

'*Jimmy!*' she cooed. 'Where are *you* off to so bright and early?'

'Hi, Summer.' He had given up trying to persuade her to call him 'Jim.' At least she didn't say '*Hi* Jimmy-wimmy!' any longer, like she did when he first moved in.

'First day back to college,' he told her. 'Another year, another fifteen antisocial illiterates.'

'Hey – *I'm* starting a new job, too. It's really good money, and the tips are supposed to be fantastic. I'm pole dancing at Le Pothole.'

'Le *What*? Le Pothole?'

'That's right,' she smiled. 'It's this new club that just

opened, on Cahuenga. It's *such* a ritzy place. You have to come see me. I could wangle you a pass.'

Jim frowned. 'Hey . . . I think I read an article about it a couple of weeks back . . . Le *Poteau*. "Poteau" – that's French for "pole."'

'Pothole, Poteau, whatever. You should still come see me. You never saw me pole dance, did you? Kiefer Sutherland said I must be fourble-jointed. Well, he looked like Kiefer Sutherland. That was when I was dancing in the VIP Club at Xes.'

'I never knew you danced at Xes. Mind you, I never went there, so it's not surprising.'

'Oh, yes! But Le Pothole is so much more lavisher. Like, the music is *ur*-mazing! And they mix this frozen mango margarita! It's like your lips have died and gone to heaven without you. And you should see my costume! It's this tiny little thong, all gold and glittery, but I have this incredible headdress with all these huge gold feathers. I look like Big Bird, but practically naked.'

'Wow,' said Jim. 'I'll try to drop by.' He could just imagine himself sitting in the front row, grinning like somebody's half-witted uncle, while Summer slowly counter-rotated her booty in his face. He wondered if there was any accepted etiquette for pushing a twenty-dollar bill into your downstairs neighbor's thong.

'So, uh, where are you headed now?' he asked her.

'Claws, to have my nails done. I'm starting tomorrow evening. Eight o'clock – *eek*! And I have to look perfect. That's what Mr Subinski said. "Summer," he said, "you have to look *perfect*."' She suddenly frowned, hefted up her breasts in both hands, and said, 'You don't think I need a boob job, do you? Maybe I should go up a cup.'

Jim shook his head. 'Oh, no. I think the good Lord has been very magnanimous to you already. In fact, more than magnanimous.' He looked up to the sky and said, 'Thank you, Lord.'

Summer gave one of her squittery little giggles and locked her front door. Jim followed her down the last flight of steps to the steeply angled driveway. 'Jimmy – you have a fantastic day at college,' she told him, and blew him a kiss.

'I'll try. To tell you the truth I'm dreading it. Maybe we should swap places. I never had a manicure before.'

'I'm having a Brazilian, too.'

'Oh. In that case . . . I think it's back to the classroom.'

She climbed into her bright yellow VW Beetle and put the top down. He waited until she had backed out of the driveway and into Briarcliff Road, and tooted her horn, and waved, and then he opened the door of his ageing metallic-green Mercury Marquis and eased himself into the driver's seat. It was only 8:25 in the morning, but the interior of the car was already uncomfortably stuffy and hot, and the green vinyl seats were sticky. He switched on the engine and adjusted the air-conditioning to Freeze Your Face Off.

While the car gradually cooled down, he lowered the sun-vizor and looked at himself in the vanity mirror. He thought that he had aged exponentially in the past five months. After his last birthday, his thirty-fifth, he had still felt young – or youngish, anyhow. Handsome in a scruffy, beaten-up way, with two days' stubble and one collar button missing from his button-down collar. Now, however, he definitely looked exhausted, and he *felt* exhausted, too. His eyes were puffy and he could see the treacherous gleam of silver through the ratty brown.

Maybe he had been teaching a year too long. Maybe he should have taken a sabbatical. He should have gone to Europe and wandered around the British Museum in London, and the Musée d'Orsay in Paris, and the Prado in Madrid. He should have climbed the Acropolis, and looked out over the orange-tiled rooftops of Athens.

He should have sat in St Mark's Square in Venice, with a glass of Barolo, listening to the tolling of church bells and watching the pigeons burst into the sky like shrapnel.

But in spite of his tiredness he had an unaccountable premonition that he was going to be needed at West Grove College this semester, more than ever. It was like feeling that he was coming down with the swine flu. No definite symptoms yet, but something was out of kilter. All through the summer vacation, he had been convinced that he was being given signals, and hints, and coded messages. It was hard to describe, but he had caught random snatches of conversation in bars, and on the street, and out on the beach, and they all sounded like fragments of the same conversation.

One evening, about six weeks ago, when he was drinking with his friend Nils Shapiro in the Blu Monkey Lounge, he had overheard a girl saying, 'shot himself in the head – just like Mia Farrow's brother, you know – like he couldn't face living any longer . . .' Then, only three days later, in the 8 Oz Burger Bar, a teenage boy at the next table had been telling his friend, 'they found him in the lake – right in the middle – with all of his clothes on – even his sneakers – and he had *rocks* in his pockets.' And early yesterday evening, when he was shopping at Ralph's, his packer had said to the check-out girl, 'stepped off the sidewalk – right in front of a four-one-three bus – driver stood on the brakes but he didn't have a hope in hell . . .'

On a hoarding on Hollywood Boulevard, where they were fitting out a new health spa, somebody had scrawled the words END IT WHAT'S THE POINT in bright red paint.

Jim had wondered if he were suicidal without knowing it, and that was why he had picked up on all of those mentions of people who had killed themselves. But he didn't *feel* suicidal, just tired and bored. Maybe he *should* go to Le Poteau tomorrow night and watch Summer pole-dance. It might be mildly embarrassing. It might be *highly* embarrassing. But it would make a change from sitting on his sagging maroon couch with Tibbles, drinking Fat Tire beer out of the bottle and eating pretzels and watching repeats of *The Mentalist*.

Tibbles appeared on the first-floor landing, and stared at him balefully through the wrought-iron railings. Jim was tempted to climb out of the car, pick Tibbles up by the scruff of his stupid neck and lug him back up to his apartment. But then he thought, *no, Tibbles needs to be taught a lesson*, the same as all of the foot-shuffling students he was going to meet for the first time today. No suffer, no grow. You make a decision, you have to learn to live with it.

He switched on the car radio. Bruce Springsteen was singing 'Part Man, Part Monkey' so he changed the station. He was allergic to Bruce Springsteen. He sometimes felt that if he accidentally met Bruce Springsteen in the street, he

would headbutt him, just for the sake of it. 'Bruce! Hi!'
Klonk! He shifted the Mercury into R and twisted around in
his seat so that he could back down the driveway. He didn't
see Tibbles running down the steps.

He had to wait for a while to allow a gardener's truck to
come laboring up the hill, its transmission whining like the
female mourners at a Mexican funeral. Then he gunned
the engine and swerved out into the street. As he did so, he
felt that unmistakable thump, crunch, and knew that he had
run over something living.

He stopped, and pressed down the parking brake. It was
probably a raccoon, or an opossum, or more likely a gopher.
Lately, a whole tribe of gophers had been digging in the
landscaping in back of their apartment building, leaving
mounds of dirt, and even a visit from a cross-eyed opera-
tive from Go-Fer Good! Inc. had failed to get rid of them
completely.

Jim walked around the car, twice. He couldn't see any
gophers. Maybe he had hit one but it hadn't been hurt too
badly, and it had managed to limp away. Just to make sure, he
knelt down in the road and looked right underneath the chassis.
It was than that he saw Tibbles, lying on his side, staring back
at him.

He suddenly felt as if he couldn't breathe. 'Tibbles!' he cried,
hoarsely. 'You stupid goddamned stupid cat!'

He reached underneath the car and managed to catch hold
of Tibbles' back legs and drag him out. He laid him down
gently on the driveway but there was no doubt that Tibbles
was dead. He looked as flat as a child's nightdress case. His
ribcage and his pelvis were crushed and his whiskers were
bloody.

'You goddamned stupid cat,' Jim repeated. 'Why the *hell*
do you think I told you to stay inside? But, oh no, you knew
better, didn't you? You always think you know better. Well,
this time, buddy, you proved that you *don't* know better. In
fact you know absolutely *squat*.'

He picked up Tibbles' disjointed body and cradled him in
his arms. Tibbles continued to stare back at him, unblinking.
Inside his fur, he felt crushed and lumpy. Jim could hear his
bones crackle.

He was still standing there when old Mrs LaFarge came shuffling down the steps, wearing a circular straw sun hat like a 1950s flying saucer and a billowing red linen dress. She had huge black sunglasses and a pointed nose, so that she looked like a giant insect. As usual, she was wearing lavender-colored desert boots.

She approached Jim and stared at him with her head tilted to one side. 'Why, Jee-*yum*!' she said, in her lispy Cajun accent. 'I do believe you weep! And what is wrong with your *petit chaton*? He don't look none too good to me at all.'

Jim had to purse his lips. He wanted to tell Mrs LaFarge what had happened but his throat was too tight and he couldn't speak. Mrs LaFarge came up closer and tickled the top of Tibbles' head with her long, clawlike fingernail. She had rings on every finger, including a ring that looked like a human skull, with rubies for eyes.

'*Oh-h-h!*' she breathed. 'He's day-*ud*! *Il est mort!* How did this happen?'

Jim nodded toward his car, with the driver's door still open and the engine still running. 'I – uh – I didn't see him,' he managed to choke out. 'I don't know why he ran out into the road. He's never done that before, ever.'

Mrs LaFarge took off her sunglasses. Her eyes were watery gray, the color of roofing slates after a rainstorm. She had a slight cast, so her right eye appeared to be looking over his left shoulder. She always gave Jim the disconcerting feeling that there was somebody standing behind him.

'You must not blame yourself, Jim. Everybody believe that cats are wise, but cats are just as foolish as any other animal, and much more arrogant than most. All the same, *c'est très triste, n'est-ce pas*? It is very sad. We must think about a funeral.'

'I can't believe it,' said Jim. 'I ran over my own goddamned cat. That has to be some kind of bad luck, right?'

'For your cat? *Oui*, for sure, very bad luck. For *you*, who knows? It may be a warning. You know what they say in Louisiana? *Si vous tuez un chat, son esprit vous attendra toujours*. If you kill a cat, its spirit will always be waiting for you.'

Jim blinked at her through the tears that were clinging to his eyelashes. 'What exactly does that mean?'

'You know something?' said Mrs LaFarge, taking hold of his arm. 'I never really knew. But my grandfather was always saying it. I suppose it means that whatever we do we cannot avoid the consequence.'

Jim said, 'I have class today. I'm going to be late. I'd better take Tibbles inside.'

'Do you want me to arrange the funeral for you? I have a friend who works for the Los Angeles Pet Memorial Park. His name is Albert. You have to have a funeral.'

'Violette, he's a cat.'

'I know. Do you want him buried or cremated? What sort of casket would you like?'

'Violette, I just ran him over and killed him. I'm very upset.'

'I understand, Jim. He was your companion.'

'Yes, he was. He was interesting. He was funny. He was intuitive. I think at times he even liked me, just a little.'

Mrs LaFarge stroked Tibbles' ears. 'All the same. *Le pauvre*. He must have a funeral.'

Jim was very close to saying something that he didn't want to say. But he took a deep breath, and said, 'OK . . . let's talk about it this evening, when I get back from college. Right now, I don't think I'm in any fit state to talk to anybody about anything.'

Mrs LaFarge leaned forward and kissed Tibbles on the nose. '*Au revoir, mon petit chaton.* Safe journey. There is a golden basket waiting for you in heaven.'

Jim climbed the steps back to his apartment and opened the door. He carried Tibbles' body through the living room, opened the sliding doors and laid him on one of the sunbeds on the balcony.

He stood there for a while, half-expecting Tibbles to jump up and give him one of his disdainful looks, and then start licking himself. But Tibbles stayed there, not moving, not breathing. He had been flattened by a two-ton automobile, and Jim had to admit that he was dead. Blood was leaking from his anus, and dripping on to the sunbed.

'Why did you have to do that, Tibbles?' he demanded. 'Why did you have to come after me?'

He turned around and punched the wall, and said '*Fuck!*' because it hurt so much.

TWO

He arrived at West Grove Community College fifteen minutes late. As he walked along the corridor, his sneakers squeaking on the freshly waxed tiles, he could hear Special Class Two from more than a hundred yards away. Shouting, laughing, hooting and playing gangsta rap. He stopped for a moment, next to the lockers, and thought: *You don't have to do this, Jim. You could turn around and walk away and never come back. By this time tomorrow morning you could be fishing for steelhead on the Umpqua River in Oregon.*

He was still standing there when the classroom door next to him opened and Sheila Colefax came out. Sheila was a petite bespectacled brunette who always dressed in pencil skirts and formal blouses, with a brooch at her neck, as if she were attending court. Jim always fantasized that she wore a black garter belt and black stockings and black lace panties underneath her skirts, and that once she had taken off her spectacles and shaken her hair loose, she would be a tigress in bed.

'Ah, Jim. Do you think you could keep your class a little quieter, please? We're trying to discuss our Spanish reading list for the coming semester and the *noise* they're making. It really is very distracting.'

'Sure. Yes. Sorry, Sheila. How was your vacation?'

'My vacation?'

'Yes. How was it? You have quite a glow about you. Did you go someplace exotic? Bali, maybe?'

'Sherman Oaks.'

'Oh. Oh, well. Staying at home, that's always pretty relaxing, isn't it?'

'Not really. I was taking care of my mother. She has Alzheimer's, and she's doubly incontinent.'

'Oh. Sorry to hear it. I'll – uh – tell my class to put a sock in it.'

'Thank you, Jim. I'd appreciate it.'

Sheila Colefax went back into her classroom and closed the door. As she did so, however, she looked back at Jim through the circular window and he was sure that she lowered her eyelashes at him. He blinked back at her, but she was gone.

Pull yourself together, he thought. *You're dreaming. She probably wears fifty-denier pantyhose up to her armpits and goes to bed every night with a mug of hot chocolate and a Mary Higgins Clark novel.*

He walked along to Special Class Two and opened the door. All of the students were out of their seats. Some of the boys were throwing a basketball across the classroom, while some of the girls were perched on top of their desks polishing their nails. Others were scuffling or pushing each other. A tall black boy in a spotted silk headscarf and impossibly droopy jeans had a huge boom box on his shoulder. He was playing a G-Unit song and mouthing along with it, with his eyes closed. Another boy was dancing and jumping and spinning on the floor.

'*Shawty you know I want dat cat – drop it now, pick it up, drop it, work dat back – hustle now, hurry now Shawty, make dat stack—*'

Jim walked across to his desk and put down his canvas bag. He rummaged inside it until he found the book that he was looking for. Then he sat down, opened it, and started to read. He said nothing, and didn't even look up.

Gradually, the class realized that their teacher had arrived. One of the boys caught the basketball and tucked it into the crook of his elbow, and when his friend said, 'Come on, man, throw it over here,' he shook his head and said, 'Wait up, OK?' Almost all of the girls climbed off their desks and sat down, although one black girl with elaborate gilded cornrows remained where she was, one long leg raised up high, polishing her toenails in purple frost.

The last to wake up to the fact that Jim had walked in was the boy with the boom box. He was still singing '*No discrimination – blacks and da Asians – even Caucasians – got dem all shakin'*' when he opened his eyes. Every other student was staring at him. Immediately, he switched off the music and

sank down into his seat, although he stuck one leg out into
the aisle, with a red Kanye West sneaker on the end of it.

Still Jim didn't look up. He continued to read, while
the class watched him in silence. Over three minutes went
by, and the students looked at each other and frowned and
shrugged and started to grow restless. The boy with the
basketball tossed it over to his friend, who caught it and
tossed it back again. Jim turned the page, and sniffed.

Eventually, one of the girls raised her hand and said, 'Sir?
Is you our teacher?'

Jim tucked a Hot Tamales wrapper into the page he was
reading, as a bookmark. He raised his head and looked around
the classroom. 'Do you *want* me to be?'

A short black boy with a polished head and glasses said,
'Aint down to us, sir, is it? If you da teach, then you da
teach, whether we likes it or not.'

'What's your name?' Jim asked him.

'Arthur, sir.'

'Arthur What?'

'That's right, sir. How jew know that?'

'How did I know what?'

'My name, sir. Arthur Watt.'

Jim thought: *This day is becoming more surreal by the
minute.* He stood up and walked around to the front of his
desk.

'Do you know something?' he said. 'I ran over my cat
this morning, before I came here. I killed him. Right now
he's lying on a sunbed on my balcony, and he's dead.'

'And what?' asked a sallow-faced boy with a large bony
nose and masses of black curly hair. He wore an orange and
brown T-shirt that was much too tight for him, with a picture
of the Jewish reggae singer Matisyahu on the front of it.
'Are we supposed to feel, like, *sad* or something?'

'No,' said Jim. 'Why should you feel sad? You didn't even
know him. But I am. I'm sad.'

'And this relates to us how?' asked the sallow-faced boy.

'I'll tell you how it relates to you. You all came to this
class because you have difficulty in communicating. You
find it difficult to express your feelings to other people. And
there are two reasons for this.

'The first reason is that you didn't pay enough attention when your grade-school teachers were showing you how to read and write. You always thought you knew better, and that reading and writing were a waste of your valuable time.

'The second reason is that you never try to put yourself into other people's shoes.'

'I wouldn't want to put myself in Mikey's shoes,' said a ginger-haired boy at the back of the class. 'They totally *stink*!'

Jim ignored him, and stood up. 'You want to know the secret of being a great communicator? Like Ronald Reagan, maybe, or Barack Obama? The secret of being a great communicator is to know what other people want to hear, and what they *need* to hear, too. I told you that I ran over my cat. And what did you say?'

He approached the sallow-faced boy's desk and stood right in front of him. The boy leaned back, looking uncomfortable.

'"Are we supposed to feel sad?"' Jim mimicked him. 'That's what you said. So tell me. Did you seriously think that saying that to me was going to make me *like* you, or make me think what a chilled-out, together kind of guy you are? Because all it told me about you is that you're a thoughtless, insensitive, self-centered idiot.'

'Hey,' said the sallow-faced boy, in a voice that was obviously much more shrill than he had meant it to be. 'Who are you calling an idiot?'

'I don't know. What's your name, idiot?'

'Leon. Leon Shulman. And if you think *I'm* an idiot, at least I wasn't stupid enough to run over my own cat and expect everybody to feel sorry for me.'

Jim said, 'You're missing the point, Leon. I don't expect you to feel sorry for me. I simply expect you to show some sensitivity, you know? So that I think – *hey, this Leon Shulman is a nice, considerate, respectful young man. In return, I'll pay him extra attention in class, and when it comes to marking his papers, I'll be more inclined to mark him up than down.*

'*That's* communication, you idiot. And that's what I've come here to teach you. But, like I said, only if you want me to. If you don't, you can carry on playing basketball and polishing your nails and dancing and fighting and listening to "Chase Da Cat", and I'll just sit here and read my book and go home when the bell rings. It's entirely up to you.'

'How did you know that?' asked the boy with the boom box, suspiciously.

'How did I know what?'

'How do you know that I was playing "Chase Da Cat?"'

Jim closed his eyes for a moment, so that he looked even more exhausted than he actually was. Then he opened them again, and said, with monumental patience, 'Tell me your name.'

'Neville Brown. But most people call me Top Dime. Or T.D. for short.'

'Well, T.D., let me tell you this. I've been teaching Special Class Two for longer than I want to remember. Students who have difficulty with the English language try to find other ways to tell people how they feel. Sometimes they do it through aggressive behavior. They carry knives, or guns. Sometimes they do it through the way they dress. Sometimes they clam up and say nothing at all. A lot of the time, they express themselves through the music they play, the way you do. And if I didn't know every hip-hop artist and every gangsta rap track that there ever was, then I wouldn't be much of a teacher, would I, because I wouldn't know what my students were trying to say to me.'

He paused, and then he said, 'Kind of ironic, wasn't it, that you were playing "Chase Da Cat" – today of all days?'

'What's "ironic"?' asked Top Dime.

Arthur's hand shot up. 'I know!' he said. 'That's like made of metal. You know – same as Iron Man.'

Jim marked the register. There were eight boys and seven girls in Special Class Two this year. He never tried to learn their names all at once, but he had to be careful because he tended privately to give them nicknames, like Squinty or Hellboy or Britney or Bart, and last year he had inadvertently come out and called a girl Hooters to her face.

The class started to grow noisy again. The girls started chattering and several of the boys began to flick paper pellets at each other.

'Tamara Wei?' said Jim. A Chinese-American girl put up her hand. She was wearing a dark green silk blouse with a cheongsam-style collar, and her hair was immaculately cut in a shiny black bob.

'Looking pretty dolled-up for college, Tamara,' Jim remarked.

'I want to be an anchorwoman, sir,' Tamara told him. 'I auditioned in July for KTLA. They said I have a terrific TV face and a terrific TV voice. All I have to do is learn to read more better.'

'OK, we'll see what we can do,' Jim told her. He stood up, went to the whiteboard behind his desk and wrote the word 'euphemism' in large blue letters. 'Do you want to try reading that for me?'

Tamara stared at it for a long time, and then slowly shook her head. 'I don't know how you would say that. I don't even know what it means.'

'It means using an inoffensive word instead of a word that could be rude or upset people. Like calling it an "image enhancement community" instead of a "fat camp." Or "wind" or "gas" instead of "fart."'

The ginger-haired boy let out a whoop and said, 'I don't believe it! Did my ears deceive me? My teacher said "fart!"'

'Oh! I'm sorry!' said Jim. 'What do you normally call it?' Jim waited until the laughter had subsided. Then he said, 'OK . . . anybody else want to try reading out this word on the board? How about you, Arthur?'

'Oopahooism? Yoopahooism?'

'Good try,' Jim told him, and then told him how to pronounce it properly. 'There . . . you actually learned something, and it's only your first class. Think what you'll know by the end of the year.'

'Yeah,' put in the ginger-haired boy. 'How to talk about poop and stuff like that in polite company, without nobody getting offended.'

'Well, you're nearly right,' Jim told him. 'The reason we sometimes use euphemisms is to spare people's feelings. But it's not just a question of respect. It makes for good communication, too. If you swear a lot, it gets in the way of what you're trying to say. It devalues your argument. Bad language makes you sound like you're ignorant, like you only know words beginning with F.'

'I know a word that don't begin with an F,' put in Top Dime. 'It begin with an M, like in M for mother, but I have to admit that it do have an F in it halfway through.'

Jim sat down. 'OK, T.D., very hilarious.' He ran his pen down the register, and then he said, 'Last name on the list, then. Kim Dong Wook? Which one of you is Kim Dong Wook?'

Everybody turned around in their seats, but there was nobody in the classroom who looked as if they might be called Kim Dong Wook.

'Guess Wooky's playing hooky,' suggested the ginger-haired boy. His real name was Teddy Greenspan but Jim had already nicknamed him Splatter because of his freckles. He was tempted to change it to Motormouth.

Jim marked Kim Dong Wook 'absent' and closed the register.

'Right, then,' he said, 'because this is your first morning I'm going to give you something real easy to do. I want you all to pretend that you're on Death Row, right? At midnight they're going to take you out of your cell and give you a lethal injection.'

'*But I'm innocent!*' howled Teddy.

'Maybe you are,' Jim retorted, 'but the governor has turned down your last appeal and you're going to die anyhow.'

'Yeah, Fanta-pants,' said Arthur. 'You shouldn't of left that bright-red hair in the toilet. The CSI knew right off it was you.'

'How would *you* like to die right now?' Teddy challenged him. 'I can give you a lethal injection, bro! I can shove a hockey stick right up your fat black ass!'

'Teddy! Arthur!' said Jim. 'What the hell did I just tell you about using bad language?'

'Hey, I apologize, OK?' said Teddy, raising both hands in surrender. 'I am beyond contrite. What I meant to say was "economy-sized Afro-American sit-upon." That's a euphemism, right?'

'That's enough,' Jim told him. 'Like I told you, I don't care if I teach you guys or not. You want to spend your time scrapping with each other, go ahead. I can find plenty to do without you. I have a great book here, and I can't wait to finish reading it.'

'Sorry, sir,' said Arthur. 'We was only messing.'

A girl in the front row cautiously raised her hand. She had a pinched triangular face with buck teeth and protuberant green eyes, so that she looked to Jim as if her great-great-grandmother might have had a fling with a stick insect. 'Please, sir,' she asked, almost in a whisper, 'why do we have to pretend that we're all on Death Row? What are we supposed to have done?'

Jim smiled at her. As far as he remembered her name was Janice Something, but he had nicknamed her Sticky. 'It doesn't matter *what* you've done, Janice. The only thing that matters is that you're scheduled to die tonight, but you're allowed one last meal, of whatever you like. Steak, ribs, lasagna, three-bean salad, anything. That's today's project. That's what I want you to do – write down a menu for your very last meal.'

'Isn't that kind of sick?' said a heavy-jawed, muscular boy with sculptured sideburns and designer stubble, and a single pirate-sized earring in his left earlobe. He wore a black T-shirt with *Marco's Gym* printed on it, and his bulging pectorals were noticeably bigger than Janice's breasts. His name was Grant Bronowski, and he had already told Jim that he was a tight end on the West Grove football team, with fifty-five catches to his credit last season – just in case Jim got the laughable idea that remedial English was more important to him than touchdowns.

Jim said, 'I'm only asking you to make-believe, Grant, that's all, and make-believe is a very good exercise for the brain muscles. More than that, when I see all of your various menus, they will give me a very clear idea of what kind of personalities you are. You know what they say? You are what you eat. Or, in this case, what you feel like eating as your very last supper.'

He went to the stationery cupboard in the corner of the classroom, unlocked it, and took out a pad of yellow lined legal paper and a boxful of blue ballpens. He walked up and down the class, tearing off a sheet of paper for each student,

and handing them each a pen. He had long ago given up
any expectation that Special Class Two would think of
bringing their own writing materials.

Teddy, however, had taken out a black plastic case with
both pens and pencils in it, as well as a pencil-sharpener and
an eraser. He also produced a spring-bound study book, with
a marbled cover.

'Glad to see you came prepared,' Jim told him.

Teddy shrugged. 'It's an English class, right? I wouldn't
show up to a swimming class without my swim shorts.'

Jim said, 'You're *good* at English, aren't you?'

'I'm OK.'

'You're more than OK. Admit it. You knew how to
pronounce "euphemism", didn't you? You knew what it
meant, too. In fact you have a pretty extensive vocabulary.
I never heard a student of mine use the word "contrite"
before.'

Teddy opened his study book and wrote *My Last Meal* at
the top of the first page. Then he looked up at Jim and said,
'You're going to ask me what I'm doing here, aren't you?
In remedial English?'

'You don't have to tell me if you don't want to.'

'Well, so what. It's all in my college records I guess. I
have kind of a problem when it comes to writing. Once I've
started, it's like I can't stop. I write pages and pages and
pages until I run out of paper.'

'You have logorrhea?'

Teddy nodded. 'Logorrhea, that's right. That's what my
shrink calls it.'

'Logorrhea is actually a euphemism for the uncontrollable
urge to write endless reams of bullshit,' said Jim. 'Believe
me, you're not the only one who suffers from it. There's
plenty of famous writers who do the same, but they get
prizes.'

Jim returned to his desk and opened up his book again. Most
of his class were frowning into the middle distance as if he
had asked them to explain Einstein's Special Theory of
Relativity in ten words or less. Only two students had their
heads down: Teddy, who was scribbling as if his life depended

on it, and Arthur, who was writing much more laboriously, but licking his lips as if he could almost taste the food that he was writing about.

At the back of the class, sitting at the next desk to Grant, was a pretty, dark-haired girl in a tight gray T-shirt. Georgia Bisocky. She was staring at Grant and batting her eyelashes flirtatiously, even though Grant remained oblivious.

Jim said, 'Georgia . . . I know Grant looks good enough to eat, but I doubt if the cooks at San Quentin have any recipes for football players.'

Georgia blushed, but Grant only looked around in bewilderment, and blinked. Jim realized then that – although Grant wasn't stupid – he was only capable of thinking one thought at a time.

Jim was reading *The Memory of Goldfish*. It was a novel about a man who wakes up every morning having totally forgotten what happened to him the day before. Jim found the idea quite appealing. To wake up, every single day, and rediscover life afresh. The trouble was, he might be nice to people he hated, without remembering that he hated them. He might eat broccoli, and he detested it.

He glanced up at the clock. Only another ten minutes to go before recess. But then there was a polite knock at the classroom door, and Jim could see somebody standing outside, looking in through the window.

'Come on in,' he called, and beckoned.

The door was cautiously opened. An Asian-looking boy came in, with straight black hair that stuck up vertically from the top of his head, and a round face that put Jim in mind of a very young Jackie Chan. He was wearing a snowy-white T-shirt and blue jeans with rolled-up cuffs.

In one hand he was carrying three textbooks, fastened together with a strap. In the other he was carrying a large brown wicker basket with a lid.

'Special Class Two?' he asked.

'That's right,' said Jim. 'And unless I'm very much mistaken, you must be the late Kim Dong Wook.'

The boy approached Jim's desk and bowed his head. 'I apologize, sir, for missing first half-hour. I was delay at pet store.'

'OK . . .' said Jim, suspiciously. He looked down at the wicker basket. He could hear something scratching inside it, something alive. 'What do you have in there, Kim? We don't generally allow students to bring livestock into college. Petty rule, really. To my mind, there's nothing like a few chickens pecking about the classroom to give it some character.'

'This is gift for you, Mr Rook,' said Kim. He lifted up the basket and set it down on Jim's desk.

Jim said, 'I'm sorry, Kim. I can't accept gifts from students. Might be seen as bribery. Maybe an apple now and again, or a slice of pepperoni pizza. But not this, whatever it is.'

'This is not gift from me, Mr Rook. This is gift from Kwisin.'

'Kwisin? Who's that?'

'Please to open it, Mr Rook.'

'Kim, I can't. You'll just have to take it back where it came from.'

'Not possible, Mr Rook. Once Kwisin has given gift, it cannot be returned.'

T.D. called out, 'Come on, sir! Open it up, why don't you? Let's see what's in there. Might be a beaver! Me, I love beavers!'

'Yeah, come on, sir,' Arthur urged him. 'Can't hurt to take a look.'

Jim stood up. 'OK,' he agreed, 'I'll open it up just to see what it is. But I can't keep it. Faculty rules.'

Kim unfastened the cord that held the lid on the basket. Then he took two steps back, and bowed his head again.

There was more scratching, and the basket rattled and creaked on top of Jim's desk. Whatever was inside it was obviously impatient to be let out. Jim said, 'This isn't dangerous, is it? It's not a polecat or anything like that?'

Kim said nothing, and his expression remained unreadable.

Jim lifted the lid at arm's length, prepared to jump backward if the creature inside the basket sprang out at him. But it didn't. Once he had removed the lid and set it down on the desk, it simply sat there and stared at him with narrowed eyes.

Jim looked at Kim and he found it almost impossible to speak. Kim Dong Wook bowed his head for a third time and said, 'Gift from Kwisin, Mr Rook. Given with gratitude and deep respect.'

'How is this possible?' said Jim. 'How the hell can this be?'

'All things are possible,' said Kim.

Jim reached inside the basket and lifted Tibbles out. Jim's heart was thumping but Tibbles seemed to be unimpressed. He gave Jim one of his usual condescending looks and then turned his head to take in Special Class Two.

'Well, I was *nearly* right!' said T.D., popping his fingers. 'It's not a beaver, but it's a pussy!'

'He's *dead*, for Christ's sake,' Jim told Kim, under his breath, so that nobody else in the classroom could hear him. 'Where did you find him? How did he come back to life?'

'Maybe not same cat, Mr Rook.'

'Of course he's the same goddamned cat!' Jim hissed at him. 'You think I don't recognize my own cat? He's still wearing his collar! Look at it! Look what it says here! *Tibbles*! That's my cat!'

'Gift from Kwisin, Mr Rook. Not dead now. Door close, door open.'

'Oh, just *look* at it!' squeaked a blonde-haired girl in the second row, sitting in front of T.D. Her name was Judii Rogers, although Jim had already nicknamed her Calamity Jane because of her tight denim vest with silver stars on it, and her tiny denim skirt, and her white boots with fringes on them. 'It's so totally *cute*! Can I take it home with me?'

Tibbles looked across at her with an expression of deep disdain. Jim said, 'That's it,' and lowered Tibbles back into the basket. Tibbles tried to cling on to the sides, but Jim forced him down, gently at first and then much harder, and replaced the lid, tying the cord securely. Tibbles gave his distinctive '*warrooow*' mew, which meant that he was annoyed, and scrabbled at the sides of the basket in frustration.

Jim felt as if he couldn't breathe. Maybe he should take the basket out of the classroom and check Tibbles again, just to make sure that he wasn't hurt. Or maybe he should dismiss Special Class Two altogether, and take Tibbles straight to Dr Hooperman, his vet.

Kim seemed to guess what he was thinking, because he said, 'Cat is perfectly healthy, Mr Rook. Same as yesterday. No need for worry.'

Billy Friedlander called out, 'Sir? Mr Rook, sir? You still want us to finish this last meal thing?' Billy Friedlander was sitting right at the back of the class. He had messed-up hair and a gray T-shirt with holes in it and gray sneakers without any laces. Jim had nicknamed him Hobo.

'I'm just getting to dessert,' said Billy. 'I was thinking about Death By Chocolate. Better than Death by Potassium Chloride, huh?'

Jim said, 'Yes, please. Everybody finish their menus. Kim – find yourself a desk and sit down, please. Here's some paper, and a pen. Your assignment is to write down what you would like to eat for your last supper, if you were on Death Row, and you were going to be executed.'

Kim took the paper and pen, but looked directly at Jim and said, 'Only in Christian religion is last supper.'

'Well, write it down anyhow,' Jim told him. 'Let's wait until the bell rings, and then you and I can have a little talk about life and death, can't we?'

THREE

Jim spent the rest of the lesson with his elbows on his desk, his book open in front of him but unread, his eyes fixed on Tibbles' cat basket. Every now and then, Tibbles let out a plaintive mew, but Jim thought that he sounded sorry for himself rather than sick. He certainly didn't sound as if he were breathing his last shrimpy breath.

Kim had seated himself at the end of the front row, nearest the stationery cupboard, next to Janice Sticky. Jim glanced at him from time to time but he didn't raise his head once.

The black girl with the gilded cornrows and the purple glitter nail-polish waved her hand at him. Her name was Elvira Thomas, although Jim had nicknamed her Cleopatra because of her sleek high cheekbones and her exotic looks. She wore dangling gold earrings that almost hung down to her collarbone, like two chandeliers.

'Sir? My last supper? What if the prison kitchens don't know how to cook it?'

'What is it?'

'It's blaff, sir.'

'Blaff?'

'It's fish, cooked in lime juice and chillies. My grandma makes it.'

'Let's assume for the purposes of this assignment that the catering staff at San Quentin know to cook just about anything. Where does blaff come from?'

'Martinique, sir. That's where my grandma came from. She's the greatest cook ever, and she can mix up magic potions, too. When I was a little girl she told me that she knew a way to walk straight through walls.'

'I've heard about that,' put in Teddy. 'It's called a door.'

Eventually the bell rang and everybody in the class came shuffling forward with their assignments. Some of them had written only four words, while others had used up half of their sheet of paper. Teddy had filled up both sides, and then written vertically up the margins, too.

Judii tottered up and gave Jim a white toothy smile. She had masses of blonde curls and shiny scarlet lip-gloss. 'I totally adore your cat, Mr Rook,' she said in her breathy, squeaky voice. 'Any time you want a cat-sitter, just let me know.'

'OK,' said Jim. 'But let me warn you that he's very temperamental.' *Not to mention immortal.*

'He won't be temperamental with me. I'll love him and I'll tickle him and I'll squeeze him so tight that he won't even be able to *breathe*.'

Kim was the last student to come forward. Jim took his paper and read what he had written. *Bindaeddeok, mi yeok guk, dak gal bi* and *in jeol mi*.

'Sounds almost edible,' he said. 'What is it?'

'Mung bean pancake, then beef and seaweed soup, then spicy chicken with vegetable, and finish with sweet rice cake with roasted bean powder.'

'OK, good.'

Kim turned to leave the classroom but Jim said, 'Wait up, Kim. You and I need to have a little talk, don't we?'

'There is no charge for basket, Mr Rook. Please fetch it back when you have taken cat home, and I will return it to pet store.'

'I'm not worried about the basket, Kim. It's the cat.'

'Like I say, sir. Cat is perfectly healthy. Same like yesterday.'

'Kim – my cat *died* this morning, before I came here. I ran him down in my car and squashed him flat as a tortilla. I *killed* him. But less than an hour later you stroll in with a cat basket and hey presto! He's not dead after all. You want to explain to me how that happened?'

'Like I say, Mr Rook, your cat is a gift from Kwisin.'

'He was lying dead on my sunbed on the balcony of my apartment. My apartment was locked. How did you get hold of him, and how come he isn't dead any more?'

'Doors close, Mr Rook. But doors also open.'

'That means absolutely nothing as far as I'm concerned.'

'With greatest respect, you will soon see that it means everything.'

Jim went over to the basket and untied the lid. Tibbles climbed out and made a performance of stretching himself. Jim picked him up, although Tibbles made it obvious that he hadn't yet forgiven him. He hung suspended from Jim's arm, his eyes closed, his tail occasionally twitching to show that he was irritated.

'You see?' said Kim. 'He is mad at you, maybe, but he is living and breathing for sure.'

'So who's this Kwisin?' Jim asked him. 'Is it a he, or a she? Or is it a bunch of monks? Or a street gang, like the Korean Killers?'

'Kwisin, sir, is *she*. She is like spirit. Like somebody who step through door. Somebody gone but still here.'

'You're talking about a *ghost*?'

Kim shrugged. 'In Korean story, spirits are different from Western story. We call them demons, but they have many different shapes. Like frog, like fox, like witch-woman. Like spider sometimes.'

'So you're telling me that Tibbles here was resurrected by a Korean demon?'

'Kwisin is grateful to you, Mr Rook. Your cat's life – that is your reward.'

'I don't get it. My grandfather served in Korea during the Korean War and he was always telling me Korean folk stories about magic bottles and fish that could talk but I never heard of Kwisin. And why should she be grateful? What the hell have I ever done for her?'

'You have not yet given Kwisin anything. But you will. And for this Kwisin is grateful. Like thank you in advance.'

Jim stared at Kim intently, but just as before, Kim's face remained smooth and round and impassive. Jim was tempted to shout '*boo!*', just to get a reaction. For a Korean, Kim had very pronounced creases over his eyes, so that it looked almost as if he were watching Jim through the eyeholes in a papier-mâché mask.

'I know that you can see spirits, Mr Rook,' he said, in a flat, matter-of-fact tone.

'*What?*'

'I know that you can see ghosts, and demons. You have the eyes.'

'What are you talking about? What eyes?'

'But it is true, yes? You can see spirits?'

Jim hesitated. He could deny it. He could simply refuse to answer. After all, he didn't know this Kim Dong Wook from Adam. He hadn't yet had the opportunity to check through his school and his medical records, and for all he knew, Kim was autistic, or drug-dependent, or a borderline schizophrenic. But he had walked into the classroom with a living, mewing, bad-tempered Tibbles, and whatever he was, and however he had done it, he had brought an undeniably dead cat back to life.

'What's going on here, Kim?' Jim asked him. 'You seem to know more about me than I know about you.'

'I have come here simply to learn, Mr Rook. My father and mother were told that you had great gift of teaching. You see not just one world, like most teacher, but both worlds.'

'Oh, yes. And who told *them* that?'

'Kwisin, Mr Rook. You cannot open a door into the spirit world without the spirits knowing about it. The spirits can see the living when they enter the world of the dead, just like you yourself can see the dead when they enter the world of the living.'

Tibbles began to struggle, so Jim dropped him down on the floor. 'All right, Kim. Let's put it this way. I *can* see things that most other people can't see. Spirits, ghosts, whatever you want to call them. Demons, too. I've been able to do it ever since I was nine years old, when I nearly died of pneumonia. But don't think for a moment that I *like* doing it, because I don't.'

'There is a saying in Korea, Mr Rook. If you are given a lamp, why would you not light it when darkness falls?'

Jim looked down at Tibbles and Tibbles looked back up at him with supreme arrogance, as if *he* had asked the question, instead of Kim.

Jim didn't answer. He was very reluctant to meddle with spirits these days, because it always seemed that there was a price to pay. Real life wasn't like that TV program *Ghost Whisperer*, in which troubled ghosts were eventually shown the way to heaven, and everybody ended up tearful and happy. Once – reluctantly – he had helped his neighbor to talk to her recently dead husband. She had wanted to make up with him because he had stormed out of the house after an argument about the way she cooked chili and he had been cremated less than twenty minutes later in a fifteen-vehicle auto pile-up on the Golden State Freeway. When Jim had raised his spirit, there had been a highly emotional confrontation, with husband and wife both shouting and crying. Eventually they had sorted out most of their mis-understandings, and calmed their anger with each other, even if they hadn't found perfect peace. That same evening, however, the woman's sixty-seven-year-old father had suffered a stroke which left him permanently speechless and paralyzed.

Almost every time that Jim had put the living in touch with the dead, similar tragedies had followed, sometimes worse. He had never been able to prove that they were a direct consequence of getting in touch with the spirit world, but he no longer offered his services as a mediator between the living and the dead, no matter how much pain and loss anybody had suffered. Two years ago, he had contacted the late wife of one of his fellow teachers. She had died of breast cancer at the age of thirty-three, and all that her bereaved husband had wanted to do was to embrace her one last time.

At 3:33 p.m., with the drapes in their living room drawn together to keep out the sunlight, the teacher had held his lost wife in his arms. She had been shadowy, barely visible, but she had been sufficiently substantial for him to feel the warmth of her body, and kiss her lips.

At 3.33 p.m., less than five miles away, their four-year-old daughter had fallen from the seventh-story balcony at her grandmother's apartment on to a concrete path, and died later that night from severe head injuries.

Jim said to Kim, 'What will I be giving this Kwisin, to make her so grateful? You could at least tell me that.'

'You will find out, Mr Rook, when we reach the right time.'

'Actually, Kim, I think I'd like to know now. In fact, I *insist* on knowing now.'

Kim shook his head slowly from side to side. 'Not possible, sir. Kwisin can show people what will happen in the future, but even Kwisin cannot tell what they will think of it. Some people much braver than others.'

'You're talking in riddles, Kim. I don't like that. I want you to talk straight. Why is Kwisin so grateful?'

'You will know soon, Mr Rook. I promise you.'

Jim stood there for a few moments, feeling increasingly frustrated by Kim Dong Wook's refusal to answer him. But then he thought: *Let this go, Jim. For now, anyhow. This will all unravel itself, sooner or later. And the last thing you want to do is antagonize this young guy.*

'OK, Kim,' he said. 'But I'm warning you now. Any more BS from you and you're out of my class.'

Kim pressed his hands together and bowed his head. 'Of course, Mr Rook. Quite understand, Mr Rook. In Korea they say, do not throw dirt into the well from which you drink.'

After recess, Jim stood up in front of the class and said, 'I'm going to read you a poem.'

'Oh, *man*,' T.D. complained.

'What's the matter, T.D.?'

'Come on, sir. I don't object if you learn us how to communicate better. You know, how to tell our fellow human beings what we're feeling inside. But *poetry*? How cissy is that?'

'T.D., rap is poetry.'

'Sure it is. But rap aint all daffodils and birds twittering in the trees and how does I love thee. Rap is like expressing your *needs,* and how angry you is. Rap is like saying this is me you dumbass and you got to respect me. Otherwise I'm going to blow your dumbass head off.'

Jim said, 'Listen to the poem first, before you make any judgments. It's called "Tomorrow Will Bring Me Roses" by Caitlin Livingston, who was a well-known poet from Marblehead, Massachusetts. And after I've read it, I want each of you to tell me what you want tomorrow to bring *you*.'

Teddy said, 'It's OK, sir. Please! You don't have to read out the poem. I already know what I want tomorrow to bring me. Britney Spears. Naked, and smothered in molasses.'

The class whistled and laughed and Teddy sat down, clasping his hands triumphantly over his head like Rocky.

Leon leaned back in his chair, stretched his arms out, and

opened his mouth in an ostentatious yawn. 'Sleep,' he said.
'That's what I want tomorrow. All day. And nobody waking
me up by trying to read me any stupid poems.'

'Hey – I want a phone call from the Raiders,' said Grant.
'Like, "We want you to wear the number eighty-six jersey
for Saturday's game against Seattle, and we'll pay you fifty
thousand dollars if you say yes."'

Elvira Thomas said, 'You know what I want? These
amazing boots by Antonio Berardi. They don't have heels.
I mean who knows how you're supposed to walk in them,
but they look so-o-o fantastic, who cares?'

'Hey, hey, hey, hold up!' said Jim. 'Before somebody tells
me they want a recording contract with Sony or a house in
Bel Air or a date with Jennifer Aniston, I want you to listen
to this poem. It's not all daffodils and birds twittering in the
trees, T.D. In fact it's pretty acerbic. Anybody knows what
that means – acerbic?'

'Is that like somebody from Serbia?' Arthur suggested.

'Good guess,' said Jim. 'But in this particular context it
means bitter and harsh.'

He started to read, and as he did so he walked slowly up the
aisle between the desks. Judii followed him with wide-
open eyes. T.D. watched him, too, but kept jiggling his
red-sneakered foot to show that he wasn't really all that interested in poetry. Teddy was already scribbling pages of notes,
while Billy was persistently tugging at one of the holes in
his gray T-shirt so that it was growing even bigger, and Arthur
was staring out of the window at the grassy slope outside,
where four or five girls from Mrs Daumier's art class were
sketching the cedar trees.

Jim read:

'Tomorrow when it comes for me
(and if it comes)
Will bring me roses, just like every other day
Your sweet apologies for everything you said and did
Tied with a silken ribbon like your lies.

'Tomorrow when it comes for me
(and if it comes)

Will bring a fog of sunshine to my room
Light up the dust upon the table and the faded chairs
That photograph of us beside the lake
So leached of color that we look like ghosts.

Tomorrow when it comes for me
(and when it comes)
The phone will ring and ring and I will let it ring
Until it stops, and never rings again
And I will sit and listen while the roses die
Petal by petal, dropping on the floor.'

Jim stopped next to Maria Lopez, a quiet, plump girl with
long black braids. She hadn't said a word all morning, except
to say 'here, sir!' when he had called out her name. She was
wearing purple jeans and a bronze satin blouse with puffy
sleeves and a necklace made of multi-colored wooden beads.
She sat with her head bowed, fiddling with her wooden-bead
bracelet as if it were a rosary, but Jim stayed where he was,
close beside her, and recited the last verse as if he were
reading it to her alone:

'Tomorrow when it comes for me
(and it will come)
Will bring me rain, and breezes, and a walk alone
And all the roses in the park will nod their heads
As if they are applauding me for breaking free.
But – back at home, a silence. No applause.
No lies, no dying roses, only me.'

Jim closed the poetry book and went back to his desk. In his
basket in the corner, Tibbles restlessly turned around and around,
making the wickerwork creak, as he tried to get comfortable.
    'So, what do you make of that?' Jim asked.
    Judii said, 'This woman is stone sick of the man in her
life because he's a lying creep and so she decides she's going
to dump him.'
    'Ah, yes. But *will* she?'
    'Yeah – she says so, doesn't she? She knows he's going
to call her but she's not going to answer the phone.'

'OK . . . but she's not going to dump him *today*, is she?' said Jim. 'The whole point of the poem is that she's talking about what she's going to do *tomorrow*. But if that faded photograph is anything to go by, she's been forgiving this guy for more tomorrows than you can shake a stick at.'

'I think there's something else, too,' Janice piped up, her cheeks flushing pink. 'At the end of the poem she goes back home, doesn't she, and it's all silent and it's almost like she *misses* him, even if he *is* a cheat and a liar.'

'That's very perceptive, Janice,' said Jim. 'She knows for certain that she's going to get her roses tomorrow, by way of him saying sorry. And she knows for certain that he's going to call her. She thinks that she ought not to answer his call, and she thinks she ought to leave him. But when she imagines what tomorrow is going to be like, all on her own, without him, she's really not so sure that she will.'

Kim said, 'What reason you choose this tomorrow poem, Mr Rook?'

'That's a strange question.'

'I am interested you want to talk about tomorrow.'

Jim thought about it. Then he said, 'I couldn't tell you specifically, Kim. I guess I was interested to find out what each of you wanted tomorrow to bring you, if you had the choice.'

'But none of us have choice. Tomorrow bring what tomorrow bring.'

'I disagree with you, Kim. We always have *some* choice. If we choose to behave well toward the people we care for – if we choose to make the best of who we are and what we can do – then all of our tomorrows have every chance of being so much more rewarding.'

'Sure,' said Leon. 'So long as we don't step off of the curb and get hit by a four-one-three bus.'

Jim stared at him. 'A four-one-three bus? Why a four-one-three bus?'

Leon pulled a face. 'How should I know? It's the only bus in LA I've ever ridden on.'

'Oh, really?' said Jim. He couldn't help thinking about that packer at Ralph's saying, '*stepped off the curb – right in front of a four-one-three bus – driver stood on the brakes but he didn't have a hope in hell.*'

He stared at Leon for a long, long moment, but Leon simply looked confused. He obviously had no idea of the significance of what he had said, and why it had made Jim react so sharply.

Jim turned back to Maria's desk. 'How about you, Maria? What would you like tomorrow to bring you?'

Maria raised her eyes. She had a round face with heavy black eyebrows that joined in the middle and a spread-out nose. 'I do not know, sir. I cannot tell you.'

'You must have some idea. How about winning the lottery? How about getting married?'

'You believe that this all Latino girls ever think about? Winning the lottery and getting married?'

'Hey, of course not. Only kidding. But surely you have *some* dream, don't you?'

'I dream only to be left alone, that is all.'

It was then that Jim saw the dark crimson bruises on her wrists – bruises that looked as if somebody had gripped her tight and twisted her arm. She had a bruise on her cheek, too, which she had covered up with foundation.

'OK,' he said. 'That's as good a dream as any other. Tamara – how about you?'

'You know what I want tomorrow to bring me, Mr Rook. An offer from KTLA. Anchorwoman for the nightly news.'

'Sure. But what about *you*? What about the way you feel about yourself?'

'I feel fine. Tomorrow I will feel fine.'

'Fine? Is that all?'

Tamara frowned at him. Her eyes flicked from side to side as if she were trying to focus on something inside of her head – something that unsettled her. 'I feel fine,' she repeated. 'I don't want to think about tomorrow. The bathroom. The bath's overflowing. There's too much red.'

'Tamara?' said Jim. 'What do you mean by that?'

'What?'

'What do you mean about the bathroom?'

'What?' She didn't seem to understand what she had said.

Jim stood up straight and looked around the classroom. Outside, the sun was shining and the girls from Mrs Daumier's art class were still drawing. Yet he was aware of a strange feeling of dislocation inside Special Class Two, as if none of his students were sure what they were doing here. It was the same feeling that Jim had experienced after a bus crash, on a tour of Italy. Nobody had been hurt, and yet afterward everybody had milled around by the side of the highway, bewildered.

'Maybe I shouldn't have asked you about tomorrow,' he said, returning to his desk. 'You all seem to have enough problems dealing with today.'

'Hey, I know what I want tomorrow to bring me!' T.D. volunteered. 'An Uzi, so I can scare the living crap out of my mom's latest boyfriend!'

'Yes, well,' Jim told him. 'When I say that you all seem to have enough problems dealing with today, that's a prime example.'

During the midday break, Jim drove Tibbles home. As he was lifting the cat basket out of the back seat of his car, Mrs LaFarge appeared at the top of the steps, carrying a huge bouquet of white lilies.

'Well, well!' she said, and she sounded more than a little disapproving. 'Bought yourself a new cat already, Jim? And Tibbles not even cold in his grave.'

Jim climbed the steps and set the basket down on the landing. 'Somebody made me a surprise offer of a new cat, Mrs L., and I couldn't really say no. Besides, I've *always* had a cat around. I have to have somebody to complain to, even if they can't answer back.'

Mrs LaFarge nodded. 'I know what you mean. It took me years to get used to living on my own, when my late husband passed over, even though he never said a single word from one week's end to the next. My sister used to call him *Bloc-de-Bois*, my lump of wood.'

Tibbles let out one of his irritated '*warrooows*'. Mrs LaFarge said, 'Aren't you going to show me? Is it a he or a she?'

'It's a he. Pretty much the same as Tibbles. Half Russian Blue and half something else. Nothing much to look at.'

'Well, come on, then. Let me say *bonjour*.'

Jim cocked his head and lifted a hand to his ear. 'Oh, I'm

sorry, Mrs L.! I can hear my phone ringing! Listen – I'll bring him down later and we can have a proper cat-warming party. Maybe you can help me think of a name.'

'Your *phone* is ringing?' frowned Mrs LaFarge. 'I don't hear anything.'

'It's my new ringtone. Sounds just like cicadas.' Jim scooped up the cat basket and quickly mounted the next flight of steps. He opened the door of his apartment, carried the basket into the kitchen and set it down on the table. When he lifted the lid, he expected Tibbles to jump out immediately, but Tibbles stayed where he was, staring at him with undisguised disgruntlement.

'OK,' said Jim, and lifted him out. 'You've had a very difficult morning. We *both* have. One minute you're squashed flat, then you're three-dimensional again. I can understand how you feel. But you have to understand how *I* feel, too. I thought I'd lost you for ever, and I was going to have to get to know some totally new cat, right from scratch, so to speak.'

He held Tibbles close and stroked his ears. 'Listen, Tibbles, I don't understand what's happened any more than you do, and even if you did you couldn't explain it to me, could you? You don't even sign. So let's agree to accept it and draw a line under it and move on, OK? Friends?'

Tibbles hesitated for a moment. Then he wrestled himself free from Jim's arms and jumped down on to the kitchen floor. He padded over to his dish and started to eat his shrimp dinner. Jim could only presume that he was forgiven.

He picked up the empty basket and left his apartment. Tibbles didn't attempt to run out of the door this time, and the last that Jim saw of him he was still bobbing his head down over his bowl.

Mrs LaFarge was standing at her window as he passed her apartment, arranging her lilies. He waved at her and gave her a smile. He thought the lilies made her kitchen look like a funeral parlor.

FOUR

As he turned into the college parking lot, he saw Kim standing in the shadow of one of the cedar trees, talking to Maria. He climbed out of his car, slamming the door twice because it didn't fit properly. Kim was making chopping gestures with both hands, while Maria nodded and nodded as if she were agreeing with him.

Jim walked up to them and held out the empty cat basket. 'Here, Kim. You can take this back now. I just took Tibbles home.'

Kim took the basket and bowed his head. 'Thank you, Mr Rook. Cat is happy to return, yes?'

'In every sense of the word, yes he is. I don't really think he knows what hit him, any more than I do.'

'Door close, Mr Rook,' said Kim, with the faintest suggestion of smugness. 'Then door open, like I say before. One day maybe door close for ever. But . . . maybe not.'

'Well, let's leave it like that for now, shall we? How are you guys? OK?'

Maria said nothing, but lowered her eyes, and looked away. Kim said, 'Maria and me, we discuss future life. Like in "Tomorrow Will Bring Roses" poem.'

'Oh, yes? You'll have to tell me about it.'

'We will, Mr Rook. But not yet. Nobody can speak about future life until they have *seen* future life. Not for certain.'

Jim looked at Kim narrowly, trying to work out what he was driving at. Kim seemed to have a philosophical agenda of some kind, like a Scientologist or a Zen Buddhist or a Zoroastrian, but Jim couldn't really work out what it was. Doors opening, doors closing – what the hell was all that about? In Zen Buddhism, the world was going to end after the Three Great Calamities – Fire, Water and Wind. In Zoroastrianism, the whole world was going to be flooded in molten metal, to purify it, and that was going to be the end

of that. The Big Sizzle. But doors closing for ever? Or maybe
not closing for ever?

As he walked up the steps into the main entrance, Jim
turned around just one more time. Maria had raised one hand
to cover her face, as if she were trying to conceal the fact
that she was crying. He stopped for a moment, but then he
decided that it would be better not to interfere, at least not
yet. *Kids. They drive you doolally.*

On his way back along the wax-polished corridor, he heard
a woman's footsteps click-clacking up behind him. When he
turned around he saw that Sheila Colefax was trying to catch
up with him.

'Oh – Jim! *Jim!* Could I have a word?'

'Hey, I'm sorry, Sheila, I swear to God, I'm doing my
best to keep the pandemonium down to a minimum, but they
don't call it a remedial class for nothing. Those kids still
need a whole lot of remediating.'

'No, no. The noise level is quite acceptable, thank you.
I'll be sure to tell you if it disturbs us.' Sheila Colefax took
off her black-framed eyeglasses and gave her head a little
shake, which loosened her hair. Jim was tempted to say,
'Why, Ms Colefax . . . without your glasses . . . you're beautiful!' but he managed to resist it. Maybe she really *was*
wearing black stockings and a garter belt.

'There's a poetry recital Friday evening at the Brentwood
Theater. The Santa Barbara School. I've been given tickets
and I was wondering if you'd like to come.'

'The Santa Barbara School?' said Jim, suspiciously.
'They're, like, *feminists*, aren't they?'

'Insofar as they have always believed that women have
as much literary fire in their bellies as men. But they're not
militants, if that's what you mean.'

Jim looked down at Sheila Colefax and realized for the
first time that her eyes had very unusual violet-colored irises,
and that she had the slightest of overbites, her top teeth
cushioned on her lower lip, which for some unknown reason
he had always found absurdly attractive. Actually, he *did*
know what the reason was: it made a woman look hesitant
and defenseless, as if she would be putty in his hands. He
had experienced quite enough relationships with women who

were domineering and opinionated and wanted to sit on top
of him every time, as if they were lurching down the Grand
Canyon on a rented mule.

'Actually, Sheila, I'm not too sure,' he told her. 'I think
I might already have plans.' Then he thought: *Excuse me,
Jim. What plans, exactly? Sitting on that springless maroon
couch with a bottle of Fat Tire beer, watching yet another
repeat of* The Mentalist, *with Tibbles rattling on your lap?*

'It was just an idea,' said Sheila, replacing her eyeglasses.
She looked a little hurt, but also as if she was used to being
hurt. 'Why don't you get back to me? I think it could be fun.'

'Fun' wasn't exactly the word that Jim would have chosen
for an evening of warm chardonnay and crop-haired women
reading out poems about getting their revenge on wife-
beaters, but off the top of his head he couldn't think of a
better one, so he said, 'Sure. Yes. I'll let you know. The
Brentwood Theater? That's on Wilshire, isn't it?'

Sheila said, 'Yes. Wilshire. I'll wait to hear from you.'
She click-clacked back to her classroom in her pencil skirt
and he stood in the middle of the corridor watching her. No
VPL. Maybe she wasn't wearing a garter-belt. Maybe she
was wearing a black lace thong. Maybe she wasn't even
wearing that.

That afternoon it started to thunder, and Jim gave Special
Class Two a list to study.

As he handed them out, he said, 'This is a list of one
hundred ideas by a writer called Michael McClure, who is
a well-known writer of what they used to call the Beat
Generation. Nineteen-sixties hippies, to you. A typical idea
in this list is "The Stars Are A Gas." Another one is "Man
Is A Panda." Yet another, "War Is One Color." It's safe to
say that none of you will understand what in hell Michael
McClure is talking about.'

'So why do we have to read it?' T.D. demanded. 'You
tryin' to prove that we all *stupid* or somethin'? We already
know we all stupid. We're not *that* stupid.'

'You won't be able to understand any of Michael
McClure's ideas at face value, but then you'll be gratified
to know that nobody can.'

'Well, if *nobody* can understand him, why does anybody have to read what he write? Especially us. What are we, like goatscapes?'

'That's scapegoats, T.D. But no you're not. This list of ideas will show you that words can be so much more than just descriptions, or explanations, or instructions. OK, words can tell you that the sky is gray and it looks like a storm's brewing up. Words can warn you that you're driving the wrong way on the freeway off-ramp, or that a candy bar may contain nuts. But words can also stretch your brain to its very limits, right to the very edge of your sanity. Come on, you know that from rap.

'Words can give you brilliant insights, even if they don't appear to have any literal meaning. Words can do unimaginable things.'

'Like say *what*, for instance?' asked Arthur, leaning on his elbow to show how unimpressed he was.

'OK – let me give you a comparison, from basketball. Think about Kareem Abdul-Jabbar's skyhook shot. If you had tried to tell people about that skyhook shot before he actually did it, it would have sounded impossible. They would have said, "*Nah* – nobody can climb straight up into thin air like they're going up a ladder." But Kareem did, using the same muscles that everybody else has, and it was amazing. It was a revelation. What I'm hoping is that some of you may find a similar kind of revelation in this list by Michael McClure. A skyhook, inside of your mind.'

Lightning flickered behind the San Gabriel mountains, and after a few seconds they heard the crumpling of thunder.

'I don't think God approves of this Michael McClure dude,' said Billy. 'I think He's trying to tell us to go back to reading *Hustler* instead.'

'Just get on and study it, Billy,' Jim told him. 'Make notes if it'll help you. Tomorrow I'm going to ask you to write ten original ideas of your own. Ten off-the-wall ideas, like these are. Not just "Eating Ten Krispy Kreme Donuts At One Sitting Will Temporarily Make You Hyperactive."'

While the class shuffled and muttered and coughed and scratched their heads over their assignment, Jim perched himself on the corner of his desk to read through the menus they had selected for their last meals on Death Row.

Leon's was the first. Lox, eggs and onions for starters, followed by a triple-decker sandwich of knockwurst, pastrami, Swiss cheese, Russian dressing and coleslaw, on grilled rye bread, finishing up with a sour cream, raisin and nut rugelach.

Although Leon would have broken the first commandment to end up on Death Row, Jim was interested to see that he was still going to make sure that his last meal was completely kosher. He might be sarcastic and defiant in class, but Jim guessed that he was very respectful to his family at home, and at the synagogue. That gave Jim a good handle on how to deal with him when he was being obnoxious. Ask him how his parents would feel if they knew that he was behaving like such a *schmendrick*. Ask him what his rabbi would say.

To Jim's surprise, Grant wanted 'Lobster ravilolli followed by roce chicken with black figgs and sore toe potatoes.' In spite of the creative mis-spellings, Jim was impressed. Grant clearly saw himself as more than just a highly successful football player. He saw himself as a highly successful and *wealthy* football player, who would be able to live a sophisticated life of luxury. His menu suggested that he had been reading celebrity magazines like *OK!* although Jim doubted if he would ever admit it. The only nagging uncertainty that he would ever play at the thirty-million-dollar-a-year level was revealed in his choice of dessert, a Twinkie. But Jim realized that there was a whole lot more to Grant than he liked to show anybody – a yearning for glamour, as well as sporting glory. A feminine side. He was the kind of guy who could knock you flat with one punch but still used moisturizer.

Then there was Kim's menu: *bindaddeok, mi yeok guk, dak gal bi* and *in jeol mi*. Jim wouldn't have been able to understand it at all unless Kim had translated it, but now he knew that it was very uncomplicated: only beef and chicken and vegetables and rice. But that was like Kim himself: although he liked to appear mysterious, he was using enigmatic words to hide a very simple secret.

Simple, but not necessarily benign. Jim had encountered enough demons to know that whatever they gave you, they always wanted something in return, and that what they wanted in return was usually more than you were able to pay. If Kim was capable of bringing a crushed animal back to life – or he knew somebody or something that could – he had to have a motive for being here at West Grove that went far beyond remedial English.

Elvira had been waving her arm for nearly half a minute to attract his attention. 'Sir? Michael McClure says here, "Men feed mustangs to dogs, and whales to cats." What does he mean by that?'

Jim said, 'So far as I can make out, he's pointing out that we nourish our domesticated pets with the flesh of wild animals. He wants us to think about the rights and the wrongs of it. Most of us humans eat animals, too – some of them tame, like cows, some of them wild, like deer. Is it morally right for us to do that?'

'I think it's morally wrong for us to eat anything that can't put up any kind of a fight,' said T.D. 'You know, like carrots. Or baked beans.'

'Carrots and baked beans don't have emotions,' Janice Sticky protested.

'Yeah, but Big Macs don't have emotions, neither. Did you ever see a Big Mac cry?'

'Just get on and finish the text,' Jim put in. 'We can talk about vegetarianism later.'

All the same, the next Death Row menu he picked up had only one word written on it, and that word was 'Lettis.'

The name on the top of the paper was Patsy-Jean Waller. Jim looked up at her. She was sitting in the front row, at the opposite end from Kim Dong Wook. All the euphemisms in the dictionary couldn't have disguised the fact that she was obese, well over two hundred and twenty pounds, with curly brown hair scraped back with a yellow plastic Alice band, and eyes that were little more than slits. She was wearing a loose brown smock to cover her enormous breasts and her protuberant stomach, and underneath she was wearing tight white leggings and yellow vinyl Crocs.

Jim stood up and went across to Patsy-Jean's desk. She was

reading the Michael McClure text with intense concentration, moving her lips as she did so, and she didn't realize for nearly half a minute that Jim was standing next to her.

'Patsy-Jean?' said Jim, very gently.

She looked up at him, and blinked, her mouth turned downward as if she had done something wrong without knowing what it was.

'I just read what you wanted for your last meal,' he told her.

She swallowed hard, and her double chins wobbled. 'Did I spell it wrong?' she asked him in a hoarse voice. 'I can never spell it right.'

'Yes, you spelled it wrong,' Jim told her, with a smile. 'But don't worry about it. By the time I'm through with you, you'll be spelling "radicchio" with your eyes closed.'

Patsy-Jean tried to smile, but it was obvious that she still felt anxious. Jim said, 'It really wasn't much of a meal, was it? Lettuce. Didn't you even want some tomatoes with it? Maybe a couple of scallions, or half an egg?'

Patsy-Jean's cheeks flushed red. 'I want God to know that I'd repented.'

'And *lettuce*? That's your penance?'

She nodded. 'I've been eating too much all of my life and it's a sin. I didn't put on the freshman fifteen when I started college. I put on about fifty.'

'What are you talking about? Eating too much isn't a sin, it's a disorder. At the very worst, it's a lack of self-discipline. People do far worse things in this world than eat too many chocolate fudge sundaes. People *kill* people, and actually get medals for it.'

Jim hunkered down beside her and said, 'Listen, Patsy-Jean, one of the things I always do with Special Class Two is have each student stand up and explain what they want to change about themselves, and why. I'm not trying to play psychiatrist, or social worker. I'm trying to teach you how to express how you feel to other people. Once you've done that – once you can clearly describe to your classmates who you are and why you eat too much – I believe that you won't be asking for lettuce for your last meal. Maybe a diet burger without the bun, and a jacket potato instead of fries, but that's not too much of a penance, is it?'

Patsy-Jean's slitty little eyes suddenly filled up with tears. Jim took hold of her hand and squeezed it. 'I'm on your side, Patsy-Jean. We're all on your side. You wait. Tomorrow you'll get roses, I promise you.'

Halfway through the lesson, Maria put up her hand, and said, 'Sir?'

Jim looked up from the notes he was jotting about Judii Rogers' Death Row supper (a KFC family bucket, all for herself, with family-size fries, but with Moët champagne instead of Coke, and an Oreo cookie ice-cream pie to finish). 'Maria?' he asked her.

'Can I leave the room, sir?'

Jim frowned at her. All the color had drained out of her face, so that the two spots of rouge on her cheeks looked almost like clown make-up, and her eyes were glassy black.

'Are you OK there, Maria? You're looking a little *peaky*, if you don't mind me saying so.'

'I'm OK,' she nodded. 'I just need to leave the room, that's all.'

'Sure you can. Do you want one of the other girls to go with you?'

'No, thank you, sir. I'll be fine.'

Maria stood up and tottered unsteadily out of the classroom, taking her gold vinyl bag with her. She had to pull at the door twice before she managed to close it. Jim checked his watch. Ten after three. He frequently had trouble with his students taking drugs – anything from their mothers' tranquilizers to crystal meth. Maria wasn't the usual type he would have flagged as a substance abuser, but she had spoken to him very aggressively when he asked her about winning the lottery and getting married, and she did have those crimson bruises on her wrists and her cheek. She obviously had *some* underlying problem, even if it wasn't simply drugs.

He carried on writing comments about the Death Row menus. Like the last meals ordered by real condemned murderers, most of them were very plain, with a predominance of cheeseburgers, steaks and fries. He wondered what *he* would order, himself, if he were about to be executed. He would have to have a large slice of his mother's key lime pie – or he would do if his mother was still alive.

Kim raised his hand and said, '*This* idea is very interesting, Mr Rook. "Each Self Is Many Selves."'

'Oh, yes?'

'Do you think he means that our self changes day by day? Tomorrow we will be different self from now? Or does he mean that we are many different selves all at once? I am child that I was, but also old man that I will be?'

Jim cleared his throat and tried to look as if he understood what Kim was talking about. 'What do *you* think?' he asked him.

'I think that life is similar to book. Beginning of story and end of story exist at same time. You can read beginning, then turn to end. Or maybe you can read end first. You can read half of book, and never finish, but end still exists. It is still there. If you wanted to, you could pick book up again and read it. Or not.'

'I don't think I'm entirely sure what you're trying to say here, Kim,' said Jim.

'I am saying that tomorrow is today, and yesterday is today. And the day we were born is today. And the day we die is today.'

'Pretty busy day we're having today,' put in Teddy, without looking up from his frantic scribbling.

Kim turned around in his chair and said, 'It is not difficult. All you have to do is open door.'

Jim was about to ask him to explain further, although he could see by the baffled expressions on the faces of the rest of Special Class Two that he had already left them way behind.

Arthur said, 'If yesterday is today, what am I doing here in class? I should still be bowling.'

'Don't worry about it,' T.D. told him. 'Tomorrow is yesterday, too, so you'll be bowling tomorrow.'

'Yes, but I'm going to be *born* tomorrow. I won't have the time to go bowling. And I won't know how to. And I'll be much too little.'

'OK, OK, that's enough!' said Jim. He checked his watch

again. Maria had been gone for over ten minutes. 'Janice . . .
do you mind going to the restroom and making sure that
Maria is OK?'

'Hey, I'll go,' Billy volunteered. 'I love those Latin looks.
Penélope Cruz, mmm-mmmh!'

'Penélope Cruz is a vegetarian,' said T.D. 'She eats things
that can't fight back.'

'Who cares? With an ass like that? You could serve lunch
for six people off of that ass.'

Jim raised both hands for quiet. 'Let's get back to Mr McClure,
shall we? We can finish our existential discussions tomorrow.
Those of us who are not going bowling, anyhow.'

He was sitting down again when Janice came back in.
'Maria's not there, sir. I knocked on all of the stalls, but
she's not in any of them.'

'OK,' said Jim. 'She wasn't looking too good, was she?
Maybe she went to the infirmary, or went home. I'll go check
in a minute.'

But he had only just lifted up his pen again when the
classroom door burst open with a shuddering crash. Judii
and Tamara both screamed, and even Leon said, 'Shit, man!'

Maria was standing in the open doorway, holding out
both of her hands as if she were pleading for mercy. She
was stark naked, and she was smothered in blood from
head to foot. Her hair was a riot of bloody black curls, and
her eyes were staring white out of a scarlet mask. She was
criss-crossed with gaping cuts and covered in huge red
bruises.

She had left an erratic trail of bloody footprints on the vinyl
floor behind her, and two bloody handprints on the door.

Her mouth was stretched wide open but she said nothing
– just stood there, with her hands held out.

Jim jumped up from his desk, went across to her and took
her in his arms.

'*Teddy!*' he shouted. 'Call nine-one-one! Paramedics and
police! Do it now! Grant – go to the infirmary and fetch
Nurse Okeke! Tell her to bring blankets and a stretcher and
a first-aid kit!'

Maria's knees gave way, and she started to sag. Her skin
was growing tacky as the blood started to congeal, and Jim

felt as if they were stuck together in some kind of unholy embrace. He lowered her gently to the floor and said, 'Kim – my coat!'

Kim lifted Jim's crumpled linen coat from the back of his chair and spread it out. Jim lifted Maria a little and laid her head down on it.

'Here,' said Arthur, 'you can cover her up with this,' and he handed Jim his Michael Jackson sweatshirt.

Maria's eyes were still wide open and staring, but she didn't seem to be focusing. She opened her lips and a bubble of blood formed between them, and then softly burst.

'Maria,' Jim urged her. 'Maria – can you hear me?'

Maria's eyes rolled toward him, although he couldn't tell for sure if she could see him.

'Maria, what the hell happened? Who did this to you? Maria!'

Maria opened her lips again and mouthed something, but there was a sudden clatter and squeak of running feet in the corridor outside the classroom, and Jim couldn't hear what it was.

'What did you say?' Jim asked her. 'What happened, sweetheart? Who did this?'

'*Door*,' she whispered. '*Door.*'

FIVE

Lieutenant Harris arrived ten minutes after the squad car and the paramedics. He climbed out of his bronze Crown Victoria and walked across to the ambulance, where Jim was standing with Dr Ehrlichman, the principal, and Nurse Okeke.

Two uniformed officers had assembled Special Class Two under the cedar tree, and were taking notes. One of them had hay fever and kept sneezing. Lieutenant Harris gave them a wave and called out, 'See you in a minute, you guys.'

Lieutenant Harris was short and almost square, bull-necked, with a gingery buzz-cut, and a gingery suit to match. 'What happened?' he asked, patting his perspiring forehead with a balled-up Kleenex. 'I picked up the call as I was driving home.'

'One of my students got herself badly cut up,' said Jim. He raised his arms to show Lieutenant Harris all the dried blood on his shirt, like a dark red map of the Balkans. 'Maria Lopez, seventeen years old. We don't know how it happened, but the paramedics are trying to make her comfortable before they take her off to the hospital.'

Lieutenant Harris peered inside the ambulance. 'Is it life-threatening?'

'I don't know. I hope not. But she has lacerations all over and she's pretty seriously bruised.'

'So how did she get that way?'

'Search me,' said Jim. 'She excused herself to go to the restroom. She took so long that I sent one of the other girls to go look for her. She wasn't there. But a couple of minutes later she came bursting in through the door totally naked and covered in blood.'

Lieutenant Harris looked around the grounds, his lips tightly compressed, as if he were searching for some kind of a sign. A burning bush, maybe, or an angel holding up a sacred text. When he turned back, he said, 'Does anything *normal* ever happen in your class, Mr Rook? Every time we get called out here to West Grove, it always involves *you*, and it's always something spooky.'

Dr Ehrlichman gave a sharp, disapproving cough. 'I'm sure there's a perfectly rational explanation for this, Lieutenant. It's my first guess that Ms Lopez was attacked at random by some intruder from outside the campus.'

The sun was bouncing brightly off the top of Dr Ehrlichman's bald head. These days he wore rimless spectacles and he had shaved off his droopy moustache, because a woman friend had told him after too many vodkatinis that he looked as if he had bought it in a joke store. As far as Jim was concerned, he now looked like a six-month-old baby that was just about to burst into tears.

'We don't yet know if she was – ah – sexually interfered with,' Dr Ehrlichman added. 'No doubt we'll discover that when the doctors have been able to examine her.'

Nurse Okeke looked unimpressed. 'Myself, Dr Ehrlichman, I am not at all certain that Maria was attacked by any intruder.'

Nurse Okeke was Ibo, from Nigeria. She was nearly six foot tall and every move she made had a complicated elegance. Her skin was intensely black, almost blue-black, and she had a haughty, sculptured face, with high cheekbones and hooded eyes. She wore a pale blue button-through overall and a pale blue cotton headscarf, folded with intimidating neatness.

'Oh, you don't think so?' Dr Ehrlichman retorted. 'Frankly, I don't see who else could have been responsible. Even the most unruly of our students isn't capable of doing anything like this. This is the work of some whackjob. Some psychopath.'

'You misunderstand me, Dr Ehrlichman,' said Nurse Okeke. 'I was not suggesting for a moment that any of our students did it. In fact I was not suggesting that *anybody* did it. To me, Maria's injuries look more consistent with some kind of accident with farming machinery. I saw similar lacerations and bruises in West Africa, when people fell in front of harvesters, or corn-threshers.'

Lieutenant Harris dabbed the back of his neck with his

Kleenex, and then blew his nose on it. 'With respect, Nurse Okeke, there probably isn't a harvester or a corn-thresher within fifty miles of here.'

'We have lawnmowers here on campus,' said Nurse Okeke. 'The blades of a lawn-mower could account for such trauma.'

'Maybe so,' said Dr Ehrlichman. 'But our lawnmowers don't happen to be in use today, do they? And even if they had been, and the unfortunate Ms Lopez had somehow managed to get herself tangled up in one of them, I am quite certain that the groundsperson involved would have raised the alarm immediately.'

'Have you informed her next-of-kin?' asked Lieutenant Harris, trying to change the subject. He didn't like speculation, or theories, or hunches. This was real life, not *Murder, She Wrote*.

Jim said, 'Maria's mother works for Sunbright. It's a domestic cleaning company in Burbank. I managed to get in touch with her boss and he's agreed to pick her up and drive her to Cedars-Sinai, so that we can meet her there.'

A black Taurus came up the college driveway and parked at an angle alongside Lieutenant Harris's Crown Victoria. Two detectives got out – a middle-aged Chinese American in a loud plaid coat, and a young woman with curly blonde hair and a turquoise suit that was half a size too tight for her.

'Ah – Wong, Madison,' said Lieutenant Harris. 'Good of you to join us.'

'We got here as soon as we could, Lieutenant,' said Detective Wong. 'A cattle truck turned over on the Ventura Freeway, and there was prime rib all over.'

'This man and his excuses,' said Lieutenant Harris. 'What was it the last time? That freak storm, with hailstones as big as baseballs? Or was it that high-wire walker at Century City who got struck by lightning and fell on your car?'

'That was true, Lieutenant, the high-wire walker,' Detective Wong protested. 'It was all over the TV news.'

One of the paramedics came over, snapping off her blue latex gloves. 'OK,' she said, 'Maria has suffered considerable blood loss but we have her on a drip and she's stabilized now. We're taking her directly to the ER.'

'Thank you,' said Jim. He felt a sudden surge of help-lessness. This was Maria's first day in Special Class Two, and he could hardly be expected to have discovered much about her. But he had seen from her bruises that she had some kind of a problem and even though he hadn't had the chance to find out what it was, he still felt responsible for her.

The ambulance sped off with its siren scribbling. Jim said, 'You don't need me here any longer, do you, Lieutenant? I need to go to the hospital and talk to Maria's mom.'

'Jim,' said Dr Ehrlichman, firmly, lifting his hand. 'I'd rather you didn't.'

'Excuse me?'

'There are legal implications here, Jim. It's quite possible that the college could be held liable for what happened here today.'

'We don't *know* what happened here today! Maria left the classroom looking a little logie, then she came back all bloody. I sure as hell didn't have anything to do with it.'

'All the same, Jim. One expression of sympathy – that's all it takes.'

'What do you mean, "one expression of sympathy"? Maria was almost killed, and I'm not allowed to be sympathetic?'

'Jim, if you say "sorry" to Maria's mother, it might sound comforting and heartfelt in the emergency room, but think what it's going to sound like in the Los Angeles Superior Court, seven months from now? I've been there, Jim. I've done it myself, and it cost the college a whole bundle of money in damages. No matter how badly you feel, and I *know* you feel badly, it's better to keep it to yourself, OK?'

Jim knew that Dr Ehrlichman was right. But he had a feeling that something was seriously out of whack. It was like an electric storm approaching. The air seemed to be congealing, and the trees sounded restless. However Maria had been injured, he was sure that she wasn't going to be the last of his students to get hurt. He didn't exactly know why, but he was highly sensitive to supernatural disturbances, and he could feel his hands tingling and a crawling sensation down his back. This morning's resurrection of Tibbles hadn't exactly put his mind at ease, either.

Lieutenant Harris and his two detectives went over to talk to the uniformed officers. Jim guessed that he might as well go home. He could call Cedars-Sinai later this evening to find out how Maria was getting on.

He was approaching the steps to the main entrance when Kim came across to him.

'Mr Rook?'

'Yes, Kim, what is it?'

'You should not worry about Maria, Mr Rook. She survive this time.'

Jim stopped. 'What do you mean by "this time", Kim?'

'I mean she survive for now.'

'When I saw you two earlier, under the tree, what were you talking about? It seemed to me that Maria was upset.'

'Maria have trouble at home, Mr Rook. She beg me not to tell anybody.'

'What kind of trouble?'

'I cannot say. She make me promise.'

'Kim, you saw the state of her. She was chopped up like a hamburger. If you know anything at all that can help us to protect her, then you need to tell me what it is.'

'She survive this time, Mr Rook.'

'So you think it might happen again?'

Kim said nothing, but stared at Jim unblinking, as if he hadn't heard him.

'Kim – do you have *any* idea what happened to her?' Jim persisted.

'It has not happen yet. No need to worry.'

'You're talking in riddles again, Kim. If you know how Maria got herself hurt, then we really have to know. Did somebody attack her? The nurse seems to think she was injured by a lawnmower, or maybe some kind of farm machinery.'

'Maria have great trouble with her stepfather, Mr Rook. He is dangerous man. I should not tell you this because she make me promise.'

'What are you telling me? That her stepfather cut her up like that?'

'No, Mr Rook. Nobody cut her up. Not yet.'

Just then, Lieutenant Harris came over. 'Hard to make any

sense of this. The crime scene guys tell me that she left blood spatters and bloody footprints only a quarter of the way along the corridor. They start about thirty feet short of your classroom door. How do you think she got as far as that without making a single mark?'

'I can't say that I noticed that,' said Jim. 'I was too concerned with trying to get everybody out of the building without treading all over the evidence.'

'But even if somebody was carrying her along the corridor, there would have been drops of blood on the floor.'

'Maybe somebody was carrying her wrapped up in a blanket, or a coat or something,' Jim suggested.

Lieutenant Harris pulled a face. 'Still doesn't make any sense.'

'Let's hope she can tell us when she comes round.'

'*If* she comes round.'

'Kim here seems to be convinced that she's going to be fine,' said Jim.

Lieutenant Harris looked around and frowned. 'Kim? Who's Kim?'

Jim turned. Kim had been standing right next to him, on the steps, but now he was more than seventy-five yards away, underneath the shadow of the cedar tree, with his classmates. Jim hadn't even seen him turn around and walk off. And how had he managed to get so far away, in only a few seconds? He was talking to Tamara and Arthur as if they were in mid-conversation.

Lieutenant Harris said, 'If you think of anything that might be helpful, Mr Rook, you *will* get in touch with Detective Wong, won't you? I think that you and he will probably get along. He's a great believer in the occult. He says that his grandmother talks to ghosts on a regular basis. Apparently they give her pretty reliable tips for Santa Anita.'

'Sure, yes,' said Jim, abstractedly. He paused for a moment longer, still staring at Kim. How the hell had he gotten over to that tree so fast? Jim felt as if fifteen seconds had been edited out of his life, and that somehow he had missed Kim saying goodbye and walking away. But how could he?

He continued up the steps to the main entrance. As he opened the door, though, he felt a chill across his shoulders. He turned around and looked up at the sky. Clouds were sliding across the sun as fast as a speeded-up movie, and the trees and the bushes were increasingly agitated, although there seemed to be hardly any wind blowing.

Nurse Okeke was coming up the steps toward him. 'Mr Rook?' she asked him. 'Is something wrong?'

'Yes, Nurse. I believe that there is.'

Nurse Okeke raised one immaculately plucked eyebrow. 'Can I ask you what it is? You're looking troubled, if you don't mind my saying so.'

Jim said, 'I think you're right, Nurse Okeke. That's what's wrong. I don't believe that Maria was attacked by any intruder, either. Maria got herself mangled by some piece of machinery. But the question is what, and how, and why – and even more important, *when*?'

Before he went home he stopped off at the Cat'n'Fiddle English Pub on Hollywood Boulevard. It was dark in the Cat'n'Fiddle, with stained-glass windows and dim Tiffany lamps. Out on the patio a jazz trio was playing 'Won't You Come Home, Bill Bailey' and he knew that he ought to go home and see Tibbles but actually he wanted his life to go on hold for an hour or two, and nothing else to happen, so that he could try to catch up with what had happened so far.

He sat up at the bar and ordered a bottle of Fat Tire Amber Ale, which he drank much too quickly, so that he couldn't stop burping. He ordered another, but this time he sipped it more slowly. He crunched a few giant pretzels, too, to see if they would help, but they kept surging up in the back of his throat, so that he had to swallow them twice.

A tawny-blonde girl in a very short miniskirt climbed on to the barstool next to him and said, in a cheerful British accent, 'You look sad, mate!'

'Sad?' said Jim. 'No, I'm not sad. I'm just trying to make sense of the world.'

'How about a shag? That should cheer you up.'

Jim looked at her. She had a chubby oval face and double false eyelashes and dark circles under her eyes, even though she couldn't have been much older than Maria Lopez, or any of the other girls in his class. Her miniskirt was covered with glittery purple sequins, and she wore purple stilettos with worn-down heels.

'A shag?' Jim asked her. 'What's that? Today's special?'

The girl gave a throaty little laugh. 'It's a *screw*, silly.'

'Oh, I get it. I thought you were offering me some weird British meal like bangers 'n' mash. Or maybe a carpet, or a seabird, or an ounce of tobacco. They're all different kinds of shag.'

'You're nuts, you are. But you can still have a shag if you want one.'

'No, no thanks all the same. A little early in the day for me.'

'What do you mean? It's never too early to cheer your-self up. What time is it?'

'Seven twenty-five.'

'What – seven twenty-five in the morning?'

'Seven twenty-five in the evening. Do you know what day it is?'

The girl stared at him for a long time and then she shook her head. 'No. Surprise me.'

'Don't you think it matters, what day it is?'

'I don't know. No. Every bloody day's the bloody same, as far as I'm concerned.'

He stared at her so intently that she gave him a quick, defensive smile. 'Something wrong, mate?' she asked him.

'No, nothing,' said Jim. 'Well, nothing that you need to worry about, anyhow. But you're right. Every bloody day *is* the bloody same. Yesterday, today, tomorrow. All the bloody same.'

He left his last bottle of Fat Tire only three-quarters finished, and handed the bartender fifteen dollars.

'Keep the change,' he told him.

'Oh . . . Mr Generous rides again,' the bartender clucked at him.

The tawny-haired girl looked at the bartender and shrugged. 'Nutter,' she said, but Jim didn't hear her because he was already halfway to the door.

When he stepped out into the parking lot, Jim looked up and the sky was a strange purplish color, with clouds flying past much faster than they should have been. Even though he could feel only the lightest of breezes, the yuccas along

Hollywood Boulevard were shaking as violently as cheer-leaders' pom-poms.

He drove back to Briarcliff Road and parked at a steep angle next to Summer's yellow Beetle. Dry leaves were scurrying around and around in front of the steps, as if they were chasing each other. He climbed up to his apartment and opened the door. It was gloomy and airless inside and there was still a lingering fishy odor from Tibbles' shrimp dinner. He switched on the lamps and the air-conditioning.

'Tibbles?' he called out. 'You there, boy?' Tibbles always trotted out to greet him when he arrived home but this evening there was no sign of him.

'Tibbles?' He went through to the kitchen, and as he did so he was sure that he heard his bedroom door closing. Not slammed – not caught by the wind – just closing, very quietly, *ker-lick*. He stood in the middle of the kitchen listening. The air-conditioning was rattling intermittently, as it always did when it started up, but he was sure that he could hear some-body moving around.

He went across to his bedroom door and opened it. He sniffed. He could smell shower gel – his own Armani shower gel that Heidi had given him for Christmas last year before they had split up. Not only that, his bed was a mess, with his red Zuni throw dragged back at a forty-five-degree angle and his pillows all twisted as if he had been wrestling with them. But this morning he had taken the time to make his bed really neatly, with double-folded hospital-type corners and everything.

He looked across at his closet. It had mirrored doors, and he could see himself standing on the opposite side of the room with a frown on his face. He went around the end of the bed and took hold of both door handles.

'O-*kay*!' he shouted, and flung the closet doors wide open. He didn't know what he had expected to find in there – a strange man who had spent the day tossing and turning in his bed and then had the brass *cojones* to take a shower in *his* bathroom, with *his* shower-gel? But there was nobody inside, only his clothes hanging up, apart from some crum-pled old T-shirts on the closet floor which he never wore any more and a paint-spattered pair of Levis which had dropped on top of them.

'Tibbles?' he repeated. 'You there, Tibbles?'

Jim came out of the bedroom and as he did so he heard the front door close. Again, it wasn't slammed, and it didn't sound as if the wind had caught it. But he had already closed it behind him when he had come home, hadn't he? It sounded more like somebody had taken advantage of his being in the bedroom so that they could make a stealthy exit.

He hurried to the front door and pulled it open. He thought he could hear footsteps pattering down the stairs, but when he went to the railing and looked down to the landing below his, there was nobody there. The streetlights were going on, all over Hollywood, and this evening they were twinkling like heliographs because the trees and the bushes were thrashing around so much.

Jim was still standing by the railing when Tibbles appeared out of the front door, and rubbed himself against his legs.

'Hey, there you are,' said Jim, and lifted him up. 'I was worried that I might have had some kind of hallucination, and that you were still, like, deceased.'

Tibbles stared at him with his green eyes very wide, which Jim took to mean that he forgave him for running him down. Or not. He never quite knew, with Tibbles. But then Tibbles licked his lips, and started to make a rattling noise like the air-conditioning, which meant that he was hungry.

'You know something?' Jim told him. 'Even for a cat you're a blatant hypocrite. What do you want? Chicken, chicken liver, tuna or turkey? I'm all out of shrimp, and besides that I can't stand the stink.'

He carried Tibbles back into the kitchen and dropped him on to the floor. It was then that he saw that the kitchen sink was crowded with dirty dishes – a large white dinner plate; a side plate; two saucepans, one with a question-mark of spaghetti still clinging to the inside and the other crusted with lava-like rings of Bolognese sauce; a dessert bowl with caramel-colored circles all around it; a coffee mug; two wine glasses; and a cheese-grater that was sprouting shreds of waxy-looking cheese.

Jim approached the sink very slowly. He picked up the saucepan that had been used to cook Bolognese sauce, and

then put it down again. This was insane. These were the
dirty dishes that had been left over from the supper that he
had cooked himself last night. He had eaten it in the couch
while watching *CSI: New York*. Tibbles had been staring at
him fixedly the whole time he was eating because Tibbles
had a most un-cat-like penchant for Bolognese sauce, even
when it was so hot that that he had to cool it off by batting
lumps of it around the kitchen floor with his paws.

What was insane, though, was that Jim had washed up all
of these dishes. The plates, the saucepans, the glasses, the
cutlery, everything. He had washed them all up and dried
them and put them back in the cupboards and shelves and
drawers where they belonged.

He checked his watch. It was 8:09 p.m., on the evening
of September 7. Yesterday, when he had cooked and eaten
his spaghetti Bolognese, it had been September 6. So this
wasn't yesterday. Not according to his watch, anyhow.

He went into the living room and switched on the TV. He
changed the channel to K-Cal 9 and the dateline on that, too,
was September 7. Letitia Brown was announcing that a forty-
two-year-old Caucasian man had been found in Covina,
minus his head. Only two hours later, a disembodied head
had been discovered six miles away, in Glendora, but it was
that of a twenty-nine-year-old African-American woman.
One head, one body, but they didn't match.

Jim looked down at Tibbles, who was still expectantly
licking his lips. 'What the hell is going on here, Tibbles? You
saw me wash those dishes. You saw me tidy everything up
before I left. Who's been here? Who's been sleeping in my
bed?' He paused, and then he said, 'Jesus. I sound like
Goldilocks.'

Tibbles, of course, said nothing. Jim opened up a can of
organic chicken for him and spooned it into his bowl. Then,
tired as he was, he lifted all of the dishes out of the kitchen
sink, filled it with hot water, and started to wash up.

When he had finished, he took a bottle of Fat Tire out of
the fridge and sat down on the couch, but he kept the television on mute. Since it was the first day of the new semester,
and the first day was always bruising, he had been planning
to reward himself this evening with a takeout Japanese supper

from Murakami, maybe some sashimi and some braised pork
belly in shoyu broth, which was his favorite. But he didn't
feel at all hungry any more. He felt disoriented and anxious
and as mashed-up inside as Tibbles had been this morning,
when he had run him over.

He was one hundred per cent certain that he had washed
up those dishes. He was equally sure that he had meticu-
lously tidied his bed. But if somebody else had been here,
who the hell was it, and how had he found the time to cook
himself spaghetti Bolognese and eat it and sleep for long
enough to mess up the bed and take a shower, too? And how
had he managed to sneak out of his apartment without Jim
catching even a glimpse of him?

Jim was still sitting with his head bowed in front of the
silent television when there was a buzz at his front door. He
waited for almost half a minute, but then there was another
buzz, and another. He cursed under his breath, put down his
bottle of beer and shuffled out into the hallway.

'Who is it?' he called out.

'It's me, Jee-yum! *C'est moi!* I brought a little treat for
our miracle cat!'

He opened the door. It was Mrs LaFarge, wrapped up in
a black candlewick robe, with a floppy hood and black
sunglasses, so that she looked like the Wicked Witch of the
West. She was holding a Tupperware box which contained
something dark and bloody. Behind her, out in the night, the
trees were surging like the ocean.

'Chopped chicken livers,' she said triumphantly. 'I know
how much he loves them.'

'You do?'

'Well, of course. I always save him a few morsels whenever I'm making my liver pâté.'

Tibbles appeared, with his tail waving, and gave Mrs
LaFarge a sweet, ingratiating mew. 'Here, Tibbles!' said
Mrs LaFarge. 'Look what your *marraine* has brought for
you! *Foies de poulet*, you lucky cat! You *very* lucky cat!'

'Mrs LaFarge . . .' Jim began.

'Pssh!' said Mrs LaFarge. 'It is nothing at all. *C'est rien.*
He has been smiled upon by God, and he deserves a treat.
All I can say is, it's a pity about the funeral. I love a funeral,

don't you? It does one so much good to cry.'

'Mrs LaFarge—'

'Pssh! When you came down this afternoon and told me that Tibbles had come back to life, I was so delighted. You are right, Jim. It *is* a miracle. And as you said, who are we to question things that we do not really understand, nor have any hope of understanding?'

Jim said, very slowly, 'I came down this afternoon and told you that Tibbles had come back to life?'

Mrs LaFarge took off her sunglasses, and prodded Jim with her finger. 'Don't pretend that you have forgotten already! What a joker you are! I don't know why you didn't tell me when you first brought him home in that basket. I know you were still worried that he might not survive, but you could have told me!'

She bent forward and tickled Tibbles under the chin. 'I am his godmother, after all, am I not? His *marraine*?'

SIX

After Mrs LaFarge had left, Jim closed his front door and stood with his back to it for a few moments, holding the Tupperware box of chopped chicken livers. Tibbles came up to him and stared at him.

'So, Tibs – *you* were here this afternoon,' said Jim. 'When exactly did I come home and go downstairs and tell Mrs LaFarge about your miraculous resurrection? I distinctly recall that I was at college all afternoon. I was conducting a class on the incomprehensible musings of Michael McClure. How could I have come back here?'

Tibbles continued to stare at him. Then, after a while, he turned away, went back into the living room, and jumped up on to the couch.

Jim found a space in the fridge for the Tupperware box. He felt light-headed and swimmy, as if he were drunk, or as if he had been smoking something that he had confiscated from one of his students. He had asked Mrs LaFarge when he had come down to tell her about Tibbles, and she had insisted that it was two thirty-five, give or take a minute or two, because she had just started watching *Guiding Light*.

'You're sure it was then?' Jim had repeated. 'You're absolutely sure?'

'Of course I am sure. I never miss one moment of *Guiding Light*, but your news was much more important. Your news was like a message from heaven.'

'And you're sure it was me?'

'Oh, you are always teasing me, Jim.'

He went into the living room and picked up the phone. He had written the number of Cedars-Sinai emergency room on the back of a folded envelope. He dialed it, and waited while it rang.

'I didn't come back here this afternoon,' he told Tibbles. 'All right, I have this gift, I can see ghosts and stuff. But I can't be in two places at the same time.'

Tibbles was already asleep, but he wouldn't have answered him, even if he had been awake.

'Emergency Room, can I help you?'

'Oh, yes. My name is Jim Rook. I'm a member of the faculty at West Grove Community College, and I'm enquiring about a student of mine, Maria Lopez. She was taken into the ER around four o'clock this afternoon.'

'Maria Lopez?'

'Yes, I'm her English teacher. She had an accident and got herself pretty badly cut up. I'm just wondering how she is.'

'Wait up a moment, please.'

Jim waited and waited. He could hear ambulance sirens in the background, and somebody shouting. Then the receptionist picked up the phone again and said, 'You're sure she was brought to Cedars-Sinai?'

'Absolutely. That's what the paramedics told me. I sent her mother there, too.'

'Well, I'm sorry, Mr Rook, there is nobody of that name here.'

'Are you quite sure about that? Maybe she was registered under another name. She's Hispanic, aged seventeen. She had lacerations and bruises all over.'

'No, sir, we have received no admissions of that description, not today. Two young Hispanic boys with serious knife-wounds, that's all.'

'OK, thanks.'

Jim hung up. This didn't make any kind of sense at all. He was sure that the paramedics had told him that they were taking Maria to Cedars-Sinai. But maybe they had decided to take her to another hospital which was closer, or which specialized in reconstructive surgery, or which would take her in if she was uninsured.

He found the card that Lieutenant Harris had given him and called Detective Wong. It took the detective nearly a half-minute to answer, and when he did his voice echoed as if he were sitting in the men's room.

'Detective Wong? This is Jim Rook, from West Grove Community College.'

'Who?'

'Jim Rook. We met this afternoon, when Maria Lopez got herself hurt.'

'Who?'

'Maria Lopez. The girl who got herself all cut up.'

'I'm sorry, Mr Whatever-your-name-is—'

'Rook. Like in the bird.'

'Well, I'm sorry Mr Rook-like-in-the-bird, I don't have the least idea what you're talking about.'

'Didn't you come out to West Grove this afternoon, with your partner? What's her name, Detective Madison? Lieutenant Harris was there, too. One of my students was seriously hurt, Maria Lopez. Either somebody attacked her, or she got herself caught up in some kind of machinery.'

There was a lengthy pause, accompanied by a hollow rattle which sounded like a toilet-roll. Then Detective Wong said, 'No, sir. I wasn't called out to any incident like that, not today. I was catching up on paperwork for most of the afternoon.'

'You *are* Detective Wong who has a red and green plaid coat?'

'That's right. But I absolutely did not come out to West Grove Community College this afternoon and I know nothing at all about any Maria Lopez.'

Jim couldn't think what else to say. He hung up the phone and stood in the middle of the living room feeling as if he were going mad. He almost felt like banging his head against the wall, just to prove to himself that he wasn't having a nightmare.

'Come on, Jim,' he told himself. 'There has to be *some* explanation for this.'

He rummaged under the couch and pulled out a dog-eared copy of the yellow pages. Then he picked up the phone again and called every hospital with an emergency room within a twenty-mile radius – starting with Kaiser Permanente on Sunset Boulevard and then working his way through Santa Monica Medical Clinic, Glendale Memorial, and even the Brotman in Culver City.

He located a Susanna Lopez, who had suffered third-degree burns in an auto wreck on the Hollywood Freeway. He also found a Michael Lopez, who worked at B&B Lumber

in North Hollywood and had cut off his thumb and two
fingers with a circular saw. Then he discovered a Dorothea
Lopez, who had suffered a heart attack at her home in Boyle
Heights, and fallen downstairs, breaking her hip. But after
ringing round eleven hospitals, he could find no trace of any
Maria Lopez.

He thought of calling Dr Ehrlichman, but by now it was
nearly midnight, and what could Dr Ehrlichman do? Even
if he knew where Maria had been taken, he would be majorly
ratty at being disturbed so late, and if he didn't know any
more about Maria than Detective Wong did, or the emergency department at Cedars-Sinai, he would think that Jim
was finally ready for the nuthouse.

Jim opened the fridge and took out another bottle of Fat
Tire. It was his last, so he would have to buy more tomorrow.
Maybe he should give it up. Maybe it contained some secret
ingredient that gave him hallucinations, because right *there*
on the shelf in front of him was the Tupperware box full of
chopped chicken livers, and that was incontrovertible proof
that somebody had told Mrs LaFarge that Tibbles had been
resurrected. Somebody who looked like him. Somebody who
knew what he knew. Somebody, for all he knew, who *was*
him. A *doppelgänger*.

While he drank his beer, he switched on his laptop and
Googled *Kwisin*. There were very few references to it (or
her, or whatever she was.) But he came across a PDF of a
memoir entitled *Folk-tales and Mysticism in Korea*, written
in the 1950s by an English anthropologist called Peregrine
Fellows.

In his chapter on Ghosts And Demons, Fellows had written,
'*Kwisin* are the ghosts of women who have not married
before their death. They haunt their relatives every night,
keening and crying for them to arrange a marriage for them,
so that they can find eternal peace. It is said that, occasionally, their relatives manage to effect this, especially if they
are able to find a man from a far-off town or village who
has not heard of the woman's passing.

'For some considerable time after her death, a *Kwisin* can
sustain a physical form, so that she will be indistinguishable

to her unsuspecting husband from a living woman. As time goes by, however, she will sleep longer and longer every night until she never wakes at all. She will, however, have found peace in the spirit world.

'If her relatives fail to marry her, however, she will increasingly take on a demonic shape, such as a dog or a fox or a hawk, and she will take her revenge on a world that has deprived her of happiness and peace by preying on the souls of those who have met a premature death, in particular other unmarried women and those who have died by their own hand.

'She will deliberately encourage the separation of those couples who are betrothed, by whispering lies to each partner about the other's faithfulness; and she will deliberately encourage suicides by showing vulnerable and depressive people that their future lives will be filled with nothing but sickness and despair.'

That was all about Kwisin. The rest of the chapter was devoted to ghosts who haunted people who were unwise enough to travel through the mountains at night; and to the ghosts of Sŏn Masters, Zen Buddhist monks who had found a way through to 'the Great Way that has no gate.'

Jim was too tired to make any sense of the higher concepts of Zen, so he switched off his laptop and snapped it shut. Tibbles had been sleeping and he opened his eyes in annoyance.

Before he went to bed Jim changed the sheets and the pillowslips. Even if the only other person who had slept in them was a double of himself, he didn't relish the idea of sharing somebody else's sweaty bedclothes. As he stood in front of the bathroom basin, brushing his teeth, he peered at his reflection intently to make sure that it was really him, but he couldn't detect any differences from the usual him. No moles, no scars, no additional gray hairs.

It took him over an hour to get to sleep. He kept hearing noises like somebody walking around the living room, and opening the fridge door in the kitchen. Twice he got out of bed to make sure that no intruders had forced their way into his apartment. Both times he found that all the windows were locked and the security chain on the front door was still fastened. Tibbles was still lying on the couch, purring like a death-rattle.

He lay in bed staring at the ceiling. If he had imagined what had happened to Maria Lopez, maybe he had imagined the whole day, from start to finish. Maybe he hadn't killed Tibbles at all. Maybe he hadn't gone to college and marked the register. Maybe he had imagined all of those new students – T.D. and Arthur Watt and Janice Sticky and Teddy Greenspan. But how was that possible?

He fell asleep, but after what seemed like only a few minutes he jerked violently and opened his eyes. The digital clock beside his bed said 2:37 a.m. and it was still dark outside. He lay there for a while, listening, wondering what it was that had woken him up. His knees and his elbows ached, and his nose was clogged up, as if he had a cold. He *felt* cold, too. In fact he was so cold that he was shivering, and he reached down the bed and dragged the red woolen throw up to his neck.

Something was wrong with him. Something was badly wrong. He lifted his head from the pillow and his neck creaked, as if he had been lying in a draft. He didn't want to get out of bed but he urgently needed to take a leak. He felt that if he didn't go to the bathroom immediately, he would wet his shorts.

'Goddammit,' he cursed under his breath. He tried to swing both of his legs out of bed but his knees hurt him so much that he could only manage one leg at a time. When his feet were on the carpet he heaved himself up and hobbled toward the bathroom door. He felt terrible. Not just aching, but exhausted.

He barely made it to the toilet, but when he did, he managed only three or four spurts. He stood there, waiting, feeling as if he wanted to pee some more, but he simply couldn't.

He flushed the toilet and went over to the basin to wash his hands. When he saw himself in the mirror, however, his knees gave way, and he had to grab the edge of the basin to stop himself from collapsing on to the floor.

The face in the mirror was that of an elderly man, at least eighty-five years old. His hair was sparse, and what there was of it was wild and white. His eyes were red-rimmed and watery, and his cheeks were sunken. There were deep lines all around his mouth as if his lips had been sewn together by head-hunters. His chin was covered in white stubble, and his neck was wrinkled.

'That's it,' he said. 'Now I *know* I'm having a nightmare.' He turned his head to the right, and the old man in the mirror turned his head to the left. He nodded his head up and down and the old man did that, too.

'I'm thirty-five years old,' he insisted. 'You are not me. I don't know who the hell you are, but you are not me.'

When he spoke, the old man moved his lips to mime what he was saying; and when he reached up and touched his cheek, the old man copied him.

'*You cannot be me!*' he shouted, although his voice was thin and strained, just like an old man's voice. '*You cannot be me!*'

He lowered his head. On the shelf above the basin he saw a green plastic mug caked with toothpaste. It contained a toothbrush with splayed-out bristles and a crumpled tube of Blanx. On the other side of the shelf there were seven or eight bottles of tablets. He reached out and picked up the nearest, which was labeled Lorazepam. He knew that Lorazepam was prescribed for panic attacks, but he had never taken it in his life.

It was then that he looked at his hand. His skin was wrinkled and liver-spotted, and his nails were chalky, with deep ridges in them. He dropped the bottle of Lorazepam in the basin, and held up both of his hands in front of his face, staring at them in horror. He was old – at least fifty years older than when he went to bed. How could he be so old? Not only that, he was *sick*, too. He picked up one medicine bottle after another, and saw that he had tablets for arthritis, high blood pressure, heart arrhythmia, ulcers and gout.

There was no doubt that they had been prescribed for him, either. Each bottle was clearly marked James Rook, although he had never heard of the doctor, S. Fabrizzi, MD, with an address on Sunset Boulevard.

Jim left the bathroom and shuffled across the corridor and into his living room. It smelled stale and stuffy, and when he switched on the lights he saw why. The windows were all covered in thick brown drapes, and the air-conditioning unit was turned off. He didn't recognize any of the furniture. There was a heavy armchair, upholstered in worn brown velveteen; a grubby yellow couch with heaps of old newspapers on it; and a cheap upright dining chair with a red vinyl seat.

The carpet was filthy and threadbare, and there were stacks of magazines and newspapers everywhere, as well as brown paper grocery sacks from Ralph's, dozens and dozens of them, all neatly folded.

Jim went across to the window and pulled back the drapes. Outside, on the balcony, there were five or six terracotta pots with dead plants in them, including a ghost-like yucca, and an ivy that trailed across the floor like the tentacles of a stranded squid.

He tried to switch on the air-conditioning, but the knob dropped off on to the floor, and when he looked closer he could see that the unit's connecting wires were frayed and hanging adrift. He left the knob where it was. His back was too stiff for him to bend over and pick it up.

He limped slowly around the room. He knew *where* he was. He was still in his third-floor apartment on Briarcliff Road, although it looked as if he hadn't redecorated it in twenty years or more. The walls were streaked with grimy gray condensation, and the chandelier was thickly furred with dust. It looked as though he hadn't thrown anything away for twenty years, either. Not just newspapers and magazines and grocery sacks, but empty boxes of painkillers and indigestion tablets, as well as carefully creased candy wrappers and envelopes and flyers from local pizza restaurants.

He knew *where* this was, but he didn't know *when*. It appeared to be sometime in his own future, but there was no way for him to tell if he was dreaming, or hallucinating, or if he was suffering from amnesia, and had lived through the past half-century day by day and year by year but had simply forgotten it all.

He turned around. He was wheezing with effort, and he made his way over to the heavy brown armchair. He was just about to sit down, however, when he realized that there was a white plastic cushion-cover on the seat, stained with yellow. So not only had he lost most of his hair, and not only was he suffering from anxiety attacks, and arthritis, and a half-dozen other complaints, but he was incontinent, too.

He stood swaying in the middle of the living room and he thought: *If this is real, if I really have arrived at the age of eighty-plus and this is what my life is like, then I'm going to go back into that bathroom and take every single tablet on that shelf.*

He started back toward the bathroom, but then he stopped, holding on to the back of the couch for support. He couldn't count on it, but there might be a bottle of Fat Tire in the fridge to wash the tablets down his throat, if they were still brewing Fat Tire after all these years. If not, he would have to make do with soda or a glass of water, or whatever he could find.

He was halfway to the kitchen when he saw a dark gray blur crossing the kitchen doorway, as if somebody had flashed past it, so quickly that they were almost invisible. He heard the front door open, and for a moment he felt the briefest of warm drafts. Then he heard it close again.

'Who's that?' he shouted, in that thin, reedy voice. God, he sounded like his own grandfather, George. 'You come back here, whoever you are! You just come back here!'

He hurried as fast as he could manage into the hallway. The security chain beside the front door was hanging loose, and still swinging. He tugged open the door, which was stiff for lack of oil. Right next to it stood an umbrella stand with four or five walking sticks in it. He lifted one of them out, a heavy ebony cane with an elephant's head carved on the top of it, and stepped out on to the landing.

'Who's there?' he called out. 'You come right back here and show yourself!'

The light at the far end of the landing was broken, so the steps that led down to the second story were swallowed in deep shadow. Jim strained his eyes to see if there was anybody there, but it was far too dark, and he suddenly realized that his eyesight wasn't too good, either.

'Whoever you are, you come out where I can see you!' he demanded.

He waited, his lungs wheezing like a worn-out concertina, but there was no movement in the darkness. Whoever it was, they must be long gone. But as he turned to go back inside, he heard a slithering, scratching sound coming from the steps.

'I hear you!' he said. 'I know you're there! You come on out!'

He felt frail, and as vulnerable as if he were made of out of nothing but folded paper. He had to grip the railing with his left hand to keep himself steady. But for some reason he felt less afraid than he had ever felt in his life. And *angrier*, too.

'Don't think you can get away, you yegg!' he shouted. 'You come back here you son-of-a-bitch and show yourself!'

For over a quarter of a minute, all Jim could hear was distant traffic, and the rumble of a faraway airliner. Then he heard that scratching again, and that slithering, as if some kind of animal were slowly climbing the steps. He held the railing tightly in his left hand and lifted the ebony cane in his right. He realized now why he wasn't afraid. He wasn't afraid because he was so old, and he didn't really care whether he lived or died. Less than a couple of minutes ago, he had even *wanted* to die.

But he also realized why he was so angry. Whoever had broken into his apartment had taken advantage of an old man's vulnerability, *his* vulnerability. His age may mean that he was sick, and feeble, and incontinent, but he still deserved respect.

'What?' he demanded. 'Are you chicken-shit or something?' He swung the cane around and around, so that it whistled, even though his elbow gave a painful *click* every time he swung it. 'Too damned scared to show yourself?'

It was then that he realized that two slanted yellow eyes were looking at him from just above the top step. He stopped swinging the cane and took two steps backward, until he was close to his open front door. The yellow eyes rose higher, as the creature climbed further up the steps. It was still in shadow, so Jim couldn't yet see what kind of a creature it was, but he could tell that it was very big, and from the way it was steadily coming nearer, it didn't seem to be afraid of him at all.

He heard claws tip-tapping along the tiled floor toward him, and he was just about to stumble back into his apartment and slam the door when the creature stepped into the light. To his shock, it wasn't a creature at all, but what appeared to be a woman. She was dressed in a shiny robe of slate-gray silk that reached right down to her feet, and which made a slithering sound as she walked. On her head she was wearing a tall black wide-brimmed hat, rather like the Puritans used to wear, but with a dark smoky veil underneath it. All that Jim could see of her face was that her eyes looked like two black smudges, more like holes than eyes, and that her skin was very white.

She stopped in front of his door, with both her hands tucked into her sleeves.

'Erm . . . hi,' said Jim. He couldn't think of anything else.

The woman said nothing. The night breeze stirred her veil, and Jim thought that he saw her face change, as if it were a white screen on which different images were being projected. For a fleeting moment, it looked animal-like, a dog or a fox.

Jim cleared his throat. 'Was that you in my apartment just now?' he asked her. He was holding his cane tightly in both hands, in case she wasn't as harmless as she looked. 'If it was, I have to admit that you scared me.'

The woman was silent for a long time. Then she said, '*Nomu palgayo. Mot chayo. Chamyonso, gumulkkwoyo.*' Her voice was high, but it was blurry and indistinct, like somebody talking in their sleep.

'I'm sorry,' said Jim. 'I don't understand you. What language is that?'

Again, the woman didn't reply. Underneath her veil, her face appeared to alter, again and again, but it could have been nothing but the smoky chiffon, stirring in the wind.

'Were you here, inside my kitchen?' he repeated. 'What were you looking for? What did you want?' He paused. 'Were you looking for *me*?'

Without a word, the woman pushed past him and into the open door of his apartment. Her silk robe slid against his hands and it was slippery and cold. '*Hey!*' he protested. He took a step back and almost lost his balance. He lifted his

cane, but what was he going to do, hit her with it? She slithered along the corridor until she reached his bedroom.

'Excuse me, ma'am, but where exactly do you think you're
going?' Jim asked her. 'You really need to get out of here,
now. Like, exit, stage right.'

She stood staring at him, as if she expected him to follow
her. Then, without any further hesitation, she disappeared
into his bedroom door.

Jim went after her. When he reached his bedroom, he saw
that she was standing on the opposite side of his bed, waiting
for him.

'I don't know what the hell you think you're doing here,'
he told her. 'I don't have anything worth stealing, so far as
I can make out.'

The woman drew her left arm out of her right sleeve and
pointed stiffly to the bed. She was wearing gray leather
gloves, but instead of having five separate fingers they were
divided only in two, and each half was very long, more than
two inches longer than a normal finger.

'You want *sex*?' Jim asked her. 'I'm a little too decrepit
for that, I'm afraid. Besides, I hardly know you.'

The woman continued to point at the bed with her gray
cleft glove. Then she raised her right glove, and pointed at
Jim.

'You want me to lie down on the bed? Is that it?'

Still the woman didn't speak, but she kept on rigidly
pointing with both arms, as if she were sending a semaphore
signal.

'I think I'm going to call the police,' Jim told her. 'It
seems to me like you've managed to escape from someplace
that you seriously need to go back to.'

He went across to the nightstand and picked up the phone.
Right next to it, there was a glass tumbler with a dental
bridge soaking in it. Until now, Jim hadn't realized that he
had three molars missing at the back of his lower jaw.

He held up the receiver and said, 'This is your last chance,
OK? If you leave here nice and quiet, I'll forget that you ever
pushed your way in here. Otherwise, I'm sorry, it's the cops.'

He waited, but the woman stayed where she was, still
pointing.

'I'm real sorry that I have to do this,' he said. 'It's not like I want to get you into any trouble. But you don't leave me any choice, do you?'

He prodded 911, but the instant he did it, the woman let out a screech that sounded like a hundred animals having their legs torn off – agonized, but hoarse with rage. It was so unexpected and so deafening that Jim staggered backward against the nightstand, and the bedside lamp toppled on to the floor.

The woman's screeching went on and on, relentlessly, and she didn't pause once to take a breath. As she screeched, she started to grow, both in height and in bulk. Underneath her veil, her face changed in shape, becoming narrower and longer and more pointed, like a fox, and behind the chiffon her eyes gleamed a septic yellow. Her black hat toppled backward, her veil fell away, and her gray silk robe burst open. Her gloves exploded to reveal four long claws on each of her hands. Now Jim could see that she wasn't a woman at all, but a huge black-haired creature – a creature that became taller with every second, until its head was almost touching the bedroom ceiling.

It had a snout like a fox, and staring eyes like a fox, and it had pointed ears like a fox, too. But it also had curved incisors and two twisted black horns between its ears. It stank of wood smoke and incense and dried blood – the unmistakable stench of hell, no matter what religion had created it.

Jim knew that it was a demon, although he didn't know its name or where it had come from or what it was looking for. He could guess, though. Almost all demons were hungry for human souls, because the more human souls they could devour, the more powerful they became, and the more pleasure they derived from their victims' endless suffering. He stood in his shabby bedroom looking up at this black bristling creature and for the first time in his life he felt as if his insides had turned to water. He wasn't afraid of dying. He didn't relish it, but everybody had to die sometime and he had woken up tonight so old and sick. What terrified him was the prospect of his soul being trapped by this demon for ever, never knowing peace, never knowing an end to darkness and cruelty and pain. What terrified him was the prospect of being dragged around for eternity, with hooks in his intestines, jolting and bumping over the rough hot cinders of hell, screaming for mercy.

The creature gave another deafening screech, although this time it sounded less like a hundred tortured animals and more like a hundred tortured men. Jim ducked down and tried to dodge toward the door, but the creature swung its arm and hit him on the shoulder, tearing through his T-shirt and ripping his skin – a blow so hard that Jim was knocked sideways back on to the bed.

He tried to scramble across the bed to the opposite side, but the creature struck his other shoulder, and then his hip, and then his chest, so that he was winded. His T-shirt was in tatters and the bedsheet was sprayed with droplets of blood.

'*Get off me!*' he coughed. '*Get the hell off me!*'

But now the creature reared up at the end of the bed, snarling and spitting, with strings of mucus swaying from its lower jaw. It was still swelling larger and larger, and it felt to Jim as if it were filling up the whole bedroom. The stench of wood smoke and dried blood was overwhelming, and it filled his lungs with every gasping breath, almost choking him.

The creature leaned over him at an impossible angle, and he could feel its bristles prickling against his legs. Wincing with fear, he looked up into its face, and it was almost laughably grotesque, as if an oriental artist had set out to create the most hideous and frightening monster that he could. It looked as if a fox had mated with a bear, and the bear had mated with a bull, and all three of them had been possessed by some mad vengeful spirit that was screaming for human blood.

He closed his eyes tight, praying that the creature wouldn't hurt him too much. The creature screeched again, and he could feel its chilly breath and its flying spit against his face.

'Oh God,' he said, between gritted teeth. 'God, take care of me, won't you?'

It was then that darkness fell on him, as if the night sky had collapsed like a huge black circus tent.

SEVEN

A voice very close to his ear said, '*Jimmy?*'
He opened one eye. It must have been at least five in the morning because the white calico blind was already beginning to brighten, and he could hear birds chirping outside his window. He opened the other eye, and turned his head, and there, lying so close to him that he could hardly focus on her, was Summer.

'Summer?' he croaked. His mouth felt parched.

'Hey . . . you're awake,' she smiled, touching the tip of his nose with her finger.

He sat up. Summer was wearing a sleeveless yellow T-shirt and a pair of white satin shorts and that was all. She wasn't wearing make-up, either. He had never seen her looking so fresh-faced and young. She looked more like a high-school cheerleader than a Hollywood pole-dancer.

'What happened?' he asked her. He held out both of his hands and turned them this way and that. No wrinkles, no liver-spots, no deeply furrowed fingernails. 'God almighty, what did I do?'

Summer smiled and sat up, too. 'You were screaming.'

'*Screaming?*' He looked down at his Mr Natural T-shirt. It was faded, but it wasn't ripped, or spattered with blood.

Summer said, 'Even Mrs LaFarge could hear you. She wanted me to call the paramedics, but I said you were probably having a nightmare, that's all. I came up here and your door was wide open and I came in and found you on the bed. You looked like you were having a fight with somebody. You know – waving your arms around, kicking your legs.'

'And screaming?'

Summer nodded. 'I didn't know you had it in you. Like, eat your heart out, what was his name? That singer. I think he's dead now.'

Jim swung his legs out of bed and found that he could do it easily. 'Was I screaming anything comprehensible?'

'Unh-hunh. You weren't cursing or nothing like that.'

'I mean, could you understand what I was saying?'

'I don't know. Something like "get off me!", and "go away!" But you were really going crazy. That's why I stayed here, to calm you down.'

'You've been here all night?'

'Pretty much. I didn't want anything to happen to you, you know, like swallowing your tongue or something.'

Jim felt as if he had the mother and father of all hangovers, although he couldn't remember drinking more than three beers last night – two at the Cat'n'Fiddle and one here at home. He looked around the bedroom. It looked just like normal. Its off-white carpet was reasonably clean, with only one red-wine stain on it, in the shape of the Baja peninsula; and it was reasonably tidy, except for a stack of books beside the bed – the books he always picked up before he went to sleep, but never managed to finish. *Swann's Way*, by Marcel Proust; *A Fire on the Moon*, by Norman Mailer; and *Midnight's Children* by Salman Rushdie.

Summer climbed off the bed and stood up and stretched. Jim said, 'I don't know what the hell could have been wrong with me. I wasn't drunk. I don't remember getting drunk, anyhow. I only had one beer in the house.'

Summer came up to him and ruffled his hair, as if he were a kid. 'Who knows? Maybe you're worried about going back to college. I get nightmares sometimes before I start a new job. Did I tell you I got a job at Le Pothole? I didn't, did I? Isn't that great?'

Jim looked up at her. 'Le Poteau? That new pole-dancing club on Cahuenga? Yes, you did. Congratulations. You start tonight, don't you?'

'No, tomorrow night. Today I have to have my nails polished, and my Brazilian Brazilled. Mr Subinski said I have to look one hundred per cent perfect. He's the owner, Mr Subinski. He's like *such* a perfectionist.'

'You didn't have your nails done yet?'

'No. I'm going this morning. Why?'

Jim stood up. For a moment he felt giddy, and he swayed.

'Hey, are you OK?' Summer asked him, laying her hand on his shoulder. 'You look like death warmed over.'

'No, I'm fine. Just a little disoriented, that's all. What day is it?'

'Tuesday.'

'Tuesday? It can't be Tuesday.'

'Jimmy, it's Tuesday. Why would I lie to you?'

'I don't know. Of course you wouldn't. Why would you? But how can it be Tuesday? Yesterday was Tuesday. I ran over Tibbles yesterday when I was backing out of the driveway, and squashed him.'

'Oh, *yuck*! You ran him over and you squashed him? You didn't tell me that!'

'I ran him over and squashed him but then I went to college and this Korean kid came in and he was carrying Tibbles in a cat basket and Tibbles was OK.'

Summer was staring at him with her little nose wrinkled up, as if he were talking to her in a foreign language. 'Jimmy, listen to me. You didn't go to college yesterday. Yesterday you went to the market. You went to Ralph's. I saw you coming back with all of your shopping. College doesn't start back until today. You told me that yourself. You said you were dreading it. Those were your actual words. Another fifteen sickos, that's what you said.'

'Sickos? Oh – you mean illiterates.'

'Ill, sick, what's the difference? You said you wouldn't mind changing jobs.'

'I remember. At least I think I do. But I thought I said that this morning, just before I left for college and ran over Tibbles.'

'But you *didn't* run over Tibbles. Look.'

Jim turned toward the half-open bedroom door, and there, watching him, was Tibbles. He didn't usually wake up this early, but he had obviously heard voices and his curiosity had gotten the better of him.

'You were right,' he told Summer. 'I think I was having a nightmare. Thanks for taking care of me. You didn't have to.'

Summer kissed his cheek. 'I know I didn't. But I like you, as it happens, and even if you're crazy you always smell nice.'

Jim looked at her, standing against the sunlit blind. She made him feel old. Not as old as he had felt in his nightmare, but she was at least ten years younger than he was.

'You want some coffee?' he asked her.

She shook her head. 'So long as you're OK now, I'd better get back downstairs.'

'Well . . . thanks again for everything. I really appreciate it. And good luck with the job.'

'You have to come see me. I could wangle you a pass. I'm really good. When I was dancing at the VIP Club at Xes, Kiefer Sutherland said I was fourble-jointed. Well – he *looked* like Kiefer Sutherland. It could have been his double.'

Jim opened the front door for her. Outside, the air was filled with a gilded mist, and it was already warm. Summer gave him another kiss and then she tippy-toed barefoot along the landing.

'Summer!' he called after her.

She turned around at the top of the steps. Her hair was shining and her eyes were bright.

'Nothing,' he said. 'Just – you know – thanks.'

He made himself a mug of espresso and switched on the TV news. There was no question about it, this was September 7, the first day of the fall semester. In other words, it was yesterday. The news was the same as it had been yesterday – an unexpected drop in share prices, an airplane crash outside of Juneau, Alaska, four people dead – but there were so many inconsistencies that Jim felt as if his life had been disassembled and put back together in a totally different order.

For instance, Mrs LaFarge's Tupperware box of chicken livers was still in the fridge, and there were no cans of Instinctive Choice shrimp left in the larder, because Tibbles had eaten the last one yesterday. Or today, or whenever it was. There were no more bottles of Fat Tire in the fridge, either. So even if this *were* yesterday, it wasn't an identical yesterday. It was more like an alternative yesterday.

Jim took a long shower, and then sat naked on the end of his unmade bed, his head bowed, cooling off and thinking. He couldn't believe that the demon who had visited him last night had been nothing but a nightmare. It had been far too real, far too frightening. Even his worst nightmares had never been as frightening as that woman who had turned into a fox-creature. He could still feel its bristles.

The creature had left no traces behind. Jim's T-shirt wasn't torn, and he had no claw marks on his shoulders and arms. But then the demon hadn't attacked him as he was now. It had attacked him as he was going to be, when he was over eighty years old. Maybe it was lying in wait for him, sometime in his future. Maybe he had been given a premonition, or a warning.

But why? And what about Maria Lopez? Had she been attacked in the future, too? But if she had, how had she managed to come back to the past, or the present, or whatever yesterday had been? And if she wasn't in the ER at Cedars-Sinai, where was she?

Woody Allen once said that mankind has reached a crossroads. One path leads to despair and utter hopelessness. The other path leads to total extinction. Jim was beginning to agree with him.

When he went to the front door, Tibbles immediately ran toward him, and stood waiting for him to open it.

'If you think I'm going to let you get out this time, you have another thing coming,' Jim told him. 'Now stay, you got it? Stay!'

Tibbles looked away, as if '*stay!*' was an order that applied only to dogs, and certainly not to him.

Jim opened the door. Tibbles made a rush for it, but Jim snatched his collar and swung him back inside.

'I don't know how many lives you have left, but you're not wasting another one, OK?'

Tibbles gave him a venomous look and stalked back into the kitchen, his tail erect.

'I'll see you this evening,' Jim called after him. 'Don't worry if I'm late. I may stop off at the Cat'n'Fiddle for a drink on my way home. Or maybe I'll go to The Happy Ending instead.'

He went down the steps. As he was walking past Summer's apartment, her door opened and she came bouncing out.

'Hi, Jimmy! How are you feeling? Gotten over the screaming meemies?'

'I hope so. Maybe I was just suffering from pre-semester stress. Anyhow, thanks for taking care of me.'

'Tibbles safely locked up? You don't want to squash him a second time even if you didn't squash him a first time.'

'No, he's safe inside. Have a good day, won't you?'

'You too. And listen, don't worry too much about those ill people. You'll be OK. You've been teaching for *how* long?'

'Now you *are* making me feel old.'

Summer kissed him on the cheek. 'You're not old, Jimmy. You're not old at all.'

'Well, thanks. That's made me feel better.'

'You're just, like, *mature*.'

He waited until Summer had driven off in her yellow Beetle before he climbed into his car. He switched on the engine and the air-conditioning, and while the interior gradually cooled down, he climbed out again and went down on his hands and knees to check underneath. He knew for sure that he hadn't allowed Tibbles to escape, but after what had happened yesterday, or today, or whenever it was, he didn't trust his own perception.

He was still on his hands and knees when Mrs LaFarge came down the steps.

'Jee-yum!' she exclaimed. 'Did you lose something? Or are you praying to Mecca?'

He stood up, smacking the knees of his navy blue chinos to get the dust off. 'Hi, Violette. No – I was just making sure that I wasn't leaking oil.'

'You are feeling better now? After last night? It is many years since I heard anybody scream like that – a fellow who cut his own hand off with a chainsaw. I was going to call for an ambulance.'

'I'm fine now, Violette. I think it was something I ate.'

'Pff! To me, it sounded much more as if you were having *un cauchemar terrifiant* – a really scary nightmare. I am an old lady, Jim. I can tell the difference between terror and indigestion.'

'Thanks for your concern, but I'm fine now. Really. I have
to get to college.'

'Ah, yes. The empty flagons will be waiting for you to
fill them with knowledge.'

Before he got back into his car, Jim looked across at Mrs
LaFarge and he had the distinct feeling that she *knew* what
had happened to him – that she knew about him running
over Tibbles and bringing him back alive. But behind her
black insect-like sunglasses her expression gave nothing
away. All she said was, '*Bonne chance*, Jim. Maybe I will
see you this evening, and you can describe to me what a
great struggle your day was.'

He backed out of the sloping drive into Briarcliff Road.
As he drove along Hollywood Boulevard he played Robbie
Robertson singing 'Somewhere Down the Crazy River' on
his stereo. 'Yeah . . . that's when time stood still . . . you
know, I think I'm going to go down to Madam X and let
her read my mind . . . but she said . . . "That voodoo stuff
don't do nothing for me."'

He turned into the gates of West Grove College and drove
straight into the space reserved for Royston Denman, the
head of mathematics, because his Mercury was eighteen feet
long and six feet wide and he could park in Royston Denman's
space without a whole lot of complicated manoeuvreing. He
collected his brown canvas bag and joined the motley tide
of students who were pouring in through the main entrance.
They reminded him of extras in a movie about teenagers
who had been taken over by aliens. Or maybe he was getting
old.

Yesterday (or today, or whenever it was) he had thought
about turning around and walking out of the college and
never coming back, but today (or tomorrow, or whenever it
was) he knew that he couldn't do that. He had to find out
what had happened to Maria Lopez. And it was equally urgent
to find out what was happening to *him*.

As he walked along the corridor toward Special Class Two,
he could hear his new students up ahead of him, laughing
and shouting and whistling, and the strutting sound of gangsta
rap music.

Sheila Colefax came out of her classroom, very flustered,
and called out, '*Jim!*'

'Yes, Sheila, I'm real sorry about the noise. Give me a
couple of minutes and I'll shut them up.'

'Oh . . . well, *thank* you,' she said. 'It *is* very distracting.'
He had obviously caught her on the back foot by being so
obliging.

She was turning away when he popped his fingers and
said, 'By the way, Sheila . . . didn't I hear something about
a poetry recital at the Brentwood Theater?'

She frowned at him. 'Yes . . . there is. But it's the Santa
Barbara School, and the Santa Barbara School is abused women,
mainly. I wouldn't have thought that it was quite your thing.'

'I don't know. I hear they have some pretty strong poetic
voices. Are *you* going?'

'Well, yes. I have tickets, but I'm going with an old friend
of mine from UCLA.'

'OK, that's fine, I just thought I'd mention it.'

He continued walking along the corridor toward Special
Class Two, leaving her standing in the doorway to her classroom, completely perplexed. About twenty yards away, he
turned, and gave her a smile, and lifted his hand in salute.
They might be frightening, these inexplicable shifts in time,
but they had their advantages, too. They gave you an edge.

He entered the classroom and it was just the same as it had
been yesterday (or today). T.D. had his back to him and his
boom box on his shoulder, and was bobbing up and down to
'Chase Da Cat', while Grant and Arthur and Billy were
throwing a basketball around, and Elvira Thomas was perched
on top of her desk polishing her nails in sparkly purple. Today
he noticed that Leon was texting, and laughing sarcastically
to himself as he did so, while Georgia was plucking her
eyebrows, and behind the upraised lid of her desk, Patsy-Jean
Waller's cheeks were bulging, as she guiltily stuffed down a
BabyRuth bar, one pudgy hand half-covering her mouth.

As he laid down his bag and his papers, however, and
looked along the front row of desks, he saw that Maria's
chair was empty. But he also saw that Kim Dong Wook
was sitting in his place, calmly reading a book. Kim was
wearing the same snow-white shirt as yesterday, when he

had carried Tibbles into the classroom in that cat-basket.

The rest of the students noticed that Jim had walked into the room, with the exception of T.D., who continued to bob and sway, and Elvira, with her gold cornrow hair, who was applying the final polish to her left pinkie. Arthur caught the basketball and held on to it, and sat down, while Leon stopped texting long enough to peer at Jim and shake his head dismissively, as if to say, 'Here he is . . . just another down-at-heel remedial teacher in a cheap linen coat and crumpled chinos and five-year-old Timberland deck shoes.'

But Jim walked directly over to Kim, and stood in front of his desk, and said, 'How is Maria?'

Kim Dong Wook pushed back his chair, stood up, and bowed his head. 'I am Kim Dong Wook. I am honored to meet you, Mr Rook.'

'You've met me already, sunshine. Don't try to pretend that you haven't. I killed my cat and you brought him back to me. But that was yesterday, wasn't it?'

'I am sorry, Mr Rook. I am sorry for what happen to your cat. But each day is every day. Today is today. Today is first day of new semester, yes?'

Jim said, 'How is Maria? More to the point, *where* is Maria? She's not in the ER at Cedars-Sinai, I know that for a fact. The West Hollywood police have never heard of her. So where the hell is she, Kim?'

Suddenly, the tension between them was so electric that all of the students in Special Class Two fell silent. Arthur smacked T.D. on the shoulder, so that T.D. turned around and realized that Jim had arrived, and that something very heavy was going down. He switched off 'Chase Da Cat' and put down his boom box and said, loudly, 'Wass happenin' man? Wass occurin' here? Somebody goin' to fill me in?'

Jim ignored him, and kept his eyes leveled on Kim Dong Wook. 'I may be many things, Kim, but I'm not green.'

'I did not suggest such a thing, Mr Rook. I know that you have much deepness.'

'Well, you're right, I do have much deepness. In fact I have more deepness than you will ever know. So you had better be careful what you say and do, because otherwise you'll be in deepness, too, and that deepness will be deep doo-doo.'

Kim's face remained impassive, so Jim leaned forward until their noses were almost touching, and said to him under his breath, 'I don't exactly know what it is that you're involved in, Kim. I'll admit that much. But I do know that it's concerned with time, and spirits, and maybe one spirit in particular. And so let me just tell you this: Special Class Two are under my pastoral care, and if anybody so much as touches one hair on their heads, they'll have me to answer to. You got it?'

Kim bowed his head again. 'Whatever you say, Mr Rook. But in Korea there is a proverb, if you speak of the fox, it will come. English translation – talk of the devil.'

Jim looked at him for a long moment, saying nothing. Kim looked back at him, and Jim was sure that he was giving him the faintest of smiles. But then Jim turned around to the rest of the class. 'Good morning, Special Class Two! My name is Mr Rook – rook like in the bird, and I want to welcome you to another inspiring year of remedial English!

He went over to the chalk board and scrawled the word *phonetic*. Then he pointed at Tamara and said, 'You want to read the TV news, don't you, Tamara? Why don't you read this word for me?'

Tamara's cheeks flushed pink. 'How did you *know* that?'

'Oh . . . I'm like *The Mentalist*. Or Sherlock Holmes. I can see that you're all dressed up and your make-up is absolutely perfect. Who comes to college looking as nifty as you? Only a girl who has dreams of being a TV news anchor.'

Tamara stared at the word on the chalk board for almost half a minute. Then she said, very slowly, 'Pah-*hon*-tic.'

'OK,' said Jim. 'Good try! How about you, Arthur?'

'That's easy,' said Arthur. 'It's "phone" like in "phone" and "tick" like in "tock." Phone-tick.'

'Nearly,' Jim told him. 'It's actually pronounced "fo-netic." And what it means is, the way a word sounds when you say it out loud, rather than the way it's spelled in the dictionary. This first semester together, we're going to study how to pronounce words correctly, and I promise you that this will help you tremendously when it comes to expressing yourself, not only when you're writing but when you're talking, too.

'Do you know how many times I've seen my students write, "It's a doggy dog world," when they really mean "dog eat dog?" And "taken for granite" when they mean "taken for granted?" And "prespire" instead of "perspire?" And "nucular" instead of "nuclear?"'

Arthur put up his hand and said, 'I don't see the problem. If the person you're talking to understands what you mean, like, what's the difference?'

'The difference, Arthur, is that you have to make your-selves a life in this world, whether you like it or not, and this world is totally hard and totally unforgiving. OK – maybe your friends understand what you mean when you say "a blessing in the skies" when you actually mean "a blessing in disguise." Maybe your brothers know that "sose" means "so as", and that the Heineken Remover is what you give to somebody in a restaurant when they're choking. But nobody else in this totally hard and totally unforgiving world knows that. And they won't show you any mercy, believe me.

'You understand what I'm saying? I'm here to give you the ability to talk sense, and to write sense, and to make something out of your lives. This is your last chance, before you go out there. *I'm* your last chance. If you don't listen to me, if you don't do what I tell you to do, you're going to leave this college like helpless little lambs, and the rest of the world will pick on you, like buzzards, and rip you to pieces.'

'Shit, man,' said T.D. 'You makin' me feel seriously *scared* here. I thought college was where you s'posed to come for reinsurance.'

'So you should be,' Jim told him. 'The world is a very scary place, and you don't even know the half of it. Especially if you say "re-*insurance*" instead of "re-*assurance*."'

Arthur howled with laughter and slapped his knee and said, 'See, bro! You need that phone-tick stuff *so-o-o* bad!'

Jim went over to the stationery cupboard, unlocked it, and took out a sheaf of lined paper. 'OK, class,' he announced. 'I'm going to give you a little warming-up assignment to prepare you for the days and weeks of drudgery that lie ahead of you.'

'Oh, no,' said T.D. 'Here come de drudge!'

Jim pointed a finger at him and said, 'That was good, T.D. A very good wordplay. If there's one thing that I always encourage in Special Class Two, it's playing with words. Making up jokes. Thinking of double meanings. Finding new ways to describe things. Now let's see if you can play with enough words to describe what you would do if you unexpectedly inherited one million dollars.'

Elvira's hand shot up. 'Buy myself a Ferrari!' she said. 'A *purple* Ferrari, to match my nail-polish!'

'Are you kidding?' said Leon, curling his lip. 'You could buy yourself at least *five* Ferraris for a million dollars.'

'OK, then, I'll buy myself a purple Ferrari and a red Ferrari and a pink Ferrari and a green Ferrari and a black Ferrari with glittery bits.'

'And you wouldn't think about giving any of that money to charity?' asked Teddy. 'You wouldn't give up just one of your Ferraris so that some children in Africa could have some clean water to drink?'

'I don't know, maybe. So long as it wasn't the purple one.'

They all sat down at their desks and Jim walked up and down the aisles, handing out sheets of paper and ballpens to those students who hadn't brought their own. He had reached the back of the classroom when the door opened and Maria Lopez walked in, carrying her gold vinyl bag over her shoulder. Jim felt a tingling jolt, as if he had been Tasered.

'Maria?' he said.

'Yes, sir? Is this Special Class Two?'

She looked perfectly well. No lacerations, no blood. Her black hair was tied up in braids, just as it had been yesterday, and she was wearing the same bronze satin blouse and the same jeans and the same multi-colored necklace of wooden beads.

'Yes, this is Special Class Two,' said Jim. He looked at his wristwatch. 'You're a little late. Eleven minutes, to be exact.'

'*Muchas apologias, señor*. My brother, he was supposed to give me a ride to college this morning but at the last minute he said he could not do it.'

'OK,' said Jim. 'It's Maria Lopez, isn't it? Why don't you

sit right down in the front row, Maria, next to Janice?' He nearly said 'Sticky' but managed to stop himself.

Maria sat down, and as she did so, Jim turned his head toward Kim. 'How are you feeling today, Maria?' he asked her, without taking his eyes off Kim. 'Fit and well? Ready for a hard day's English?'

Maria looked puzzled, because she didn't really understand what he meant. But she nodded and said, '*Sí, señor*. I am ready.'

Jim laid a sheet of paper on the desk in front of her. 'I have my own pen,' she volunteered, holding it up to show him. Still he kept his eyes on Kim, and Kim continued to stare back at him. They were like a mongoose and a snake, sizing each other up across a clearing in the jungle. Neither of them had to say anything. Both of them knew what had happened yesterday, although Kim had the advantage of knowing *why* it had happened, and what was going to happen next.

'Right!' said Jim, loudly. 'You have thirty minutes to write down what you do if you were given a million dollars. Don't worry about spelling or punctuation – not today, anyhow. If you want to buy a yacht, but you're not so sure how to spell it, I'd rather you wrote down "y-o-t" than change it for something else that you think you *can* spell, like "SUV." I want to see what you're good at, but I also need to see what you're having trouble with. I want to get an idea of who you are and what you want out of your life.'

He sat down, opened up his bag, and took out *The Memory of a Goldfish*. He had left his Hot Tamales wrapper at page 27, but when he opened it up, he realized that he hadn't actually read this far. Even though he could remember coming to college yesterday, and sitting here with this book open in front of him, he couldn't remember anything that had happened in the last three and a half pages.

'*I woke up. When I opened my eyes I discovered that there was a woman lying next to me, with her arm resting on my chest. She had coppery hair and white skin and more freckles on her face than stars in the sky. She exuded that strange smell that red-headed women often do, half metallic and half animal. I lifted her arm away and sat upright, and said, "Who are you? What are you doing here in my bed?"'*

Maybe he *had* read this page, and maybe it had subconsciously inspired him to have a dream that Summer had been lying next to him, when she hadn't been there at all.

He turned back a page. '*"I think I'll go down to Madam Georgina, and ask her to tell my fortune," I said. But she said, "I don't agree with any of this mumbo-jumbo."'*

That was so close to the lyrics of the Robbie Robertson song that he had been playing in his car on the way to college that it was eerie.

He looked around the class. They were all writing with intense concentration, although some of them were writing very slowly, and mouthing the letters out loud as they wrote them. The only student who wasn't writing was Kim Dong Wook, who was staring at him with that same suggestion of a smile.

Jim felt suddenly very cold, as if all the blood had drained out of him. Outside the window, he could see Mrs Daumier's drawing class, sitting on the grassy slope, but a large cloud must have slid across the sun, because the slope was almost in darkness.

EIGHT

Jim was sitting in the faculty lounge at lunchtime, talking to Walter Armbruster, the history chair. Walter was a bulky, wide-shouldered African-American, with grizzled gray hair and a taste for jazzy silk neckties. As usual, he was complaining about the sandwiches that his wife had made for him.

'She *knows* I hate turkey. How long do you think we've been married? Seventeen years! And she *still* makes me goddamned turkey. Worse than that, turkey with cranberry sauce!'

'Maybe she's trying to punish you,' Jim suggested. 'Think about it: is there something you've done to upset her? Maybe you forgot your anniversary. Maybe she's lost some weight and you haven't noticed.'

Walter opened up one half of his sandwich and inspected its contents. 'Look at that. It's not even fresh turkey. It's *pressed*. It probably contains more preservatives than Tutankhamen.'

Jim picked up the other half and took a bite. 'It's OK. It doesn't *taste* like turkey. In fact it doesn't taste of anything at all – so what's your problem?'

'Well, you're welcome to it,' said Walter. 'One more turkey sandwich and I'm calling a divorce lawyer. What's wrong with pastrami now and again? Or a little Swiss cheese? But what do I get? Goddamned turkey, every goddamned day. Yesterday, turkey. Today, turkey. And guess what I'll get on Thursday?'

Jim said, 'You didn't come to college yesterday, Walter.'

Walter blinked at him through his thick-rimmed eyeglasses. Then he said, 'No, I didn't, did I? I went to the Watsons next door, for a barbecue.'

But then he rubbed the back of his neck and said, 'Was that yesterday? Or was that the day before? I have the strangest feeling that I *did* come to college yesterday. But I couldn't have done, could I? The fall semester only started today.'

'Do you think you might have been here yesterday?' Jim asked him.

'How could I?'

'I don't know, Walter. But I have the feeling that I was here yesterday, too.'

Walter gripped his shoulder, and squeezed it. 'You know something, Jim? I think you and me have been in this teaching game far too long. The kids have got to us at last, and we've finally lost it. Next stop the funny farm.'

'Well, maybe you're right,' Jim told him. 'But I still think that something seriously weird is going on.'

'Something seriously weird such as what?'

'I'm not sure. But it's like the days aren't behaving themselves. Somebody or something is playing around with time, or playing around with our *perception* of time.'

'Say, *what?*'

'I can't explain it, Walter, not yet. But I do have an idea *what* and *who* is causing it, although I don't have the slightest idea *why.*'

'White man speak in conundrums,' said Walter. 'Listen – do you want this other sandwich, because I sure don't. I'd rather go to the commissary for meatloaf and green beans.'

'You're kidding me. Do you have some kind of a death-wish?'

Jim took Walter's sandwich and went to sit on the patio outside. He saw three of his own students sitting on the grass nearby – Georgia and Judii and Grant. Georgia was staring at Grant wide-eyed, her lips parted, as if he had just arrived from heaven by way of Muscle Beach, while Judii was applying bright-red lip-gloss and pouting at herself in a hand mirror, which intermittently flashed as it reflected the sun.

A few yards further away, under the shade of the cedar tree, he saw Patsy-Jean and Billy sitting on the circular bench that surrounded its immense gnarled trunk, and Kim sitting on the ground in front of them, cross-legged, straight-backed. Whatever Kim was saying, he was using the same karate-style chopping gestures with his hands that he had been using when he was talking yesterday to Maria, and both Patsy-Jean and Billy were leaning forward and listening to him with rapt attention.

Jim watched them for a while, and then got up and walked up the slope toward them, eating the last of his sandwich as he did so. Actually, Walter was right. The pressed turkey filling was disgusting. He threw the crusts across the grass, and two quail immediately fluttered down and started pecking at them.

He approached Kim and Patsy-Jean and Billy and said, 'How's it going, guys?'

Kim looked up at him, one eye closed against the sunlight. 'Hello, Mr Rook. We talk about our future lives – which paths will unfold ahead of us.'

Patsy-Jean said, 'Kim says that in Korea they actually have ways of seeing what's going to happen to you in maybe ten years' time.'

'That's right,' said Jim. 'I heard about that, too. Doors open and doors close, don't they, Kim? Or is it the other way around? Close, open – open, close. Whatever it is, you guys need to be cautious. It's tough enough, living your life one day at a time, without knowing what's going to happen before it's happened.'

'Would you not like to see what *you* will be doing in ten years' time, Mr Rook?' Kim challenged him. 'Or maybe thirty years' time? Or forty? Or fifty?'

By the way Kim was looking at him, even with one eye closed, Jim was sure that he knew exactly what he had experienced last night – how he had woken up to find himself old and arthritic and incontinent, and how he had been visited by that spooky woman in that smoky veil. Maybe Kim himself wasn't capable of manipulating time, shuffling the days like a deck of cards, but Jim was convinced that he was acting as an agent or a channel for some influence that was. Kwisin, perhaps, the fox-demon that had appeared in his bedroom, or some spirit even more terrifying.

He said, 'As far as I'm concerned, Kim, ignorance is bliss. If I'm going to be healthy and rich in fifty years' time, that will be great. If I'm going to be sick and poverty-stricken, then I don't want to know about it, not yet. What's the point of worrying about something I can't change?'

'There is always one way to change it, Mr Rook,' said Kim.

'Oh, really? And what's that?'

'Everybody has choice. Everybody has free will.'

'How can you say that, when you believe that our lives have already happened, and that every day is simply waiting for us to come along and experience it?'

'We all have the choice not to go further,' Kim replied. 'To close one door, but not to open the next.'

The bell rang. Students reluctantly began to pick themselves up from the grass and amble back to their classes.

Jim said, 'I don't understand what you're saying, Kim. What do you mean, "not to go further"?'

'Simply that,' said Kim. 'If you do not like what you see on the other side of the door, then you have the choice not to go through it. Not to go further. To stay forever in the same day.'

'Are you saying what I think you're saying?'

Kim stood up. 'I have to go to class, Mr Rook.'

Jim almost snapped at him not to be so goddamned impertinent. It was *his* class, after all. But he knew that he needed to stay in control, and not allow Kim to needle him.

'Sure,' he said, checking his wristwatch. 'You don't want your teacher giving you a hard time for turning up late, do you?'

That afternoon, he read out the essays that his new class had written on 'What I Would Do If I Unexpectedly Inherited A Million Dollars.'

Jim called them 'essays' even though most of them were only three lines long, and five of them were written in block capitals without any punctuation, while one of them had even been written in text-speak. 'I wd pa drs 2 keep me 6Y 4eva. Life s Hrd n sux bt dth stinx.' ('I would pay doctors to keep me sexy for ever. Life is hard and sucks but death stinks.')

Out of all of them, Leon had the most fluent handwriting, and it was joined-up, too. 'I would take my whole family on a trip to Israel. When I got back I would buy my own apartment and invest in a half-share of my cousin Levi's comedy club.'

'That's a very generous thought, taking your family to Israel,' said Jim.

'Yeah, but I'd leave them there. They suck. All of them. Especially my grandparents.'

Billy wanted to move to Oregon and open his own riding stables 'someplace near mountins with snow on the tops and fresh air.' Ella dreamed of buying '1000s & 1000s of dress's & julre & like that & do a tv show like Paris & be a *'

Janice Sticky, to Jim's surprise, had ambitions to open her own unisex grooming salon on Rodeo Drive, while Teddy planned to travel all over the world and write about 'bizarre customs' such as Maasai wife-sharing rituals and 'frogs blended in a Mixmaster with white beans and honey which Peruvians drink instead of Viagra.' Georgia would invest her inheritance in producing a movie, so that she could 'get freinds with A-listers such as eg Brad and Aneglina and Matt Demon and be on the cover of OK magazine every week.'

Arthur wanted to run an exclusive VIP nightclub and own a gold Humvee, or maybe a pair of Humvees, one gold and one silver. T.D. had ambitions to start his own record label, Top Dime Disks. Maria said she would like to buy a beach-house somewhere in Baja, and two Afghan hounds, so that she could live in 'idolic peace.'

When he came to Patsy-Jean's paper, however, and read what she had written, Jim glanced up at the clock and said, 'Hey – we seem to be over-running our time here.'

'Hey, sir, you didn't read mine yet,' Grant complained.

'Yes, I know. I'm sorry. I'll have to finish discussing these some other time. Before we finish this afternoon, I want to read you a poem and I want you to come back tomorrow and tell me what you think about it.'

He went back to his desk, opened up his top drawer, and dropped their papers into it. Patsy-Jean's was on top. In thick black capitals, she had printed: IF I HAD $1 MILLION I WOULD PAY SOMEONE TO KILL ME.

He locked his drawer and picked up his poetry book. He found the poem that he wanted to read to them, and then he stood in front of Patsy-Jean's desk. He looked around. He could see that Special Class Two were growing restless. It was their first day back at college, and they were already tired and mentally ragged. It was always harder to teach them to concentrate than it was to teach them the rudiments of grammar.

'OK,' he said. 'This is a very short poem, but that doesn't mean it makes no demands on your brain. It's called "Beyond the Horizon," and it was written by a young Russian poet called Kiril Vasiliev in 1957.

'It's hard to believe it, but in the Soviet Union in those days, it was very risky to write a poem like this, because it didn't scan and it didn't rhyme and it wasn't all about Lenin, or tractors.'

Billy put up his hand. 'Sir – what's "Lenin"?'

Teddy turned around in his seat with his nose wrinkled up in disgust. 'Are you some kind of ignoramus, or what? Haven't you ever heard of the Lenin Tower of Pisa?'

Jim said, 'Ignore him, Billy. Lenin's a *who*, not a what. Go home. Google him. This is English, not History. Now here's the poem.'

He read 'Beyond The Horizon' directly to Patsy-Jean, looking into her eyes as he did so, searching for some clue to her state of mind. She didn't look in any way distressed, or desperate, but then Jim remembered what his own mother had been like, on the day that *she* had committed suicide. Two months after she had discovered that she had terminal ovarian cancer, she had taken thirty-five paracetamol and drunk a whole bottle of Smirnoff. But when Jim had talked to her at breakfast that morning, she had seemed so calm, so much at peace with herself. *Blissful*, even. It had been the calm of a woman who had made her choice; and had chosen to go no further. Jim read:

> '*All of us vanish*
> *eventually*
> *beyond the horizon*
>
> *But you have vanished*
> *beyond the horizon*
> *like the passing day*

While I am still rising and falling like
  the shadow of a cloud
over the dunes

The wind is rising –
the grass is dancing
where have you gone?

When I reach the horizon
will you be there?

Or will I see only another horizon
and then another horizon
and then another
beyond which you will vanish
successively
and forever?'

T.D. said, with exaggerated seriousness, 'You know somethin', sir. There just ain't no answer to that.'

Jim closed the book. 'Maybe it doesn't seem like it, not
at first. But then maybe there is.'

'Seems to me like there's two too many horizons,' put in
Teddy.

'That's a good point,' said Jim. 'What Vasiliev is saying,
in effect, is that we can never reach the horizon, no matter
how far we travel. It's always beyond our reach. It's very
short, this poem, and it's very simple, but it raises all kinds
of fascinating questions about the way we see our lives
unfolding, and the way we think of time passing us by, and
the way we relate to other people.'

'I think it's really sad,' said Janice.

'Yes,' said Jim. 'It's quite a lonely poem, isn't it? It has
an overwhelming sense of loss. You feel that the love of
Vasiliev's life has disappeared, and he's not at all sure that
he's ever going to be able to find her again.'

The bell rang. Jim said, 'OK . . . we'll talk about this some
more tomorrow. Meanwhile, I want you to think about other
things that affect us but we can't control. Like the weather,
for instance.'

'Or growing older,' said Kim.

'Yes, Kim. Like growing older.'

He went into the Cat'n'Fiddle for a drink before he returned home. He sat up at the bar, loosened his necktie and ordered a bottle of Fat Tire. He was served by the same bartender who had served him yesterday evening, but then he wasn't at all sure that he had really been here yesterday evening. Even if he had, the barman seemed to have forgotten that he had stiffed him out of a tip, because he was friendly and chatty and pushed a large bowl of complimentary pretzels across the bar.

'You teach, don't you?' asked the bartender.

'That's right. English.'

'English? Like Shakespeare, right?'

'Sure. Some Shakespeare.'

'I always wanted to be an actor, you know. I mean that's why I came out to Hollywood in the first place. I was an extra in *War Of The Worlds*, with Tom Cruise. I had to run down the street and get melted by the Martians. Then Portal Pictures were doing this remake of a Korean horror flick, and I got a walk-on part as a doorman. I even had a couple of lines of dialog.'

'That's great,' said Jim. 'That's very good. What were they?'

'Excuse me? What were what?'

'The lines. The lines you had in this Korean horror flick.'

'Oh! I had to stop this woman going through this door and say, "You really don't want to go any further, ma'am. You don't want to go through this door, I promise you."'

'That was it?'

'Yes. But I had to say them real meaningful. Like, I had to give the impression that if she decided to go through the door, she'd be in real serious shit, if you know what I mean.'

'What was it called?' Jim asked him.

'What was what called?'

'The Korean horror flick. What was it called?'

The bartender shrugged. 'I don't know. They never finished it. I think they ran out of money or the talent got sick or something. I never found out. The working title was *Demon's Door*.'

'What was the storyline?'

The bartender slowly shook his head. 'I'm not too sure. All I had to do was wear this green doorman's uniform and reach forward and take hold of this door handle and say, "You really don't want to go any further, ma'am. You don't want to go through this door, I promise you." And the director told me that I had to sound – what was the word? *Portentous.* Would that be right? I mean, you're an English teacher.'

'Yes,' said Jim. 'Portentous. It means "ominous, portending evil." It can also mean "pompous" but I doubt if your director wanted you to sound like some self-important windbag.'

'Portentous,' the bartender repeated, with satisfaction, almost as if he had coined the word himself.

'But . . . you don't know what you were being portentous about?'

'Excuse me?'

'You don't know what was on the other side of that door? You don't know why you were warning that woman not to go through it?'

The bartender shrugged. 'I never saw the whole script, only the page with my lines on it. The director said, "Read the lines and sound portentous," and that was it.'

'OK,' Jim told him. 'Thanks. I think I'll have another brew.'

'Sure thing.'

Outside, the jazz trio began to tune up. A few scattered scales on the piano, a few random squiggles on the alto sax. A throaty-sounding woman sang, 'I went down to St James' Infirm'ry . . . saw my baby there . . .' It was then that the tawny-haired girl in the glittery purple mini-skirt came out of the darkness and perched herself on the stool right next to him, crossing her legs.

She sniffed, and ran her finger under her nose, and said, 'You look sad, mate.'

'Me? No, I'm not sad. A little confused, maybe. But not sad. And before you ask me if I feel like a shag, how would you like a drink?'

'You're a bit bloody cheeky. Vodka and tonic, if you don't mind.'

Jim beckoned to the bartender and ordered her drink. Then he turned back to her and said, 'Do you recognize me?'

'Why, are you famous?'

'No, not at all. I just want to know if you've ever seen me before.'

The girl frowned at him. 'Can't say I do, mate. But I don't usually come in here till later.'

'Did you see me in here yesterday evening, round about this time?'

The girl continued to frown. She opened her mouth as if she were about to say something but then she closed it again.

'I was right here,' said Jim. 'I was sitting on the same stool.'

The girl said, 'No . . . no, I couldn't have seen you. I didn't come in here yesterday. Alex! Did I come in here yesterday evening?'

The bartender thought about it, and then said, 'I don't think so. But, you know. Every evening is pretty much like every other evening.'

Jim said, 'OK, then. Forget it. It doesn't really matter.'

The girl lifted her glass and said, 'Cheers for the drink. Do you still want that shag?'

'Thanks for the offer, sweet cheeks, but it's a little early in the day for me. I have to be going.' Jim climbed off his stool and made sure that he left a twenty on the bar. Next time he came in, the bartender might remember that he hadn't left him a tip.

When he unlocked the door of his apartment, he was surprised that Tibbles didn't come running out into the hallway to greet him, like he usually did. 'Tibbles!' he called out, as he closed the door behind him. 'Where are you, you idle moggie? I bought you Instinctive Choice shrimp! And tuna, too! And some dry crunchy things which are supposed to stop you getting gas!'

He went into the kitchen and put down his sack of groceries on the counter. Then he walked through to the living room. 'Tibbles! Where the hell are you? You haven't been sleeping on my pillow again?'

He went into his bedroom, but there was no sign of Tibbles

there, either. He thought: *Don't tell me he managed to escape this morning, when I was closing the door. I'm sure that I locked him inside.*

He returned to the living room. It was nearly eight o'clock now and it was growing dusky outside. He walked over to the windows to draw the drapes, but as he did so a huge crow flapped into the air, right outside, and let out a raucous *skrrarrrkkk!* He said, '*Shit!*' out loud and stepped back with his heart thumping.

The crow flew off, but only as far as the apartment block on the other side of the yard, where twenty or thirty more crows were perched on the rooftop, cawing and shuffling and pecking at the tiles. Jim went out on to the balcony. Flocks of urban crows gathered here almost every afternoon during the winter months and made a nuisance of themselves, like a gang of bikers, but he had never seen them so early in the year.

It was then that Jim saw what had attracted them. Lying on his back on the sunbed next to him was Tibbles, dead and crushed, his fur matted with dried blood, just where Jim had left him after he had run him down. The crows had already taken his eyes, so his sockets were hollow and empty, and they had torn at his abdomen, too, and pulled out yellowish strings of intestines.

A warm tide of bile and beer suddenly flooded into Jim's mouth, and he tilted himself over the railing to spit it out into the yard below. He stayed there for a few moments, his head bowed, his eyes watering, his stomach clenching. Then he slowly stood up straight and looked down at Tibbles' ravaged remains in horror and disbelief.

If this was the Tibbles he had killed, where was the living Tibbles that Kim had brought him in a cat basket? Where was the Tibbles he had fed this morning, before he left for college? How could a dead cat come to life again, when it must have been dead all the time? From the condition it was in, Tibbles' body must have been lying here for at least twenty-four hours. It already smelled strongly of sweet, decayed flesh, mingled with rotten shrimp.

Jim swung round toward the crows, clustered on top of the apartment block.

'Get the hell out of here!' he screamed at them. 'Go on, you bastards! Get the hell out!'

A few of them fluttered up into the air for a few seconds, but then hopped back on to the tiles, cawing at Jim in defiance. He picked up the trowel he used for his houseplants and flung it at them as hard as he could, but it fell short of the roof and landed with a clatter on to the balcony of one of the third-story apartments opposite. Almost at once, a white-haired woman opened the balcony door to find out what the noise was about, and with an explosive rustle of wings, the crows all flew away.

'What in the blue blazes is going on?' the woman called out. 'Did you just throw something at my winder?'

'The crows, ma'am!' Jim called back. 'I was just trying to scare them off! They do so much damage! Sorry if I startled you!'

'Huh!' said the woman. 'You be more careful in future, that's all I can say! You can't go throwing stuff at people's winders, willy-nilly! Something's going to get broke!'

'Yes, ma'am! Sorry, ma'am!'

NINE

Jim went back inside his apartment. From the bottom of his bedroom closet he lifted out a cardboard box full of old bank statements and letters and Polaroid photographs and assorted souvenirs, like a snow globe from Milwaukee and a luminous plastic Statue of Liberty. He found two pictures of his mother, sitting on the beach in Sarasota, Florida, and a black-and-white picture of his grandfather, Roland Rook, when he was serving with the 34th Infantry in Pusan in 1950. As usual his grandfather was grinning and giving the thumbs-up, and as usual he had his arm around a pretty Korean girl. Jim looked at it for a while, remembering his grandfather's laugh and his gravelly voice. Then he emptied all the contents into two shopping bags and carried the empty box out on to the balcony.

The crows were returning already, some of them sitting on the roof and others circling slowly in the air. There was no point in him shouting at them, and he didn't want to risk throwing anything else. He didn't want to upset the neighbors any more than he had to.

He set the box down on the floor of the balcony and snapped on a pair of red household gloves. 'Tibbles, I don't know what to tell you about this. I still can't understand what happened. One minute you were alive and then you were dead and then you were alive again and now you're dead again. Does that make any kind of sense to you? Because it makes no sense to me. None whatsoever.'

Tibbles stared up at Jim with empty eye sockets, and his teeth were bared in a vicious-looking snarl, as if he were furious with Jim for killing him and then leaving his body to the mercy of the crows.

'I can't give you much of a funeral,' Jim told him. 'I can't afford the Pet Memorial Park. Besides, you were only a cat, after all. I know that doesn't sound very appreciative. You

were a pretty interesting cat, as cats go. But you would have
made a very boring human.'

He lifted Tibbles' floppy, decaying body into the cardboard box and closed the top. The smell was so ripe and so
cloying that he almost brought up some more beer, but he
took a deep breath and quickly sealed the box with brown
parcel tape, and after a few minutes the smell faded. In the
morning he would take the box to college with him, and ask
Dunstan the janitor to throw it into the incinerator.

He slid the balcony door shut, locked it, and went into the
kitchen to open up another bottle of Fat Tire. When he returned
to the living room, he tugged the drapes across the windows.
He didn't want to sit looking at that cardboard box knowing
that Tibbles was lying dead inside it, rotting, and that he was
to blame.

He felt bruised. Mystified, confused, angry and *bruised* –
as if he had been comprehensively beaten up by some berserk
assailant who wouldn't tell him why he was doing it.

Yesterday he had lived through a day that may or may not
have happened. Today he had lived through a day in which
yesterday was mostly forgotten, but not completely – even
if it *hadn't* happened. And he wasn't the only one who had
some kind of phantom memory of it. Walter Armbruster had
felt that *he* had turned up at college, too – and even the girl
in the Cat'n'Fiddle had had to think twice about where she
had been the evening before.

Then there was Maria. Yesterday she had been a bloody
mess, lacerated to ribbons, today she was completely
unscathed. And Tibbles: dead, resurrected, now dead again.
Jim could have banged his head against the wall in sheer
bewilderment.

He took a shower and put on his faded Walt Whitman
T-shirt and his blue-and-white stripy shorts. He heated a
pepperoni pizza in the oven but only managed to eat two
slices of it because he kept thinking about Tibbles' empty
eye sockets. He put the rest in the fridge even though he
knew that he would only throw it away tomorrow.

He watched TV for a while, a long documentary about
Gnawa music in Africa – a mystical kind of music which
was used to raise *djinns* or spirits. It was warbling and

monotonous, punctuated by hollow knockings from iron castanets called *qraqabs*, which sounded like somebody hopelessly trying to get out of a metal coffin.

After twenty minutes, he realized that he wasn't really listening, so he switched off the television, went to the front door and stepped out on to the landing. It was a warm, blowy night, and the yuccas were gossiping to each other as if they knew that he was worried, and in trouble. *Did you see what happened to his cat? Did you hear what happened when he went to class today?*

He was almost tempted to shout at them to shut up, but then he realized that shouting at trees would really show that he had lost his marbles.

He held on to the railing and closed his eyes, feeling the breeze on his face. Whatever was happening to him and Special Class Two, he had to find out what it was and straighten it out. He was afraid to go to bed in case he woke up fifty years older, and even if he managed to get some sleep he was afraid of what the morning might bring. What if the sun rose tomorrow but it was still the first day of the fall semester, all over again?

He opened his eyes again. As he turned to go back into his apartment, however, he saw a figure standing on the opposite side of Briarcliff Road, just at the point where it began its steep curve down to Foothill Drive. It was the woman in the black wide-brimmed hat with the veil, and the shiny gray robe. She was standing quite still, by the cast-iron railings which ran along the frontage of number 5754. Beneath the brim of her hat her face was in deep shadow, so that he couldn't see if she had a fox-like snout or not, but her posture was strange, slightly leaning forward with both hands held up in front of her, like a four-legged animal sitting up on its hind legs and begging.

Maybe he should go down and confront her, ask her what the hell she wanted. On the other hand, what if she turned into that bristling beast again, and what if, this time, he didn't escape so lightly?

He was still watching her when he saw one of his neighbors from further up the road, Wilbert Funkel, climbing the hill with Charlie, his Boston terrier. Wilbert was in his mid-fifties, with heavy-rimmed spectacles, a thinning white pompadour, and a red and yellow Hawaiian shirt. As they came closer to the woman in the hat, Charlie started to yap and growl, and turn around and around in circles, until he became hopelessly tangled up in his leash and almost tripped Wilbert up.

'Charlie! What the Sam Hill has gotten into you, you stupid mutt?'

But even though Wilbert pulled Charlie's leash in shorter and shorter, until he was making a high-pitched strangling sound, Charlie continued to spin around and throw himself furiously at the woman in the hat, his eyes bulging and his mottled tongue hanging out.

'Charlie! You behave yourself!' Wilbert snapped at him, and whipped the terrier's nose with the end of his leash. But Charlie was beyond all control now, and flecks of foam were flying from between his lips. Jim had never seen a dog in such a frenzy, even a rabid pit bull that had terrorized West Grove Community College for over an hour before the dog catchers finally arrived.

What was so extraordinary, though, was that Wilbert himself obviously couldn't see the woman at all, and had no idea why Charlie was jumping and spinning and frothing at the mouth.

'Wilbert!' Jim shouted. 'Wilbert! It's Jim Rook! Get Charlie away from there, as quick as you can!'

Wilbert looked up. He couldn't see Jim at first, but then Jim waved at him with both hands. 'Get Charlie away from there, Wilbert! Otherwise he's going to get himself hurt!'

Wilbert called back, 'I can't work out what's wrong with him, Jim! He's just gone crazy!'

'Get him away!' Jim repeated. 'There's something there that's driving him out of his mind!'

Wilbert tried to drag Charlie further up the road, but Charlie kept hurling himself up at the woman in the hat and snapping at her as if he were trying to pull off her hat and her veil.

'What the hell is it?' shouted Wilbert. 'Why is he acting this way?'

Charlie jumped up again, but this time the woman in the

hat caught his collar. He made a noise that sounded like a scream, and thrashed from side to side, but the woman held him high up in the air in her right hand, and lifted her veil with her left.

Wilbert took two or three staggering steps back, and dropped Charlie's leash. To him, it must have appeared that Charlie was suspended in mid-air, supported by nothing but his trailing leash, like a bizarre version of the Indian rope trick.

'*Wilbert!*' Jim bellowed at him. 'For Christ's sake, grab his leash and pull him away!'

But Wilbert was too stunned to do anything except stumble further back. As he did so, he lost his footing and fell heavily on to the tarmac, so that his heavy black eyeglasses flew off. 'Hold on!' Jim shouted, then ran along the landing and hurtled down the steps. He ran along the next landing, and then the next, and as he ran past Mrs LaFarge's front door she opened it up, her hair all pinned up in curlers, and said, 'Jee-yum? What in heaven's name is *happening* out here?'

Jim ran across the road but he was seconds too late. The woman in the hat ducked her head forward and Jim thought he glimpsed a long, fox-like snout. He heard a sharp, decisive crunch, and then Charlie's body dropped with a thump on to the road, right next to Wilbert's eyeglasses.

The woman dropped her veil and Jim heard another crunch, and then another, and then she whirled around with a slithery noise from her gray silk robe, and she was gone, as if she had never been there.

'Oh, Jesus,' wept Wilbert. 'Oh, Jesus, what's happened? Charlie! Look at Charlie! Jesus, Jim, he doesn't have a head!'

Wilbert crawled across the road on his hands and knees. He picked up his eyeglasses and put them on, even though the lenses were spattered with blood. Charlie was lying on his side. He was still wearing his collar, but his head had gone, leaving nothing but an inch of bloody windpipe. Wilbert reached out for him, but then he lifted up both hands in despair and disgust.

'I don't understand it. What's happened to him? Where's his head?'

Jim said, 'Come inside, Wilbert. We'll call the police.'

'No, no. I don't want to leave him here on his own, I can't! Poor little guy. He never did no harm to nobody.'

'OK, then. I'll go up to my apartment and call the police while you stay here. But be careful. We don't want the same thing happening to you.'

Wilbert was too shocked and distressed to answer. He knelt in the road, rocking backward and forward, with tears sliding down his cheeks. 'Poor little Charlie. I don't understand it. Poor little guy.'

Jim ran up the steps to his apartment. Panting, he went through to the kitchen, lifted the phone off the wall and punched out 911.

'*What's your emergency, please?*'

'My neighbor's dog has been killed.'

'*Your neighbor's dog has been killed? Was it hit by a car?*'

'No. It was decapitated. Right in the middle of the street.'

'*Decapitated?*'

'Beheaded. Something took his head off.'

'What, exactly?'

'I don't know. I really couldn't tell you.' *A spirit. A demon. A woman who can turn into a fox-monster.*

'*OK, sir. We'll try to get somebody out to see you. Can you give me your name and address, please?*'

Jim told her. Then he hung up the phone, feeling both frightened and stupid. He couldn't possibly explain to the police that Charlie had been beheaded by a demon, especially since Wilbert hadn't been able to see it – or her, or whatever it was.

He went back outside. When he looked down from the landing, however, he couldn't see Wilbert. *Oh, shit*, he thought. *Don't say that the demon has come back and taken him, too*. He hurried down the steps and across the road. There was no sign of Wilbert anywhere, and there was no sign of Charlie, either. There was no splatter of blood on the tarmac, either.

Jim looked around. The trees and the bushes were churning in the breeze, and a fine flurry of dust stung his eyes.

'Wilbert!' he shouted. 'Wilbert, where the hell are you? *Wilbert!*'

Damn it. He should have insisted that Wilbert come up to

his apartment with him when he called 911. Now he would not only have to explain what had happened to the police, he would also have to explain it to Dorothy, Wilbert's wife. Or widow, as she probably was now.

He was still standing there when he heard somebody call out, 'Hi, Jim!' Out of the shadows and the whirling yucca leaves came Wilbert, trudging up the curve. Beside him, on his leash, trotted Charlie.

Jim said, 'Wilbert! Are you OK?'

Wilbert stopped and stared at him through his thick-rimmed eyeglasses. 'Sure, I'm fine! The old thrombophlebitis cleared up. How are things with you? New semester started yet?'

Charlie approached Jim and started sniffing at his feet. Wilbert tugged him back on his leash and said, 'Charlie! That's impolite!'

'You're OK, though?' Jim asked him. 'And Charlie – he's OK, too?'

'Sure,' said Wilbert, cautiously, as if he suspected that Jim might have had one too many Fat Tires. 'We're just taking our evening constitutional, that's all. Well, I call it our evening constipational, because Charlie never manages to do what he's supposed to, do you, Charlie?'

Charlie looked up at him with his bulging Boston terrier eyes and barked.

'Fine, OK then,' said Jim. 'Have a good evening, won't you? And give my best wishes to Dorothy.'

Wilbert and Charlie continued to walk up the road. Charlie kept turning his head around to look back at Jim, and Wilbert had to tug on his leash to keep him going. *Well*, thought Jim, *at least he still has a head*. The question was, for how much longer? Just because he was still alive now, that didn't mean that he wouldn't be killed tomorrow, or the day after, the same as Tibbles. The days were overlapping and repeating themselves but who could tell which day was which, or whether any of these grisly events would really happen? Maybe they were nothing but a threat. But a threat of what?

It was past midnight when the police arrived. When the bell rang, he opened his door and was confronted by a huge female officer with sandy hair and freckles who was almost four inches taller than he was. She shone a flashlight into his face and said, 'Mr Jim Rook? You reported that your neighbor's dog had been killed.'

'I'm sorry. Yes. I made a mistake. Sorry. I should have called you.'

The officer opened her notebook. 'You reported that the dog had been beheaded? Is that right?'

'I made a mistake. I looked down from my landing here and saw my neighbor walking his dog up the road and it was just a trick of the light. The shadows, you know. It looked like the dog had lost its head.'

'But it was still walking up the road?'

'Well, yes.'

'Wouldn't that have indicated to you that it probably still had its head on?'

'I told you. It was an optical illusion. I made a mistake.'

The officer looked at Jim for a long time. From the expression on her face, Jim had the distinct feeling that she would happily have seized him by the neck and lifted him clear off the floor.

'Sir,' she said, 'have you been drinking?'

'Only a couple of beers, that's all.'

'Well, I suggest that next time you have a couple of beers you go to bed and sleep it off and don't waste our time with your optical illusions. OK? Otherwise we might feel it necessary to take you down to the drunk tank, and I promise you that's no illusion.'

'Yes, Officer. My apologies.'

The policewoman left and Jim went back into his living room. For some reason, he had never felt so lonely in his life. He had dozens of friends and casual acquaintances. He rubbed along pretty well with almost the entire college faculty, except for Phil Magruder the English chair who was narrow-chested and always wore a bow-tie and kept an empty pipe clenched between his teeth as if he were one of the literati. Sheila Colefax had even invited him to a feminist poetry reading, hadn't she? Or else she was about to. But he had never felt so keenly that his ability to see ghosts and demons and other supernatural presences had set him so much apart. It didn't help that Tibbles was dead, and that he had killed him.

Eventually, at 1:30 in the morning, he grew so tired that he crawled into bed, and dragged the red Zuni bedcover over his face. At first he found it difficult to sleep, and rolled himself from one side of the bed to the other, winding himself up in the bedcover tighter and tighter until he looked like a huge red chrysalis.

He recited Walt Whitman to himself. Not the slogan on his T-shirt – 'Nothing can happen more beautiful than death' – which was a famous Walt Whitman quote, but the poem about the child who went forth every day 'and the first object he look'd upon, that object he came, that object became part of him for the day, or a certain part of the day, or many years, or stretching cycles of years.'

He slept. He didn't dream, or if he did, he wasn't aware of dreaming. But then he heard a shifting, scratching noise, and he woke up instantly, listening. He lay there for nearly a minute, in the darkness, his heart slowly thumping. He tried to untangle himself from the bedcover but he was twisted up in it so tightly that he could barely move. Eventually, he managed to roll over and pull himself free, and sit up.

He didn't ask if there was anybody in the room with him. He knew that there couldn't be. The front door was double-locked and chained, the balcony window was locked. But he was sure that he had heard scratching, and rustling, and when he listened harder, he was sure that he could hear breathing, too. Quick, furtive breathing that was actually more like an animal panting.

He reached across to the night-stand and switched on the light. Almost instantly, the bulb popped, and he was in darkness again. But not before he had seen that she was standing at the end of his bed, in her Puritan-style hat and her veil and her silky gray robe.

He didn't shout out. He didn't challenge her. He tumbled off the bed and wrenched open the bedroom door and ran down the hallway and pulled back the chain and opened the front door and sprinted along the landing and catapulted himself down the steps. He reached Summer's door and pressed the bell and hammered on the window with his fists.

'Summer! Summer! You have to let me in! *Summer!*'

At first there was no answer. *Oh God, don't tell me she's pole-dancing all night, or a customer has taken her back to his place for some extra-curricular fun and games.* He was sure he could hear the rustling of silk along the landing above him, and the scratching of claws.

'*Summer!* For Christ's sake, Summer, let me in!'

TEN

There was no alternative. He would have go downstairs and seek refuge with Mrs LaFarge. But just as he was making his way back along the landing, Summer's door opened up and she appeared, her hair tousled, blinking. She was wearing nothing but a red sleeveless T-shirt and a white thong.

'Jimmy?' she said in a foggy voice. 'What *time* is it, Jimmy? What's going on?'

'Is it OK if I come in?' Jim asked her. 'I don't want to impose on you, but it's back. That thing that made me scream last night.'

'Jimmy . . . you had a nightmare last night. It wasn't a *thing*.'

'Summer, please let me in. I swear to you that it wasn't a nightmare. It was an actual thing. And tonight it's come back.'

'OK,' said Summer. 'But you can't do this every night, Jimmy. Now I have this job I really need my sleep. You think that pole-dancing is like falling off a log? Pole-dancing is very exhausting.'

'Just tonight, please,' said Jim. 'I promise you I'll sort it all out tomorrow.'

Summer said, 'OK, sure,' and opened the door wider so that he could come in. He had never been inside her apartment before. The living room had purple-painted walls and a white leather couch and a coffee table in the shape of a Spanish guitar. Over the fireplace hung a large poster for a Prince 'Purple Rain' concert, with the Purple One himself sitting astride a motorcycle.

'You need a drink or anything?' asked Summer.

'No, really, I'm fine. I'll just crash on the couch if that's OK.'

'Oh, don't be insane. Come to bed. You're not going to jump on me, are you?'

'Summer, the couch is perfectly OK, I promise you.'

'It's all *leathery*. I wouldn't sleep on it. Come to bed.'

Jim followed her into the bedroom. The bed was a king-sized four-poster, with a purple satin quilt and a purple velour headboard. Jim thought it looked as if Summer had bought it second-hand from an Elvis impersonator. At the far end of the bedroom there was a dressing table with a triple mirror, crowded with dozens of half-used lipsticks and countless pots of moisturizing cream and eyelash tongs and squeezed-out tubes of blusher. Surrounded by all this chaos sat a stunned-looking teddy bear in a purple rollneck sweater.

Jim looked around. The bedroom walls were clustered with all kinds of souvenirs and oddities, like Venetian carnival masks and drinking horns and mirrors with frames made out of seashells.

The bedroom smelled strongly of some industrial-strength perfume, which Jim couldn't identify, but he could tell that it had musk in it, and bergamot. If he had been asked to give it a name, he would have called it Democrat Congressman's Mistress's Boudoir.

Summer bounced into bed and patted the quilt next to her. 'Come on. We don't have all night.'

Jim sat down on the side of the bed and said, 'You're sure about this?'

'Jimmy, you're a college teacher. If I can't trust you, who can I trust?'

'OK,' he said. 'So long as you're sure.'

He swung his legs around and pulled up the quilt to cover himself. Summer switched off her bedside lamp and they lay side by side in darkness. Outside, the wind continued to whistle and fluff, and somewhere a wind chime was jingling wildly, as if hundreds of Buddhist monks were hurrying down the road with their *tingsha* cymbals.

After a long while, Summer turned toward Jim and said, 'Are you asleep, Jimmy?'

'Nearly,' he told her. Then, 'No.'

'So what is it, this thing that you're so scared of?'

'You wouldn't believe me if I told you.'

'Try me. My last boyfriend said that I would believe anything.' She paused, and then she said, 'He was right, I guess. I truly believed that he wasn't cheating on me with that fat Mexican waitress.'

Jim said, 'The thing is, Summer, I can see all kinds of stuff that other people can't see. I nearly died when I was a kid, and ever since then I've been able to see ghosts, and spirits, and demons.'

'You're *kidding* me! You're kidding me, right? Like *Ghost Whisperer*?'

'Not really. Not at all, in fact. Ghosts and spirits usually hang around because they have a bone to pick with some-body who's still alive, or else they don't realize that they're dead, so most of them are either vindictive or stupid.'

'You're kidding me, though, aren't you? Come on – you can *really* see ghosts? What do they look like?'

'Pretty much like they did when they were alive. Less substantial, I guess. The only difference is, nobody can see them. Except me, of course, although I'm sure there must be at least a handful of other people who have the same ability.'

'But that thing in your apartment?'

'That's not a ghost, that's a demon. When it first appeared last night, it looked like a woman in a black hat and a veil. But it grew bigger and bigger, until it looked like some enor-mous kind of animal, like a wolf or a fox.'

'You *are* kidding me, aren't you? I mean, you're just saying this to scare me, like one of those campfire stories.'

Jim shook his head, although he knew that she couldn't see him in the darkness. 'I think it's a Korean demon, and that one of my new students is involved with it somehow. Maybe he brought it here. Or maybe it's the other way around. Maybe the demon has taken control of the student and is using him as kind of a front man.'

'So – let me get this straight – upstairs in your apartment – there's an actual real actual demon?'

'That's right. Maybe it's gone now, but take my word for it, it was real enough when it appeared at the end of my bed, and I wasn't going to take any chances.'

He told Summer everything, although he tried not to make it all sound too melodramatic. He told her how Charlie's head had been bitten off. He told her about Maria and all her cuts and bruises. He told her how Tibbles had come back to life after being crushed, but was dead for a second time.

He tried to explain to her how the first day of the new semester seemed to have happened and yet not to have happened, but how several people had memories of it. Or feelings of *déjà-vu*, anyhow.

'I had that once,' said Summer, nodding to show that she understood what he was talking about. 'My mom took me to Disneyland when I was about seven and when we went into Mickey Mouse's house I was sure that she had taken me there before. But my mom swore to me that she never had.'

'Well, you know what kids' imaginations are like,' said Jim. 'You'd probably seen it in a cartoon, and fantasized that you were really there. When I was a kid, I convinced myself that I knew Huckleberry Finn, and that he and I used to play together and go fishing together, even though I didn't even have a fishing pole. He always used to thrash me at marbles.'

They lay in silence for a further few minutes, and then Summer unexpectedly reached out in the dark and flicked the tip of Jim's nose. Jim had been listening for any scratching noises from upstairs and it made him jump.

'Hey!' he protested. 'What was that for?'

'Nothing. Just being playful, that's all.'

'There's a Korean demon in my apartment and you're being playful?'

She leaned over him and breathed warm spearminty breath into his face. 'You know something, you're such a great guy. You're great-looking, you're funny. You give off this what's-it's-name. This charisma. But it's like you're this old man already, when you're not.'

'I'm older than you.'

'I'm twenty-two, twenty-three next birthday.'

'Exactly. And I'm thirty-four. That means I'm twelve years older than you are. When I was reading *Twenty Thousand Leagues Under the Sea* you were still waking up three times a night for ten ounces of warm formula.'

'Well, I couldn't forget that you're a teacher, too.'

'Exactly.'

'The trouble is, *you* never forget that you're a teacher, either.

You seem to think that because you're a teacher nobody can teach you anything. Especially somebody younger, like me.'

'No, I don't.'

'Yes, you do.'

'Don't.'

'Do.'

'OK, then,' said Jim. 'I'm always open to new ideas. Why don't you expand my horizons for me?'

'You really want me to?'

'Sure. Go ahead. I can't sleep, anyhow.'

Summer switched on her bedside lamp. She climbed off the bed and said, 'You go to a club, you see pole-dancing, you think there's nothing to it, just holding on to a pole and waggling your tush. Well, look at this.'

She took hold of one of the bedposts, hoisted herself up, and spun right around it with one arm flying free. Then she held on to it with both hands and jumped up, spreading her legs wide apart.

For the next three or four minutes, she spun and circled and even hung upside-down. As she clung on to the bedpost Jim sat up in bed watching her in amazement. The bed creaked and swayed every time she swung herself around, but she performed with such fluidity and grace that it was easy to believe that she was completely weightless.

Eventually she swung around one last time and landed on the bed, almost on top of him, so that he bounced up two or three inches. She was panting a little, but Jim was perfectly aware that if he had tried to copy her, he would have been ready for CPR by now.

'You see?' she said, and kissed him. 'And that was only round the bedpost. If you could see me with my proper pole . . .'

'I'm speechless,' Jim told her. 'I don't think I've ever seen anything like it.'

She kissed him again, and then again. 'Every single move has a name. Like the first move I did, that was an Angel. Then I went into an Explosion. Then a Backwards Showgirl. Then the Full Moon . . . that was when I was upside-down and kind of curved – you know, like the moon.'

She kissed his forehead, she kissed his eyelids. She

squeezed his cheeks together in one hand and kissed his lips. He did nothing to stop her. In fact, he began to kiss her back. She tasted not only of spearmint toothpaste but of pink lip-gloss, too, and her hair smelled of apricots.

'You know what, Jimmy-wimmy?' she whispered, and her face was so close that she was out of focus. 'When you drive out of that college every afternoon, you need to stop being a teacher and you need to be yourself. Every time you talk to me, you make me feel like I'm sitting at a desk. Try to find out who you are, because one day you'll wake up and find that you've been teaching for years and years and the only person who hasn't learned anything is you.'

Jim said, 'You are wise beyond your years, my child.'

'There you are, you see! You're still doing it! You need to forget about your poems and your quotations and all of that literature stuff. You can't go through your whole life talking with other people's voices, even if what other people said was exactly what you wanted to say but you just couldn't think of the words. Look at your T-shirt.'

Jim peered down at it. 'It's Walt Whitman.'

'I don't care if it's Walt Disney. It's not Jimmy Rook.'

Jim didn't exactly know why, but the way in which she called him 'Jimmy Rook' gave him an unexpected feeling of pleasure and almost relief, as if 'Jimmy Rook' were another person altogether – somebody much more relaxed and less self-conscious; somebody who wasn't endlessly harassed by ghosts and demons and anxieties about his students. He could imagine a whole crowd of young people hanging around a diner, and one of them suddenly saying, 'Hey! Look who it is! It's Jimmy Rook! Hi, Jimmy!' and Jimmy Rook walking in, smiling and strutting and high-fiving, everybody happy to see him.

'You're really somebody, Summer,' said Jim. He touched her lips with his fingertip. 'I looked at you and I talked to you, but up until now I had no idea who you are.'

'That's the whole point. You don't know who *you* are, either. Maybe it's time you tried to find out.'

She laid one hand on top of his shorts. His instinctive reaction was to take hold of her wrist and firmly lift it away.

But she was right. She was much younger than him, but she wasn't one of his students, and tonight he wasn't the teacher. Tonight he wasn't the demon hunter, either. Tonight he was Jimmy Rook.

'Goodness!' she said, in a little-girly voice. 'I do believe there's something growing inside of these shorts!'

She gave him two or three squeezes, and then said, 'I wonder if it's a beanstalk? I sure hope so. I could climb it all the way up to the clouds and find the giant's castle and bring back the goose that lays the golden eggs or whatever. You know how good I am at climbing up poles.'

'Do you know what, Summer?' Jim told her. 'You're nuts.'

'Oh, no,' she said, in a deep, mock-serious whisper. She took hold of his waistband and tugged his shorts halfway down his thighs. 'Look what I got here. *Your* nuts!'

It was a stupid joke, but they both laughed so much that they accidentally knocked their foreheads together.

'Ow!' said Summer. 'I shall have to spank you for that! Or spank your monkey, anyhow!'

She took hold of his hardened penis in her hand, her long manicured nails digging into the skin, and rubbed it slowly and lasciviously up and down. Jim lay back on the pillow and watched her, because all she wanted him to do was watch her. She was the teacher now.

She kept on rubbing him, gripping him so tight that the glans of his penis flushed dark purple, and the eye gaped with every stroke like a landed fish.

'Now you can tell me a poem,' she said.

'What?'

'Tell me a poem. Go on.'

'Summer, for Christ's sake . . .'

'Tell me a poem or I'll stop.'

'I thought you said I was supposed to forget about being a teacher.'

'Don't tell me a poem like a teacher. Tell me like Jimmy.'

So, as she slowly rubbed him, he recited the next few lines of the Walt Whitman poem that he had been reciting to himself in bed.

'*The early lilacs became part of this child, / And grass, and white and red morning-glories, and white and red clover, and the song of the phoebe-bird, / And the Third-month lambs—'*

'That's so beautiful,' said Summer, even though she didn't once take her eyes off his penis. 'That could almost make me cry.'

Without another word, she dipped her head down and took his penis into her mouth, and very gently sucked it. Her fine blonde hair tickled his thighs, and he reached down and stroked it. He wanted to continue reciting the poem but he had forgotten it, all of it. Come to that, he had forgotten every poem he had ever known. He had forgotten *everything* he had ever known. The way that Summer was making him feel now, all knowledge was irrelevant.

He started to feel a tightening sensation between his legs, but it was then that Summer sat up, and licked her lips, and smiled at him, and crossed her arms so that she could take off her T-shirt. Her breasts tumbled out of it, and Jim could see that he had been right: the Lord *had* been magnanimous. They were enormous, but very buoyant, almost afloat, with pale strawberry-pink nipples, crinkled and stiff.

Jim sat up and pulled off his T-shirt, too. Walt Whitman's white-bearded kisser wasn't exactly a turn-on. He kicked his shorts off his ankles and took Summer into his arms. God, she felt like an angel. He nuzzled her and ran his fingers down the curve of her back and for the first time in a very long time Jim felt completely carried away, as if a huge warm wave had lifted him out to sea. No anxiety, no responsibility, nothing but soft skin and pleasure.

Summer started to sit up again, but Jim said, 'My turn,' and firmly pushed her on to her back. He knelt beside her and tugged off her tiny white-lace thong. Then he parted her thighs and opened the freshly waxed lips of her vulva with his fingertips. It was like opening up some exotic pink fruit, filled with clear sweet juice. Her clitoris peeped out and he licked it with the tip of his tongue.

'Oh, Jimmy-wimmy,' she breathed, one hand gripping his bare shoulder. 'You can teach me now, if you feel like it.'

He licked her again, and again, and at the same time she took hold of his bone-hard penis in her hand and slowly stroked it.

There was silence between them for a while. Jim continued to lick her until her back began to arch and she began to breathe faster and deeper. He could feel every muscle in her body begin to clench. He could almost feel what it was like to be her, with that clockspring tightening inside her. She was so juicy now that he was almost drinking her. His penis was dripping, too, so that her fingers were slippery.

He was happy. There was no other word for it. He was so excited that he was practically delirious, but most of all he was happy. He was Jimmy Rook, making love to a beautiful young blonde, and she was huge-breasted and long-legged and silky-haired and she was funny, too, and that was all he cared about.

But then for no accountable reason Jim Rook made one of his cutting observations inside his mind and immediately spoiled it all, just the way he had spoiled almost every other relationship he had ever had with a woman. Jim Rook thought, *Look at me, dipping my head up and down, lapping up Summer like Tibbles lapping up his milk.*

The thought totally threw him. He lifted up his head, breathing hard, but his penis started to soften. Summer kept rubbing at him, but the more forcefully she rubbed the softer he became. He stayed where he was for a moment, with his eyes closed and his head tilted back, but then he dropped sideways on to the pillow next to her, wiping his mouth with the back of his hand.

'What's wrong, Jimmy?' she said, frowning at him through a fine curtain of blonde hair. 'Don't tell me you've suddenly gone all guilty on me. I *am* old enough, you know. I'm even old enough to drink.'

He took hold of her fingers and squeezed them together, and then kissed her fingertips. 'I'm sorry, Summer. It's not you. You're beautiful and you're bright and you don't even know how wonderful you've been tonight, you really don't.'

'Then what is it? You've suddenly remembered that you're a faggot?'

Jim shook his head. 'I'm not a faggot and I know you're old enough. It's *me*. It's me and my ghosts – me and my goddamned demons. There's always a little nasty niggling imp in the back of my mind who won't trust anybody or anything, and won't take anything at face value. Like, is this really real, or are you dreaming it?' He didn't tell her what he had thought about Tibbles.

'You do like me, then?' Summer asked him.

He brushed the hair away from her face and kissed her. 'Hey – a little more than *like*.'

'Then where do we go from here? Do you want us to go back to bumping into each other on the landing, every now and then, and saying "hi, how's it hanging?" and nothing else?'

Jim looked into her eyes. He had always known they were blue, but he had never realized before what a complicated collection of blues they were, like broken fragments of corn-flowers and sapphires and sky, all jumbled up together in a kaleidoscope. She was right: he always spoke to people as they were sitting behind a row of desks, and even though he cared about them, he never looked at them closely enough. Not as close as this.

'No,' he said, clearing his throat. 'I don't want to go back to that.'

She put her arm around him. 'In that case, Jimmy-wimmy, maybe we should try again. Tell your nasty little imp to stay in his box for an hour or two, and we'll see what we can do with Mr McFloppy.'

'OK. I'll try.'

She kissed his arm. 'You're real *skinny*, you know. You need to build up your upper body. Maybe I should take you to the gym. But we can start by exercising your love muscle, can't we?'

She took hold of his penis again, and stretched it out like saltwater taffy.

Jim said, 'Careful . . . it does have a breaking-point!' Summer giggled and yanked it even harder. Just as she did so, however, they heard a loud crack, like breaking glass, followed by a high, despairing scream. Then there was another scream, and another, and each scream was so different from the last that they sounded like a chorus.

'Jesus, what's that?' said Jim. He scrabbled for his shorts, bunny-hopped into them, and hobbled toward the bedroom door, still pulling them up. Summer reached for her T-shirt but she couldn't find her thong in the tangled bedclothes so she went across to her closet and pulled out a short denim skirt.

Jim opened the front door. At first he thought that the automobiles parked on the opposite side of the street were on fire, but then he realized that the orange flames that were dancing in their windows were reflected from Mrs LaFarge's apartment downstairs. He ran barefoot down the steps to the landing below, with Summer following close behind him.

Flames were leaping out of the window, as well as thick showers of sparks, which whirled up into the yucca trees. It looked as if the interior of Mrs LaFarge's apartment was already a furnace. Shielding his face with his upraised arm, Jim could see a couch blazing from end to end, and two blazing armchairs. The television had imploded, and flames were pouring out of the empty screen. A large framed photograph of Mr and Mrs LaFarge on their wedding day was slowly being scorched black from the bottom upward, so that the happy couple looked as if they were sinking into a tarpit.

Jim couldn't see Mrs LaFarge anywhere. He shouted at Summer, 'Call the fire department! I'm going to see if Violette is still inside!'

'Jimmy! You can't! It's too dangerous!'

'Call the fire department! And tell them we'll probably need paramedics too, while you're at it!'

Summer hurried back up to her apartment. Jim stood in front of Mrs LaFarge's front door for a moment, trying to decide if it was a good idea to kick it open or not. The fire was burning with a loud hollow roaring noise, punctuated by the crackling of broken glass.

He had almost decided that it would be safer to wait for the fire department when he heard another scream, so distorted that it barely sounded human. Then another, more of an agonized wail. He didn't have any choice. He stepped back as far as the railings, and then he took two quick steps toward the front door and kicked it.

He heard the frame splinter, but the door stayed shut. He stepped back again, took a deep breath, and then rushed at it again, kicking it so hard that he was jarred by the impact all the way up to his hip.

The door burst open. Inside, the hallway was filled with fire, from floor to ceiling. Standing in the center of this fire, her arms spread wide as if she were being crucified, stood Mrs LaFarge, wearing nothing but flames.

ELEVEN

'Violette,' he said, or at least he thought he said it. But then he screamed out, '*Violette!*'

He edged toward the doorway, knees bent, ducking down low and keeping one arm raised up in front of his face. Even so, the heat was too fierce for him to approach within less than four feet of it, and he could still feel his cheeks scorching.

Besides, there didn't seem to be much point in trying to rescue Mrs LaFarge from the flames. Her skin was already blackened all over, and in several places it had split wide apart to expose her glistening red flesh, like the black crust of a lava flow splits apart to reveal the molten magma underneath. Deep in several of these crimson crevasses he could see her blood actually *bubbling*.

But it was the look on her face that gave Jim the greatest feeling of dread. It was blackened, too, like a minstrel moneybox, and all of her hair was burned into crispy clumps. It was difficult to tell if she could still see, but she appeared to be staring at him, unblinkingly because her eyelids had shriveled up into little knots. She had no eyebrows, either, so her stare was expressionless – or it would have been, if she hadn't been smiling at him so widely. There was no question about it. Jim was pretty sure it wasn't the heat, shrinking the skin on her face like some kind of horrific face-lift and distorting her lips. She was actually *smiling*, almost as if she were enjoying her immolation.

The pain she had suffered must have been unbearable – for the first few minutes, anyhow. But by now most of her nerve endings must have burned away, so she was feeling hardly anything at all. She looked ecstatic – beatific, even – as if this was something she had always wanted.

Jim stayed where he was, watching her. The last of her blood hurriedly boiled away, with a snap and a crackle and a *pippety-pop-pip*. Then, as the remaining fats of her body flared up, she actually *sizzled*, with the same sound as a hamburger patty on a hotplate. The flames that were crawling all over her body gradually jumped up higher and higher until they completely engulfed her head. A strong warm draft was drawn in through the doorway and it warbled and moaned like a ghost train.

Every breath that Jim took was filled with the eye-watering smell of charred human flesh. He cupped his hand over his mouth and his nose but it made no difference, and he couldn't stop himself from retching. In the distance, he could hear patrol car sirens scribbling and wailing, and the stentorian bellowing of fire trucks, but all he could do was watch as the flames that engulfed Mrs LaFarge's remains gradually died down.

Just as the first firefighter came hurrying up the steps, her blackened figure fell apart and collapsed on to the hallway rug, her skull rolling one way, with smoke pouring out of her eye sockets, her arms and legs falling across each other like pick-up-sticks. Jim leaned against the railings, his stomach clenching and unclenching, but unable to vomit anything but strings of half-digested cheese because he had eaten only those two slices of pepperoni pizza.

Three more firefighters appeared, unreeling a hose as they came. Almost immediately they started blasting away at Mrs LaFarge's apartment with a high-pressure jet of water, so that the blackened coats hanging in the hallway flapped like vampire bats in a thunderstorm, and the burning chairs in the living room tumbled over and over.

One of the firefighters laid a hand on Jim's shoulder and shouted in his face, 'Are you all right, sir? You didn't inhale any smoke?'

'No, no.' Jim coughed. 'I didn't go inside. By the time I got down here, the whole apartment was burning like a goddamned crematorium. Too late to do anything.'

'OK, sir, let's get you out of here. I think the fire marshal will want to ask you a few questions.'

'That's fine.' *Cough*. 'Whatever.' *Cough*.

The firefighter helped Jim down to the parking space in front of the apartment block, where a bulky fire marshal with short-cropped gingery hair and a gingery yardbrush moustache was standing with three or four firefighters, looking up at the fire with an expression of professional detachment.

'Are you hurt in any way, sir?' he shouted as Jim approached. The pumper close behind him was roaring so loudly that Jim could hardly hear him.

'I'm OK, thanks. I didn't try to be a hero, I'm afraid. I saw Mrs LaFarge but it was too late by then. I couldn't have saved her.'

'You live here?'.

'Top floor. My name's Rook.'

'You live alone?'

'Just me and my cat. Well, just me now. My cat died a couple of days ago.'

'How about this Mrs LaFarge?'

'Violette? She lived alone, too.'

'When did you first become aware that Mrs LaFarge's apartment was on fire?'

'I don't know. About twenty minutes ago, I guess. We heard glass breaking and then we heard somebody screaming.'

'*We?*'

'Me and the young lady from Apartment Two. We were having kind of a late-night get-together.'

The fire marshal looked down at Jim's stripy undershorts and said, 'Sure you were.'

It was almost 10 a.m. before the firefighters finally left. They criss-crossed the front of Mrs LaFarge's burned-out apartment with yellow tapes and warned Jim and Summer not to go inside, because an arson investigation officer would bring a dog round later to sniff for accelerants.

'You think this fire was started deliberately?' asked Jim.

The fire marshal shook his head. 'Hard to tell. I can't see any of the typical signs that somebody used an accelerant here. All the same, it started very quick and it burned very hot, so it wasn't like your victim left a cigarette smoldering on the couch or something like that.'

'Apart from which, she never smoked.'

They were still talking when two firefighters came down the steps, carrying a black body bag on a stretcher. Jim and the fire marshal watched as they took it over to a khaki van from the coroner's office and slid it inside.

'You don't know anybody who might have borne a grudge against her?' asked the fire marshal.

Jim said, 'Absolutely not. She was kind of a busybody, but she was harmless enough.'

'Well . . . I've known people set fires for all kinds of petty reasons,' the fire marshal told him. 'Maybe their neighbors played their music too loud, and refused to turn it down. Maybe they let their dog poop on the grass verge. A couple of months ago there was a family of five who got burned to death up in Canyon Oak Drive because the guy next door objected to the smoke from their barbecue. He didn't mind the smoke *per se*, but he was Jewish and he was angry that the smoke came from pork wieners and wasn't kosher.

'The trouble is, even in this town, people don't understand how quick a fire can get out of control. A whole house can go up in forty seconds flat.'

He turned to leave. As he did so, Summer came down the steps. She linked arms with Jim and said, 'How are you feeling, Jimmy?'

'Sad. Upset. They don't make ladies like Violette any more.'

They went back up to Summer's apartment. Every room reeked of smoke, so she threw all the windows open. 'How about some coffee?' she asked him.

'No . . . I'd better get back upstairs and see if that demon woman's gone.'

'What if she hasn't? What if she's still there, waiting for you?'

'I'm pretty sure that she's not. She's trying to scare me, that's for sure, but I don't think she's actually going to hurt me. Not just yet, anyhow.'

'So . . . why do you think she wants to scare you?'

'I don't know for certain, but I get the distinct feeling that there's some kind of game being worked out here – like chess, but with living people instead of pawns. The only trouble is, I don't know who I'm playing against and I don't know what the stakes are and I don't even know if I'm black or white.'

'You know what I think?' asked Summer. Completely unselfconsciously, she stepped out of her short denim skirt and walked through to the bedroom to hang it up again. 'I think this demon woman is trying to make you feel that your life just isn't worth living.'

'What do you mean?'

'She showed you what you're going to be like when you grow really old, didn't she? Sick, half-blind, pissing your pants. You said yourself that you felt like taking every pill on your bathroom shelf.'

'So?'

'So you're talking about playing a game of chess, right? It's like any game; you only want to play it because you think you have a chance of winning, even if you know that your chance of winning is practically zilch.'

'OK . . . so you're saying . . . what?'

Summer came and sat down beside him at the kitchen table, resting her chin in her hand. She looked almost like a medieval saint – Saint Summer of the Enormous Breasts. The morning sunlight reflected from the red Formica surface and made her hair shine in fraying golden filaments.

'I think this demon woman wants you to give up hope,' she said. 'If tomorrow turns out to be total shit, that's one thing, right? But if you know *today* that tomorrow is going to turn out to be total shit, you're going to think to yourself, why the hell bother? Why go on? My grandmother, she would never go to a fortune-teller or read her stars in the paper, and do you know what she used to say? If it's bad, and it's true, it'll happen anyhow, and there's nothing you can do about it; but if it *isn't* true, and it doesn't happen, then all you've done is worry yourself sick for no reason. Either way you've wasted your money.'

Jim sat looking at her for a very long time without saying anything. Then he said, 'You're not just a pretty face, are you? That is a very, very shrewd analysis.'

'A what?'

'A very intelligent way of looking at all this crap.'

'I don't know about that,' smiled Summer. 'I'm just speaking from bitter experience. The first boyfriend I ever lived with, Bryan, he was like insanely possessive and if he saw me even *smiling* at another guy he used to beat me black and blue. He used to call me when I was at work and say, "I know you've been seeing this schmuck behind my back and when you come home I'm going to make you wish you'd never been born."'

'So why *did* you go home?'

'Ask me and every other woman who gets knocked about. You go home because it's home, and you don't have any place else to go. You go home because you think that your boyfriend must love you, because he's so jealous. But in the end you lose all hope that tomorrow is going to be different. It's like that game of chess that you're never going to win. In the end, finally, you quit.'

Jim stood up. 'I'd better go. I'm over an hour late for college already. Maybe I'll catch you later.'

'Jimmy, you don't have to.'

Jim took hold of her hand. 'Summer – let me tell you this. Sometimes, without any warning at all, somebody arrives in your life who changes it for ever. They change *you* for ever. They do it because they have a totally different point of view on life. It's like they hold up a mirror so that you can see yourself from a different angle altogether, and you think, *my God, do I really look like that?*'

'Are you talking about me?'

'I don't know anybody else who can do the Backwards Showgirl.'

Jim trudged back upstairs and unlocked his apartment door. He pushed it open, but before he ventured inside he stood on the worn-out welcome mat outside, listening. He couldn't hear anything, apart from the breeze in the bushes, but that wasn't any guarantee that the fox-woman wasn't standing behind his bedroom door, waiting to jump on him and bite off his head, like Charlie's, leaving him with nothing but a bloody windpipe.

'Hello?' he called out. 'Anybody there?'

He waited and waited. A truck came grinding up Briarcliff Road, with three Mexican gardeners sitting in the back. They looked up at him and for some reason one of them crossed himself. It was almost as if a priest had given him the last rites, and Jim couldn't think of anything that could have unnerved him more.

Inside the hallway, on the floor, lay a lavender-tinted envelope. Jim picked it up and squinted at the spidery handwriting on the front. *Jim Rook*, it said. *Apt #3. Je vous attendrai, mon ami.*

He went through to the kitchen first. Everything appeared to be normal, and untouched. No fox-woman. Tibbles' bowls were still lying on the floor, even though the milk in his saucer had turned sour and lumpy.

Jim used a cheese knife to open the lavender-tinted envelope. Inside he found a lavender-tinted sheet of paper, with deckled edges. There were five lines of handwriting on it, and it was signed *Violette*.

'*Mon cher Jim*,' she had written. '*I came to pay you a visit this evening, but sadly you were not here. However I met your friend, and your friend showed me what is to become of me in two years' time. I prefer not to wait for what is inevitable, and so I have decided to embrace my fate now. Tonight I am joining my beloved Antoine and I shall be truly happy at last. I am sad to leave you, mon cher Jim, but my spirit will always be waiting for you, like a cat's spirit.*'

Jim frowned. '*I met your friend*,' Mrs LaFarge had written. What friend? As far as Jim was aware, only the fox-woman had been here, and whatever *she* was, she was very far from being a friend. But the fox-woman had shown Jim how much he was going to deteriorate as he grew older, both physically and mentally, and it seemed likely that she had shown Mrs LaFarge *her* future, too. At some time, sooner or later, Mrs LaFarge was fated to be burned to death.

Jim went through to the living room. He stood there for a while, with one hand on the back of his armchair, feeling exhausted. It was still gloomy in there, but there was no sign of the fox-woman. Eventually he crossed over to the windows and drew back the drapes. Out on the balcony he could see the battered cardboard box in which he had placed Tibbles' rotting remains. Hundreds of crows were still clustered on the roof of the apartment block opposite, and they gave him the feeling that they were watching him, waiting to see what would happen to him next. They had pecked out Tibbles'

eyes and pulled out his intestines. Maybe they were waiting
to do the same to *him*.

His phone warbled and made him jump. He picked it up
and cleared his throat. 'Jim Rook.'

'Mr Rook? This is Doris Handy, Mr Rook. Dr Ehrlichman
wants to know if you intend to honor us with your presence
today. Apparently Special Class Two is beginning to sound
like the Battle of Shiloh. Dr Ehrlichman's words, not mine.'

Jim said, 'I'm sorry, Doris. I meant to call in, but things
have been totally crazy. We had a real bad fire at my apartment building last night, and I've been helping the fire
marshal to figure out what happened. Listen – I'm just going
to take a shower and I should be into college around eleven-
thirty at the latest. Could you ask Bob Nussbaum to take
over for me, if he's free? Tell him I'll buy him a bottle of
Hevron Heights. Tell him I'll buy him a bottle of Hevron
Heights and a Canter's knish.'

'I'll ask,' said Doris disapprovingly.

Jim hung up. Then he prowled around his apartment,
checking in the bedroom and the bathroom and all of the
closets to make sure that the fox-woman was no longer there.
He even got down on to his hands and knees and looked
under the bed. After all, even kids know that boogie-persons
always conceal themselves under the bed.

He undressed, wearily, and took a long, hot shower. He
dressed in a black shirt, as a gesture of respect for Mrs
LaFarge, and khaki chinos. Then he slid open the window
to the balcony and picked up Tibbles' cardboard coffin. As
he carried it inside, he looked across at the crows and shouted
out, '*Get the hell out of here, you sons-of-bitches!*'

The crows shifted and cawed and ruffled their tatty black
feathers but none of them flew away. Jim locked the balcony
window behind him and closed the drapes. It would probably be dark by the time he got home tonight.

He took the cardboard box into the kitchen and put it down
on the counter. He opened the fridge and looked inside to
see what he could find to make sandwiches. Half-a-dozen
slices of bologna, well past their sell-by date, with dark
curled-up edges. Two Kraft processed cheese slices. A wrinkly
apple that looked like it needed Botox. A jar of pickled

beetroot. He would have to have lunch at the college commissary today, even though he hated it. All the food they served
up was so goddamn *healthy*. Everything that wasn't sprinkled
with wheatgerm was covered in pine-nuts, and everything gave
him gas.

He closed the fridge door, but as he did so he heard a
sharp scratching noise from inside the cardboard box. He
froze, and waited, and listened. There was no way that Tibbles
could have come back to life again. His eye sockets were
empty and half of his guts had gone. But on the other hand,
he had been crushed almost totally flat when Jim had run
him over, and he had come back to life then, hadn't he? It
really depended when *then* really was. Had it been yesterday,
or the day before, or was it going to be tomorrow?

He heard the scratching noise again. He went up close to
the box and said, 'Tibbles?'

A long silence. Then a few light scratches, followed by a
sudden flurry.

'Tibbles? Are you in there? You haven't come back to life
again, have you?'

This time the scratching was furious, as if Tibbles were
desperate to be let out of his coffin. Jim quickly untucked
the flaps at the top of the box, and folded them back. This
was only a cat, after all, even if he was supposed to be a
dead cat. He looked inside and saw Tibbles lying on his
back, his eyes still blind, his upper lip still curled in a snarl,
his stomach a tangle of bloody fur and rope-like intestines.

'Tibbles?' Jim coaxed him, but there didn't seem to be
any question at all that he was dead. 'Tibbles, I'm sorry,
dude, but you have permanently gone to swallow the great
furball in the sky.'

Tibbles didn't move. Jim couldn't understand how he could
have made those frantic scratching noises. Maybe his muscles
had been relaxing. Cats generally went into rigor mortis
about four hours after death, and their rigidity lasted between
eighteen to thirty-six hours, but it all depended on the ambient
temperature, and how the cat had died. Jim had learned that
from the vet, when Tibbles' predecessor had been killed.

Jim was closing the last flap of the box when Tibbles'
stomach exploded, and a huge crow came bursting out, its

feathers bloody and shreds of intestine hanging from its beak. Jim shouted out, '*Jesus!*' and toppled backward against the fridge. The crow attacked him with its claws and its beak, its wings beating wildly. It scratched and pecked at his upraised hands, and it seemed to be determined to go for his eyes.

'Get away, you bastard!' Jim yelled at it. But his shouting seemed to excite the crow even more. Its wings flapped faster and faster, and it lunged its head forward again and again. It pecked Jim just below the left eye with its beak, and then it raked him with its claws across his right cheek. No matter how hard Jim slapped at it, it kept on attacking him, more and more ferociously, until he began to feel that he was never going to be able to beat it off.

He backed away until he reached the far side of the kitchen, where all of his pans were hanging up on hooks underneath the cupboards. The crow continued to lunge at him, and now it started to let out harsh triumphant cries in the back of his throat, as if it felt that it had beaten him. It darted with its beak at his forehead, close to his eye, and he felt as if he had been jabbed in the face with a pointed stick. A fine spray of blood flew across the kitchen worktop.

Next time the crow came at him, however, Jim ducked and spun around and swung his arm, so that he knocked it halfway across the kitchen. It struck the side of Tibbles' cardboard box with a hollow thump. Immediately, he made a grab for his heaviest cast-iron griddle.

The crow cawed furiously at him and came whirling back, more like a black windmill than a bird, but Jim was ready for it. Gripping the griddle in both hands, he hit the bird with a devastating backhand that sent it smashing into the tiles between the faucets. It croaked and dropped into the sink, and although it made a feeble effort to climb out again, it eventually fell back and lay on its side, its legs still quivering but its eyes closed.

Jim picked it up by one of its claws and dropped it into the pedal-bin. 'Sorry,' he said. 'No funeral for you, you ghoul.'

He was shaking and he had to take a deep breath to steady himself. He dabbed his cheek with his fingertips and found

that he was still bleeding, so he went back into the bathroom
and dabbed tea tree oil on his face in case the crow had been
infected with psittacosis or crowitis or whatever unpleasant
disease crows could pass on to humans.

Back in the kitchen, he slung his brown canvas book bag
over his shoulder and picked up the box with Tibbles' body
in it. He took a quick look in the pedal-bin before he left,
but the crow was still lying there with its head in an empty
yogurt pot and it was definitely dead.

He left his apartment and double-locked the front door
behind him, although he doubted if any number of locks
would keep the fox-woman out, if she wanted to come back
in. The morning was still windy, with tumbling gray clouds.
As he passed Summer's apartment he was tempted to ring
the doorbell and find out how she was, but he decided to
leave her alone for the time being. She was probably sleeping,
after last night's shenanigans, and she had to go to work this
evening, to do some Full Mooning and Cradling and
Exploding and all the other pole-dancing moves she had to
make.

For a moment, though, he stopped outside her door, and
pictured how she had looked last night and everything that
had happened between them, and it gave him a warm feeling
that he hadn't experienced in a very long time, and made
him smile.

On the landing below, crunching over broken glass, he
stopped for a moment outside Mrs LaFarge's apartment, too.
All of the windows were empty and above each of them the
pink-painted stucco was stained with banners of black soot.
Inside, he could make out the skeletons of Mrs LaFarge's
furniture, and wallpaper that was streaked with runnels of
dirty gray. The stench of burning was still so strong that he
had to pinch his nose between finger and thumb to stop
himself from breathing it in.

He was about to leave when he realized that there was a
figure standing in the far right-hand corner of the living
room. The figure was completely motionless, and when he
had first seen it he had mistaken it for a hat stand. But it
was a woman, with a broad-brimmed hat on, and even though

he couldn't see her face very clearly, she appeared to be staring at him. For one chilling second he thought that it might be the ghost of Mrs LaFarge, but the woman's hat was a different shape from the 1950s flying-saucer style that Mrs LaFarge had habitually worn.

'Excuse me – who are you?' he called out. 'Ma'am? What are you doing in there? Didn't you see the fire department tapes here? Nobody's allowed inside.'

The woman gave no indication that she had heard him. She didn't answer and she didn't move. Jim didn't know what to do. Maybe he should call the police and tell them that there was an intruder in Mrs LaFarge's apartment. On the other hand, the woman looked very much like the fox-woman, although she was standing in silhouette against the bright gray light from the balcony window and he couldn't be entirely sure. If she *were* the fox-woman, the likelihood of her still being here when the police arrived was remote, and Jim would simply look like a crank and a time-waster.

Right now, he knew that he had to appear as credible and as sane as possible, especially with Lieutenant Harris and Detective Wong and Dr Ehrlichman. After the terrible injuries that Maria had suffered – whether they had been real or illusory – he was convinced that Special Class Two were all in critical danger – and that *he* was, too. He needed all the support he could get, even if he had to be economical with the truth, and not try to insist that anything supernatural was going on.

He knew the fox-woman was plaguing him, for whatever reason, even if nobody else was likely to believe him. And although he didn't know why, he felt that he was the key to whatever was happening, as if he were the key to a clock that kept losing time.

He was still standing outside Mrs LaFarge's apartment when he heard Summer calling out, 'Jimmy! What you doing, Jimmy-wimmy?'

He looked up. She was leaning over the railing wearing nothing but a blue-and-white striped shirt, with the collar turned up, and the top four buttons undone. Her hair was a riot, pinned up with grips. Up above her, the clouds were beginning to break, and the sun shone to give her a halo.

'I was just on my way to college,' he told her. 'I was

taking a look inside of Violette's apartment and I thought I
... Um, I was taking a look, that's all.' He decided in mid-
sentence that it was better if Summer didn't know that the
fox-woman was inside. That's if it *was* the fox-woman, and
not some vagrant, or some looter, or some ghost.

'You going to come see me at the Pothole tonight?' Summer
asked him.

'Maybe. I'll try. I have a whole lot of classwork to catch
up with.'

'Well if you can't make it I'll knock on your door when
I come back from work and I'll show you my Eye Opener.'

'Wow,' he said. He wished he wouldn't say 'wow.' It made
him sound like a fifteen-year-old.

He looked back into Mrs LaFarge's apartment. The figure
was still there, but now that the sunlight had brightened he
could see that it wasn't a figure, after all. It *was* a hat stand,
with a broad-brimmed hat perched on top and a pale gray
coat hanging underneath it.

He stayed there for a few moments, staring at it. Jesus,
he couldn't even trust his own eyes now. Or maybe he could.
Maybe it *had* been a woman, and then changed back again.

He went down to the parking area, opened the trunk of
his car and carefully stowed away the cardboard box with
Tibbles' body in it. Then he climbed into the driving seat,
but he didn't leave immediately. He sat behind the wheel for
over two minutes, looking up at the balcony outside Mrs
LaFarge's apartment. He was half-expecting to see a gray
figure in a wide-brimmed hat come hurrying out. But nobody
did, and after a while he turned the key in the ignition and
backed out into Briarcliff Road.

He switched on the radio and it was playing 'The Dark
End of the Street' by Percy Sledge.

'*At the dark end of the street ... hiding in shadows where
we don't belong ... living in darkness, to hide alone ...*'

As he turned into the gates of West Grove College, a large
cloud drifted across the sun, so that the campus suddenly
looked as grainy and colorless as a black and white movie.
Jim felt a sudden surge of deep misgiving, as if the cloud
were an omen that something hideous was going to happen.

TWELVE

When he walked into Special Class Two, there was no sign of Bob Nussbaum, whom he had asked to stand in for him, and the classroom was in chaos.

He went over to his desk, but the shouting and the whistling and the throbbing of gangsta rap didn't abate. Arthur and Billy and Grant kept passing their basketball, one to the other. Judii was talking on her cellphone and swinging her necklace around and around, while Tamara was peering into her compact and fixing her turquoise eye make-up. Behind her upraised desk-lid, Patsy-Jean was listening to her MP3 player with her eyes tight shut and at the same time burrowing her podgy little hand into a giant-sized bag of Golightly sugar-free tropical fruit candies.

Only Teddy appeared to be doing any work. He was hunched over his desk, scribbling furiously, but God only knew what he was scribbling about, because he never stopped scribbling from the moment he sat down at his desk to the moment the final bell rang. Kim was sitting with his head in his hands, absorbed in a copy of the Korean edition of *Men's Health*. He didn't even look up when Jim came in.

Next to Kim, Maria was doing nothing at all, staring at the blackboard as if she were expecting some kind of doom-filled message to materialize on it, like *mene, mene, tekel upharsin*, the writing on the wall which had warned King Belshazzar of the imminent end of the Babylonian empire. Jim noticed that she had a fresh crimson bruise on the right side of her mouth, and her lip was split. He would have to take her aside at the end of class and talk to her about it, or at least arrange for her to talk to Nurse Okeke.

He perched on the edge of his desk, waiting for the music and the chatter and the basketball-throwing to die down. Over three minutes went by, and the noise continued, so he went across to the stationery cupboard, unlocked it, and took

out a tub of yellow Play-Doh. Then he went back to his desk
and took a scarlet roman candle out of his bag. He stuck a
large blob of Play-Doh on his desk, and pressed the roman
candle into it. Then he took out his Zippo lighter and lit it.

Almost immediately, the roman candle started to fizz and
send up a shower of orange sparks, as well as pouring out
smoke. Everybody in the class stopped what they were doing
and stared at it in disbelief.

'Sir! You just litten a *firework*, man!' said T.D. 'What you
done that for?'

'Just amusing myself,' Jim told him, taking off his coat.
The smoke was already so thick that he could hardly see the
back row of the classroom. 'If you don't want to learn
anything when you come to this class, that's fine by me. You
do what you feel like doing and I'll do what *I* feel like doing.
Today, I feel like lighting fireworks.'

'Sir, that really *stinks*!' protested Judii. 'Isn't it like some
cancerous health hazard or something?'

'Most likely,' said Jim. 'But what do you care? You obviously don't want to be here anyhow.'

'I had to talk to my friend Roxanne,' said Judii, holding
up her cellphone. 'I met this really boom boy last night and
I didn't know if he was interested in seeing me or not. Like,
if he *does* want to see me, that could affect my whole entire
future, you know?'

'Oh, that's OK, then,' said Jim, raising his hand in acknowl-
edgement. 'I wouldn't like to think that you were doing
anything unimportant, like finding out what a noun is.'

Teddy put up his hand, although Jim could barely see him
through the smoke.

'Sir? I know what a noun is, sir!'

'I know *you* do, Teddy. But a considerable number of
students in this class of ours haven't the foggiest idea. Not
that it matters. They're not interested in finding out. They're
quite happy being ignorant and illiterate, and if they're quite
happy being ignorant and illiterate, who am I to spoil their
happiness?'

The roman candle fizzed faster and louder and now a foun-
tain of sparks was shooting right up to the ceiling tiles. Janice
Sticky started coughing, and then Leon and Arthur and T.D.

joined in, hacking and spluttering and wheezing and staggering around the classroom clutching at their throats.

'Mr Rook, we're dying in here!' said Arthur.

At that moment, the roman candle exploded with a deafening bang, which made every student in the classroom jump
in fright.

'Shit, man!' T.D. protested. 'Almost gave me a freakin'
heart attack!'

'So long as I have your attention,' said Jim. 'Billy, Georgia,
you want to open those windows at the back there? I think
we could all use some fresh air.'

Just as they opened the windows, the smoke alarm went
off, a penetrating *meep-meep-meep* that made it impossible
for his students to hear what Jim was saying to them next.
He made his way down the center aisle, shouted '*Excuse
me!*' to Tamara, and climbed up on her desk. Then he reached
up and pried the cover off the smoke alarm, and took out
the batteries.

'Right,' he said, climbing back down. 'Let's get down to
some serious grammar. That's if everybody's willing.'

Reluctantly, Special Class Two shuffled back to their desks
and sat down.

'So can anybody tell me what a noun is?' Jim asked them.
'Except for you, Teddy, that is.'

Billy put up his hand. 'Is it like something you don't do
too often? Like people say to you, how often do you go to
Burger King? And you say "noun then."'

'Interesting try,' Jim told him. 'But if you don't do something very often you say that you do it "now and then."
Three words. Now. *And*. Then.'

He looked around the class. 'Anybody else? No? You
shouldn't be afraid to have a shot at it, just because you
might make a complete idiot out of yourself.'

Nobody else put up a hand, so Jim picked up an antique
book with a green cloth binding and held it up in front of
them. 'You see this? This book was written by a guy called
Gilbert Dargent, who was born in 1889. There's a chapter
in it all about his time at school, and in those days they used
to teach their English students with a rhyme. I still don't
know of an easier way to learn what a noun is, or a verb,

or any of the other parts of speech. Learn this rhyme, and nobody will ever think that you're an ignorant illiterate jackass again.'

'Hey, nobody don't think that about me anyhow,' T.D. retorted.

'That's because nobody you happen to know right now can tell the difference between a noun and a verb, either. But one day when you go out into the big scary world you'll meet people who do. And wouldn't you feel more confident if you knew that "hat" was a noun that you wear on your head and not the past tense of the verb "hit."'

'I knew that,' said T.D., petulantly. 'Who ever says "I *hat* that dude right in the mouth?" I mean, who says that? Everybody knows it's "hitted."'

Almost all of the other students laughed and jeered at him. T.D. turned around in his seat, furious. 'What?' he demanded. 'Fit, fitted. Knit, knitted. Hit, hitted. Don't you know *nothin'*?'

'OK, OK,' said Jim. 'Here's the rhyme. You may think it sounds old-fashioned. You may think that it sounds like a rhyme for nursery-age kids. But believe me, I know dozens of adults who aren't too sure about nouns and verbs, and that includes some teachers, too.

> '*A noun is the name of anything,*
> *A hoop or garden, school or swing.*
> *An adjective describes a noun,*
> *Small shoes, bright eyes, new gloves, green gown.*
> *A verb tells us what people do,*
> *They dance, she walks, he laughed, it flew.*
> *An adverb tells how things are done,*
> *We quietly talk, they quickly run.*
> *An interjection shows surprise,*
> *As "Oh! How pretty. Ah! How wise."*'

Jim walked up and down the classroom, handing out copies of the rhyme to every student. When he reached Teddy's desk, Teddy raised an eyebrow as if to say, 'Why are you giving *me* one?' But Jim leaned close to his ear and said, 'Go on, Teddy, take it anyhow. It won't do you any harm, and if the rest of the class think that *you* need it, too – well, it won't make them feel quite so dumb.'

Teddy nodded, and took it. Jim had learned one thing about his students over the years. Most of them may have been borderline illiterate, but very few of them were stupid or insensitive. Behind all of their bravado, and in spite of their apparent indifference, they were all deeply aware that every one of them was fighting the same desperate fight.

'What I want you to do now is open your copies of *To Kill A Mockingbird* to page one hundred nine. I want you to read the whole page very carefully, and make a list of every noun you come across, and every adjective, and every verb, and every adverb. And any interjections, if you can find them.'

He glanced up at the clock. 'OK, you have a half-hour. I have to leave the classroom for a while, but I don't want any more messing around, and by the time I come back I expect you to be pretty much finished. Janice – you can be the class snitch. Anybody does anything stupid or disruptive, I want to know about it.'

Jim left the classroom and walked along the empty corridor. Outside, the wind had died down, the clouds had frittered away, and it was hot and sunny. Off to his right, one of the groundskeepers was mowing the wide grassy bank between the main college building and the swimming pool, with a tractor and a front-mounted cutter. The grass cuttings glittered in the sunlight.

He crossed the parking lot and opened the trunk of his car. He wondered if he ought to open the cardboard box and take a last look at Tibbles, just to make absolutely sure that he was dead, but the smell was enough to convince him that he must be. He lifted out the box and carried it around the side of the main building. He went down the concrete steps that led to the basement and pushed his way inside. It was hot and noisy down there, and he could hear the incinerator rumbling.

Halfway along the corridor, to the left, he turned into the boiler room. Dunstan the janitor was in there, in his brown dungarees, breaking up cardboard boxes and tossing them into the open door of the furnace.

'Hi there, Mr Rook!' he greeted him. 'You aint s'posed to be down here, sir. Health and safety regulations. Don't want you getting scorchified or nothing.'

'That's OK, Dunstan. I was wondering if you could burn this box for me, that's all.'

'Sure thing, if you want me to. But you could've just dropped it in the dumpster out back.'

'As a matter of fact, Dunstan, there's something inside it. My cat, Tibbles. He died, and I wanted to have him cremated.'

'Your *cat*? This isn't no pet crematorium, Mr Rook. Not so sure I'm allowed to incinerate animals. Health and safety regulations.'

'Oh, come on, Dunstan. Do me a favor here. I didn't want to bury him in my back yard. Too many goddamned gophers. Give them five minutes and they'd dig him back up again.'

Dunstan took the box, sniffed it, and wrinkled up his nose. 'Smells pretty far gone to me, Mr Rook. How long's the poor little critter been dead?'

'I'm not entirely sure, to tell you the truth. Couple of days, maybe. I seem to have been losing track of time lately.'

Dunstan set the box down on the floor and used a long black poker to open the door of the incinerator even wider. The wave of heat was so intense that Jim had to step back a few paces.

'Losin' track of time – that's been happenin' to me, too,' said Dunstan. 'I kept thinkin' it was Wednesday but it was Tuesday. I called up my daughter yesterday evening to wish her a happy birthday but she told me that I'd made a mistake and her birthday was tomorrow, which is today. It feels to me like things are happenin' before they're happenin', if you can understand what I mean, but then they haven't happened after all. Not yet, anyhow.'

He gave the incinerator a few sharp pokes, so that the fire roared even hotter, and then he dropped the poker with a clang and bent down to pick up Jim's cardboard box. He was just about to hurl it into the flames, however, when he stopped himself, and held it up high, close to his ear, and shook it.

'What's the matter?' Jim asked him. 'He's in there, all right. You smelled him yourself.'

Dunstan lowered the box on to the floor again. 'Are you absolutely sure he's passed away, Mr Rook? Because I could swear I felt him move.'

'Dunstan, he's as dead as a doornail. His body was lying on my balcony and the crows were pecking at it. He must have slid across the bottom of the box, that's all.'

Dunstan knelt down and bent his head forward, listening intently. 'I'm sure I can hear scratching. There's *something* alive inside of this here box, even if it ain't your cat. Maybe one of your gophers got in there, too.'

'Dunstan, please! Just burn the goddamned box, will you?'

Dunstan pulled off his thick gray work glove and opened one of the flaps at the top of the box. 'No harm in checkin', Mr Rook. We don't want to go incineratin' some poor critter while it's still livin' and breathin', do we?'

'He's *dead*, Dunstan, for Christ's sake. The crows pecked out his eyes and half of his goddamned guts.'

Dunstan took no notice, but lifted the other three flaps and folded them back. As he did so, there was a hideous screech, like a hundred knives scraping on a hundred dinner plates. Tibbles came bursting out of the box and leaped on to Dunstan's face, clawing furiously at his forehead and his cheeks and his eyelids. Dunstan fell backward on to the floor, screaming, and trying to fight Tibbles off.

'Ahhh! My eyes! It's scratchin' my eyes! Lord in Heaven, get it off of me!'

Dunstan pulled Tibbles away from his face and threw him sideways across the boiler room. Tibbles rolled over and over, but immediately got back on to his feet and came flying at Dunstan with his teeth bared and his fur sticking up as if he had been electrocuted. Jim saw that Dunstan's hands were smothered in blood, and that the bib of his dungarees was spattered with blood, too. Dunstan tried to roll himself over so that Tibbles wouldn't jump on his face again, and it was then that Jim saw his right eyeball hanging out its socket like a glass eye, staring at nothing.

Tibbles jumped on to Dunstan's shoulder and started clawing at his left ear and the side of his face, screeching and spitting as he did so. Jim picked up the poker that Dunstan had dropped on to the floor and hit Tibbles so hard that Tibbles hit the opposite wall, and dropped down behind a stack of discarded Mazola boxes.

Jim knelt down beside Dunstan and turned him on to his back. Dunstan was moaning, 'My eye . . . my eye, Mr Rook. That critter pulled out my eye.'

'Don't try to touch it,' Jim told him. 'I'm calling nine-one-one right now.'

He reached into his shirt pocket, where he usually kept his cellphone, but his pocket was empty. He remembered then that he had taken it out and put it down on his desk, because he had been meaning to call Summer.

'Please, Dunstan, try to stay still,' he said. 'So long as you don't touch your eye you should be OK. I don't have my cell with me. Where's the nearest phone?'

Dunstan was quivering with shock. 'It's down the end of the corridor. Is that cat gone? What did you do with that cat, Mr Rook?'

'I don't know. I can't see him. I think I must have knocked him out. I don't know how he could have jumped up and attacked you like that. I was sure he was dead. Listen – wait here while I go to the phone. I won't be long.'

Jim stood up and headed for the door. As he did so, however, Tibbles came slinking out from underneath the Mazola boxes. He came creeping across the boiler-room floor, keeping very low, like a lion stalking a wildebeest, but what horrified Jim was that his eye-sockets were empty, and that his pale and bloody intestines were dragging across the concrete beneath his belly. He had to be dead, and yet he wasn't.

'*Tibbles!*' Jim shouted at him. The cat hesitated, and blindly lifted his head, but then he continued to advance toward Dunstan, and he started to creep faster and faster, as if he were confident that his prey couldn't escape.

Jim threw himself across the room and grabbed Tibbles with both hands. Tibbles screeched and struggled and clawed at him, but Jim lifted him up and carried him over to the furnace. There was a moment when Tibbles was twisting so violently and scratching at him with such fury that Jim thought that he was going to drop him, but he managed to seize his tail and swing him around and around like a slingshot. Tibbles hissed in rage; but at the point of maximum velocity Jim let go of him and he flew into the open door of the furnace and instantly flared up.

Jim picked up the poker, so that he could close the furnace door, but as he bent over, Tibbles came hurtling back out of the flames, blazing from head to tail, and screaming like a child. He went after Jim in a fiery zigzag, jumping up on to the leg of his pants and clinging on with his claws. Jim hit him with the poker, again and again, and eventually Tibbles dropped off on to the floor, although he was still writhing and hissing and trying to get back on to his feet.

Now Jim beat Tibbles relentlessly, until he had beaten all of the flames out, and smashed his smoking carcass so completely that he had to be dead. Jim was panting by the time he had finished, and coughing from the smell of burning cat fur, but he didn't feel guilty, or cruel. Whatever had sprung out of that box and taken Dunstan's eye out couldn't have been Tibbles. It had been some demonic apparition, some demon's familiar, like a witch's cat.

He picked up a shovel that was leaning up against the wall and scooped Tibbles' charred and flattened body into the furnace. Then he closed the furnace door and locked it, so that there was absolutely no chance that Tibbles could leap out again.

'OK, Dunstan,' he said, unsteadily. 'Hold on, feller. I'm going to get you some help.'

Still coughing, he made his way along the corridor to the telephone, lifted the receiver and punched out 911 to call for an ambulance.

'Please hurry. The guy's in shock.'

As he hung up, he looked out of the basement window and saw a girl walking past, wearing purple jeans and a bronze satin blouse. Although she was too high up for him to be able to see her face, he recognized at once who she was. Maria Lopez. But what was she doing, walking around outside, when she should have been in class, trying to compile a list of nouns and verbs and adjectives and adverbs?

It was then that he began to get an inkling of what was happening. Maria was wearing the same jeans and the same blouse that she had been wearing on the first day of the new semester, or what had seemed like the first day of the semester. And she had left the classroom today at exactly the same time as she had left the classroom on that day, too. Today, though, something was different. Today, one of the groundskeepers was mowing the grass.

Jim ran back to the boiler room. Dunstan was sitting up now, although his eye was still hanging out on his cheek. His face was a dirty gray color, and he was trembling.

'The paramedics are going to be here in just a few minutes,' Jim told him. 'Right now, though, you're going to have to forgive me. I have to do something really, really urgent.'

'*Please*,' Dunstan begged him. 'Please don't leave me.'

'I have to, Dunstan. It's one of my students. She's in serious danger.'

Dunstan reached out to him in a mute appeal for him to stay, but Jim said, 'I'm sorry, Dunstan, I really am.' He ran off along the corridor, pushed open the door, and vaulted up the steps. He could hear the lawnmower, but he couldn't see it yet. There was no sign of Maria, either. He hurried around the corner of the building, just in time to see Maria walking out of the shadow of the cedar tree, and up the grassy bank that led to the swimming pool.

'Maria!' he shouted, and ran toward her as fast as he could. 'Maria! Stop!'

He took a short cut by running up the steps in front of the main entrance. As he did so, one of the doors opened and Sheila Colefax appeared, wearing a pink sweater the color of Pepto-Bismol.

'Oh, Jim!' she exclaimed. 'I was looking for you!'

'Later!' Jim blurted, and ran down the steps on the other side.

'It's about that poetry reading!' Sheila called after him, in a weak, hopeless voice. 'If you still want to come—'

'Maria!' Jim shouted, yet again. 'Whatever you're thinking of doing, don't do it!'

Somehow, both time and distance seemed to be distorted. Although Jim was running after Maria as fast as he could, he didn't seem to be able to catch up with her. She always seemed to be thirty yards ahead of him, and even though he

was shouting at her she didn't show any indication that she
could hear him.

She was more than a third of the way up the grassy bank
when she took off her bronze satin blouse and tossed it aside.
Underneath she was wearing a black bra, and without any
hesitation she reached behind her with both hands and unfastened it, and tossed that aside, too. As he came running
up the bank after her, Jim could see that her bare back was
covered in dark red bruises.

Now the grass-mowing tractor was less than twenty yards
away. The groundskeeper was wearing ear protectors, and
he was twisted around in his seat with his back to Maria,
watching the stripes that the mower was leaving in the vivid
green grass.

Maria, don't! said Jim, inside his head. The clattering noise
of the tractor was too loud now for her to be able to hear
him, even if she had wanted to listen. She drew off her brown
leather belt, and then she hesitated and hopped and half-
stumbled for just a moment as she took down her purple
jeans. Jim thought he might be able to reach her, but the
harder he struggled up the slope, the further away he seemed
to be. It was like a nightmare, like *Alice Through the Looking-
Glass*, in which you had to run as fast as you possibly could
just to stay in the same place.

He could see Maria and the lawnmower coming together
with a terrible inevitability, like two converging lines on a
radar screen. '*Maria!*' he screamed. '*Maria!*' but still she
took no notice.

When she was less than twenty feet away from the lawnmower, Maria pulled down her large black stomach-control
panties and threw them aside, so that she was naked, apart
from her wooden-bead necklace. Her dimpled buttocks, too,
were covered in bruises. Still she kept walking – even faster
now, if anything. Jim prayed that the groundskeeper would
turn his head around and see her, but the groundskeeper was
obviously too concerned with making sure that he was
mowing a perfectly straight stripe.

Maria reached the path in which the lawnmower was
heading only seconds before the lawnmower itself. Although
she was quite a plump girl, she lay down on the grass with

fluidity and grace. She crossed herself, and then she stayed there with her arms by her sides, her feet together, facing upward and looking at the sky.

Jim roared, '*Stop! Stop! Stop!*' so harsh and so loud that he felt as if he were tearing the skin from the back of his throat. He willed his legs to run faster. If he could have willed himself to fly, and scoop up Maria in his arms, and lift her away from the lawnmower's approaching blades, he would have done that, too.

But he knew that he was going to be too late, and he knew that time was playing confidence tricks, and that when Maria had staggered into Special Class Two on the first day of the new semester, naked and lacerated and covered in blood, it had been *this* day, and that what they had seen had simply been a warning that *this* was coming.

THIRTEEN

He closed his eyes tight, but he couldn't stop himself from hearing the crunching and the grinding and the squealing of gears as the lawnmower's blades were jammed with arms and legs and hair and flesh.

The lawnmower stopped. The groundskeeper switched off the tractor engine. In the sudden quietness, Jim opened his eyes and saw Maria underneath the machinery, still alive, staring up at him through the cutters as if she were looking through the bars of a prison cell at the world outside.

The groundskeeper jumped down from his tractor cab and came up to Jim with his mouth hanging open in shock. He was only young, no more than twenty or twenty-one, with ginger hair and spots and a straggly goatee like Shaggy Rogers from *Scooby-Doo*.

'Man,' he said. 'I never saw her, man. I mean, like, what was she *doing* there, man? I mean, Jesus H. Christ.'

Jim knelt down on the grass and took hold of Maria's bloodied hand. Half of her thumb and her index finger and her middle finger were missing.

'Maria?' he asked her. 'Can you hear me, Maria?'

She closed her eyes and then opened them again. 'Yes, sir,' she whispered. A bubble of blood formed on her lips and then softly popped. 'I can hear you.'

Jim bent down to see how the lawnmower blades had bitten into her. She was seriously cut up. Her left shoulder was split right down to the whiteness of her bone, and the left side of her stomach was gaping like a bloody mouth, but as far as he could see she wasn't trapped. He turned around to Shaggy and said, 'Can you lift this thing off her? We really need to get her out.'

'Sure. Sure thing. Jesus.'

'Just go easy, OK? It doesn't look like she's tangled up or anything, but we don't want to hurt her any more than she's hurt already.'

'OK, sure. I got you.'

Shaggy climbed back into his tractor and started up the engine again. Then, very slowly, he raised the hydraulic arms so that the lawn-mowing unit rose upward, and Jim could gently pull Maria out from under it. She left a wide trail of glistening blood on the grass.

'Right,' said Jim, when Shaggy had switched off the tractor and come back to see what he could do. 'Go tell Nurse Okeke what's happened. Tell her that I've called for the paramedics already, because Dunstan's been hurt, in the boiler room. His eye has come out of its socket. But as soon as the paramedics arrive, tell them they're needed up here first. They'll probably need to send another ambulance for Dunstan.'

The groundskeeper blinked at him.

'Did you get all of that?' Jim demanded.

'I think so, yeah. Go tell Nurse Okeke. Tell her to come up here real quick.'

'That's right. And don't forget to tell her about Dunstan, too.'

'Dunstan's been hurt. His eye's come out. In the boiler room.'

'That's it. You got it. Now *go*!'

Jim watched Shaggy cantering wildly down the slope toward the main entrance. Then he turned back to Maria. She was still conscious, still looking up at the sky. To his surprise, she was smiling.

'What happened, Maria?' Jim asked her. 'Why did you want to hurt yourself like that?'

She turned her head a little so that she could focus on him. 'Mr Rook? Is that you?'

'Yes, Maria, it's me. I just want to know why you lay down in front of that lawnmower. You're not *that* unhappy, surely?'

'It doesn't hurt,' Maria reassured him. 'I can't feel anything, anyhow.'

'But why? You're much too young to think about ending your life. You have so much ahead of you. So many years, so much happiness.'

Maria shook her head, and coughed up blood. 'I

saw myself. I saw what was going to happen to me.'

'What do you mean?'

'I saw myself in the future. I saw myself in two, maybe three years' time.'

'How did you know it was the future?'

'I don't know. I just did. I knew that I wasn't at college any more, and I had a job at Dillard's.'

'So what happened that upset you so much?'

'When I woke up, Barto was there, in my room, and not just Barto. All of these other men, too. I didn't know who they were.'

'Barto? Who's Barto?'

'My stepfather. He always treats me mean. He always wants me to *do* things for him, and if I say I don't want to, he beats me. Last week he beat me so bad that I was sicking up blood.'

Jim heard an ambulance siren whooping in the near distance. 'Maria, that's the paramedics. Lie still, OK? You're going to be fine. We're going to get you all patched up and then we're going to sort your life out, too.'

Maria shook her head. Her bloody hand was growing very cold, and her eyes were filming over. 'It is too late, Mr Rook. I can do nothing. Barto will never leave me alone. He wants me every night. My mother, she can't help me. He beats her, too, just as bad.'

'Maria, once you're better, we can go to the police. We can have this Barto locked up, so that he never touches you again.'

'I saw the future, Mr Rook. I woke up and I saw what was going to happen to me. Barto and all of these other men, in my bedroom, maybe five or six men, and Barto said to them, "Here she is, do whatever you like to her, and I mean *whatever*." I know this is going to happen to me, Mr Rook. I know this is going to happen to me for sure, and I would rather die.'

Jim turned and saw the ambulance speeding up the college driveway. It circled around and stopped in front of the main entrance, its lights flashing. Jim saw Shaggy and Nurse Okeke and Dr Ehrlichman talking to the paramedics. He waved to them and shouted, 'Here! Quick as you can!' Nurse Okeke waved back to him, although she was probably too far away to have heard him. The paramedics climbed back into their ambulance and started to drive it up the grassy slope toward them.

'Hold on, Maria,' Jim told her. 'I promise you, you're going to be OK.'

Maria smiled. 'You cannot save me, Mr Rook. The only way to change the future is not to go there.'

'Maria, listen to me – that is absolutely not true. You can never tell what's going to happen to you until it happens. From now on, your life is going to be different. I swear to God, that stepfather of yours is never going to hurt you again, because if he does I will personally beat five colors of crap out of him myself.'

'Kim told me,' said Maria.

'Kim? Kim told you what? What does Kim have to do with it?'

'I told Kim what I saw and he said I *couldn't* change it, no matter what. He said the future has happened already.' Maria coughed more blood, and then she said, 'How can you change something that has happened already?'

'You shouldn't have taken any notice of Kim,' Jim told her. 'Kim talks a whole lot of Korean BS. This is where your new life begins, Maria, and you're going to be happy and successful and you're never going to let a scumbag like Barto ever hurt you again.'

The ambulance had reached them now, and jounced to a halt next to the tractor. Two paramedics climbed out, a man and a woman, and came hurrying across the grass.

'How the hell did this happen?' asked the woman, kneeling down beside Maria and opening up her first-aid bag. 'How are you feeling, honey? Can you hear me?'

Jim stood up to give her some space. 'Please help her. Her name's Maria Lopez. She walked into the lawnmower on purpose.'

'Any idea why?'

'She's been abused by her stepfather. That's what she told me, anyhow. I guess she couldn't take it any more. Did the groundskeeper tell you about the janitor? He's down in the basement, in the boiler room. Some cat went crazy and took his eye out.'

The male paramedic nodded. 'We've called for back-up already, and in the meantime your nurse has gone to take care of him. How about you, sir? Are you OK?'

Jim held up both hands and realized that they were criss-crossed with clawmarks and sticky with blood. His shirt and his pants were stained with blood, too.

'I'm fine,' he said. 'Just a few scratches, that's all.'

The female paramedic looked up at him. She had red hair, green eyes, and freckles across her nose. 'We need to contact Ms Lopez's next-of-kin. Her mother, I guess, after what you've told us about her stepfather.'

'Sure,' said Jim. 'I'll do that now. Where are you going to be taking her?'

'I'm not sure yet. I have to contact the coroner.'

'The coroner? Why the coroner?'

'I'm sorry, sir. Ms Lopez is dead.'

'What?'

The paramedic turned Maria's head sideways, and it was only then that Jim could see that the back of her skull had been chopped open by one of the grass-cutting blades and that her brain was exposed.

'She wouldn't have suffered,' said the paramedic.

'What do you mean?'

'I mean that death would have been pretty much instantaneous.'

Jim took two or three steps backward. How could Maria have died instantaneously, when she had been talking to him, and smiling? He felt giddy, and he saw stars in front of his eyes, as if he were going to faint. The male paramedic saw that he was losing his balance and took hold of his arm.

'Why don't you sit down, sir? Sit down right here on the grass and put your head between your knees.'

Jim stared at him. He was tempted to tell him that Maria had been conscious, and lucid, and that he never would have known about her stepfather's abuse if she hadn't been able to speak to him. But now that she was dead, there was really no point, and he only would have made himself look like a fool.

He realized what had happened. He had seen Maria's spirit, before it had left her body, which had made it seem as if she were still alive. It had happened to him before, two or three times, when he had visited elderly people on their deathbeds. They had gone on talking to him long after they had died, especially when they had obviously felt that they had some important secret to tell him, which they had never told anybody else. They hadn't yet grasped the fact that they were dead, and that there was no need for them to panic, because they would have the rest of eternity to tell him, if they wanted to.

As Jim walked down the slope toward the college, another ambulance arrived, and he saw Nurse Okeke come around the side of the building and beckon the paramedics toward the basement. Class must have finished now, because several students were trying to push their way out of the main doors, but two members of the college security staff were ushering them back inside.

Jim mounted the steps. Dr Ehrlichman was standing at the top, waiting for him.

'Maria Lopez,' Jim told him. 'She's dead.'

'Oh, God, that's terrible. Young Billman here said she walked right into his lawnmower. He didn't see her until it was too late.'

Jim nodded. 'That's just about what happened.'

'She didn't do it *deliberately*, did she? Well, I suppose she must have done. But what a ghastly thing to do. Do you think she was high on something?'

'No. I don't know. I guess the medical examiner will tell us, eventually.'

'You're not hurt, are you?' Dr Ehrlichman asked him. 'You look like hell.'

Jim wiped sweat and blood from his forehead with the back of his hand. 'I need to get myself cleaned up, that's all.'

'What about Dunstan? How did *that* happen? Something about some rabid cat scratching out one of his eyes.'

'Let me get changed,' said Jim. 'Then I'll tell you all about it.'

'I've asked Ms Handy to call the police.'

'Of course you have. I'll talk to them, too, when they get here. But this isn't something that the cops can help us with, believe me.'

Dr Ehrlichman frowned at him as if he expected Jim to explain what he meant, but he didn't, because he couldn't. Not yet, anyway. He needed to have a talk with Kim Dong Wook.

He made his way through hundreds of noisy milling students to the staff changing rooms. He took off his clothes and bundled them up. Even his pale tan loafers had bloodstains on them, like maps of Korea, and he would probably have to throw them away. He didn't want to be reminded of the way that Maria had killed herself, every time he looked down at his feet.

He took a long hot shower. Afterward he sat for almost twenty minutes with one towel around his waist and another towel covering his head, trying to empty his mind of all the bloody, jumbled images that kept flickering across his consciousness like some endless horror movie.

He was still sitting there when a deep voice said, 'I'm real sorry about this morning, Jim.'

'Oh, Bob! What happened to you? I thought you were going to take over Special Class Two for me. I was here by twenty of twelve so it wouldn't have been for long.'

'Hey – I did take a look in for you.'

'You took a look in? What good did that do? Special Class Two, they're like an ongoing prison riot.'

'Exactly. That's why I didn't take over for you. I value my life too much.'

'Oh well,' said Jim. 'Forget it. Remind me never to rely on you again, that's all.'

There was a long pause. With the towel over his head, Jim wasn't sure if Bob Nussbaum was still there. But then Bob said, 'Dan Kelly told me what happened to Maria Lopez. Pretty horrific.'

'Yes,' said Jim, picturing the way that Maria had looked at him and said *how can you change something that has happened already?* 'Pretty horrific.'

'And Dunstan, having his eye taken out by some stray moggy. That was pretty horrific, too.'

'Yes,' Jim agreed. 'That was pretty horrific, too.'

An hour later, he sat down in Dr Ehrlichman's office with Detective Wong and Detective Madison and explained how

Maria had killed herself and Dunstan the janitor had nearly been blinded.

'Do you have any idea why Maria would have wanted to take her own life?' asked Detective Wong. He kept twiddling an elastic band around and around his fingers, which Jim found highly irritating.

'I think you need to talk to her stepfather,' Jim told him. 'Some bozo called Barto. Maria told me that he regularly abused her and beat up on her if she refused. She was covered in bruises. You only have to look at her body and you can see them for yourself. You'll probably find evidence of sexual abuse, too.'

'When exactly did she tell you about this abuse?'

'Yesterday,' Jim lied. 'I saw bruises on her wrists and asked them how she had come by them. Today she came to class with a split lip.'

'And she alleged that her stepfather was responsible?'

'Like I say, you need to talk to him. And her mother. Maria said that this Barto hits her mother, too.'

'OK, Mr Rook. We'll look into that. Now, what about the janitor having his eye scratched out? What's his name, Dunstan?'

'My cat did it. I think Dunstan has told you that already.'

'Your dead cat?'

'I thought he was dead.'

'You thought he was dead so you brought him to college to have him cremated?'

'Yes. I couldn't afford a proper funeral.'

'But he wasn't actually dead?'

'I believed that he was, but apparently no, he wasn't.'

'What gave you the impression he was dead?'

'He wasn't breathing and he wasn't moving and he had started to decompose.'

Dr Ehrlichman said, 'This was strictly against college regulations, Jim. I hope you understand that.'

'You mean there's a specific West Grove regulation which says you can't cremate cats in the college incinerator?'

'You can't cremate *any* animal in the college incinerator. Especially if it's still alive.'

*   *   *

The college was closed for the rest of the day to show respect for Maria's passing. After he had been questioned for nearly an hour by Detective Wong and Detective Madison, Jim went back to Special Class Two and stood for a while in front of Maria's desk. He had been warned. They had *all* been warned, everybody in the class, but he was the only one who had been capable of remembering what they had seen – Maria, stumbling into the classroom covered in blood. He was determined that it wouldn't happen again, and that no more of his students would feel such despair about their future that they would be tempted to kill themselves.

He would have to keep a close eye on Patsy-Jean, especially after she had written IF I HAD $1 MILLION I WOULD PAY SOMEONE TO KILL ME. He didn't know much about her home life – not yet, anyway – but she was clearly embarrassed about her weight. She had been stuffing herself with Golightly candies, after all. Although they were very sweet, they contained no fat, no salt and no sugar, and a whole bag was only three hundred calories.

Jim walked to the back of the class and looked out of the window at the grassy slope where Maria had been killed. The tractor and the lawnmower were still there, surrounded by cops and photographers and CSI. He went across to Teddy's desk. Unusually, Teddy had left his notebook on top of his desk. Up until now – however many days of this semester had or hadn't gone by – he had put it into his rucksack and taken it home with him. The notebook had a dark red marbled cover and a sticker on the front with *Verbal Death by Theodore Greenspan* printed on it in black ink.

Jim opened it up and started to read. So far, Teddy had filled over a hundred pages in tiny, crowded handwriting. Although he was such a stickler for correct English, this narrative was written with almost no punctuation whatsoever, an endless stream of words that ran on page after page:

> because i woke up in the middle of the night a few
> minutes after two pm and i thought of a story and it
> was a story about a man who gets lost in the woods

and when he is lost in the woods he finds a house and
so he knocks on the door and the door opens and theres
an old woman in the house leastways she looks like an
old woman she wears a black cone-shaped hat and a
veil over her face but she smells strange quite funky
like a dog or a fox.

she says to the man sit down and have some soup
so he sits at the table and she serves him an earthen-
ware bowl with a lid and when he lifts the lid he sees
all kinds of disgusting things floating in the soup like
clumps of human hair and rubbery fat and connective
tissue and even a human penis all soft and shapeless.

and when the man turns around he sees that the
woman has grown bigger and bigger and she isnt a
woman at all but a huge hairy animal so he tries to
escape but the huge hairy animal tears him wide open
and sucks out his soul which is like a shadowy reflection of him.

i tried to write this story but i couldnt think of the
words to tell it and I couldnt hold my pen without dropping it and I realized that something had gone wrong
with my brain like maybe alzheimers and i couldnt
string two words together I couldnt even think how to
write one word getting all the letters in the right order.

it was like id lost everything i was and all i wanted
to do was kill myself it was only when i woke up in
the morning i found out it wasnt true but beside my
bed was a piece of paper with OCNE MAD WOLST
in big spidery writing on it and I knew that when i was
struggling to write in the middle of the night i had tried
to write *once a man was lost* but couldnt manage it.

Jim was still reading when he became aware that there was
somebody else in the classroom with him, watching him. He
looked up and saw that it was Kim, standing in the far corner,
his arms folded, a smile on his face as if he felt very pleased
with himself. He was wearing a very white shirt with the
collar turned up, and pale-blue Levis with the cuffs rolled
up. His black hair was gelled to stick up vertically from the
top of his head.

'Good afternoon, Mr Rook, sir. I see you have found another student who has looked into his future.'

Jim held up Teddy's notebook. 'It's a story. It's fiction. Nothing more than that.'

'What Maria saw, was that a story, too?'

'It wasn't real, if that's what you mean. The tragedy was that she believed it.'

'What her stepfather was doing to her, Mr Rook – that was real.'

'I'm sure that it was. But she could have found a way to change it.'

Kim walked down the aisle on the opposite side of the classroom, until he was standing next to Grant's desk. 'She *did* find a way to change it. Now she will never suffer again, ever.'

'There has to be some other way for a person to change their future except by killing themselves.'

Kim grinned, showing very white teeth. 'Once you are born, Mr Rook, your fate is already determined. The road to Anseong-ri goes only to Anseong-ri.'

'Tell me something,' said Jim. 'Give me the truth. Are you behind all of these switches in time? Was it *you* who showed Maria what was going to happen to her? Are *you* responsible for what Teddy's written in here? And how about me? I woke up in the night thinking that I was over eighty years old – hairless, toothless and wetting the bed. Did *you* do that? Who are you, Kim Don Wook? Maybe more to the point – *what* are you?'

'I am only a student, Mr Rook. Nothing more. And, no. I did not do any of those things. This is the truth that you ask me for.'

'You know about this fox-demon, though. What's her name?'

'Kwisin, Mr Rook. You have seen her, yes?'

'You bet your ass I've seen her. She's turned up in my apartment twice already, and I suspect that she had something to do with the woman downstairs setting fire to herself. Not only that, she bit the head off my neighbor's Boston terrier.'

'The dog is dead?'

'The dog is still alive. But I'm beginning to understand what's going on here. You can show us the future, and when we see how crappy it's going to turn out, we commit suicide. And what happens to people who take their own lives, in almost every religion on the planet? They forfeit their place in whatever heaven they believe in.'

'Yes, Mr Rook, that is so.'

Jim approached Kim and looked him directly in the eyes. He had never seen irises so black. He could have been wearing those totally black contact lenses they use in werewolf movies.

'So,' said Jim, 'if their souls can't go to their respective heavens, where *do* they go?'

'There are always spirits who are prepared to welcome wandering souls, Mr Rook. The more souls that any spirit can gather in, the stronger that spirit becomes. You know that.'

'Not only spirits, Kim. Demons.'

Kim's black eyes glistened. 'Some people call them spirits. Other people describe them as demons. It depends which side you are on.'

FOURTEEN

Late that evening Jim was cooking himself a chicken and garlic stir-fry when his doorbell buzzed. He turned down the gas under the wok and went to the front door, but he didn't open it.

'Who is it?' he called out.

'It's only me, Jimmy! Not some demon! One of my customers gave me a bottle of champagne and I thought you might like to share it with me!'

Jim opened the door. It was Summer, in a very short scarlet dress. She held up a bottle and said, 'See?'

'That's great,' said Jim. 'Why don't you come on in?'

Summer came tripping into the kitchen in her high-heeled sandals and said, 'Phew-*eee*! Garlic, or what? Lucky for me I'm not a vampire!'

Jim took the bottle and looked at the label. It was Cloudy Valley sparkling wine, which usually retailed around $4.99 a bottle, and it was warm. Some champagne. Some customer.

'Let's put it in the freezer for a while,' he suggested. 'How about a glass of red to keep us going?'

'OK.' Summer looked into the living room. 'She hasn't come back again, then? That Korean fox-demon-woman thing?'

'No. Not yet, anyhow. But one of my students was killed today. You remember I told you about that girl Maria, and how she came into the classroom with all of those cuts and bruises, and then the next day she was OK?'

'Jimmy, you're *scaring* me. I know you told me all of that stuff but it's not really real, is it?'

'You don't know how real. She committed suicide right in front of me. She walked right into a lawnmower and got herself all cut up just like she was before, only worse.'

'Oh, my *God*. Oh, my God I'm so sorry. You must be, like, *devastated*.'

Jim took hold of her hand and squeezed it. 'Let's put it this way: I'm a little upset, to say the least.'

'I'd better go then. I only came up here in case you thought that demon woman was going to come back, and you felt like you needed someplace safe to sleep.'

'I'll be fine. Even if she does come back, I've made up my mind. I have to face up to her.'

Summer put her arms around his neck, and looked up at him with her big blue eyes. 'That's OK. But I thought you might want to finish what we started. I hate to leave things hanging, if you know what I mean.'

He kissed her. 'Yes. Me too. But right now I really need to work out what the hell is going on and what I'm going to do about it.'

'All right. Maybe I'd better keep this champagne for later, when we have something to celebrate.'

'No, let's drink it now. Who cares if it's warm? Every day is worth celebrating, don't you think? Even if it wasn't the day you thought it was.'

He was woken up the next morning by an earth tremor, which made him feel as if somebody was moving his bed underneath him. It was followed a few minutes later by another, stronger tremor, and he heard a loud clatter from the kitchen as his skillet dropped off its hook.

He swung himself out of bed and switched on the television news. There was no mention of the tremor so far, nor any earthquake warnings. But as he went through to the kitchen to make himself some coffee, the entire apartment building shook and all the bottles inside his fridge rattled noisily and the pictures on the walls swung off-center.

He opened his front door. All across the neighborhood, car alarms were honking. It was 7:20 a.m., but the sky was still dark, with gray clouds unraveling across it in an endless woolly stream. The wind was up again, too, and the trees were tossing wildly from side to side as if they were trying to uproot themselves.

He went down the steps and met Summer just as she was coming out of her front door, wearing nothing but a pink T-shirt and panties.

'Did you *feel* that?' she said. 'I thought I was having a nightmare at first but then I woke up and I was bouncing up and down on my bed like that *Exorcist* movie.'

'That must have been nearly a five, that last one,' said Jim. He noticed that there was a fresh crack in the stucco, underneath her kitchen window. 'Why don't you come upstairs? I'm just making some coffee. If we get any more tremors we can sit in the doorway together and drink it.'

Summer went back to find herself a purple satin robe and then she followed him to his apartment. By now the tremors were being reported on Channel 2 news. The second tremor had been measured in downtown Los Angeles at 4.7, although it had been felt no further away than Camarillo to the north and San Juan Capistrano to the south.

Jim and Summer sat on the couch together and drank coffee and ate chocolate-chip cookies, which was the only food that Jim had in his cupboard, apart from seven cans of cat food, two cans of garbanzo beans and one can of Pride brand chicken'n'dumplings.

Summer said, 'I was beginning to think that you were a little crazy. I mean, not that I minded or anything. I've gone out with people who are a whole lot crazier than you are. But you're *not* crazy, are you?'

'No,' said Jim. 'I genuinely wish that I was.'

'You'll work it out,' she told him, laying her hand on his knee. 'I know you will.'

'Well, I'm glad you have that much confidence in me. You're the only one in this room who has.'

An hour passed and there were no more tremors, although the sky remained overpoweringly dark and the wind was blowing so hard that dust-devils were dancing up and down the street. When they had finished their coffee Jim took a shower and dressed and collected his books and his papers together. Today he was going to be asking Special Class Two to give him their thoughts on time, and if there was any period in history they would prefer to have lived in, rather than today. He always asked his class to do this, every year, but given what had been happening in the past three days, it seemed grimly appropriate.

He knocked on Summer's door before he left.

'Hey – have a good day's pole-dancing. I'll try to catch you later.'

'You take care, Jimmy,' she told him. 'Don't do anything dangerous.'

'I'm only going to teach some kids how to read and write.'

'That's what you say.'

He drove to West Grove College and parked. It was so dark that it could have been the middle of the night, and he could see snakes' tongues of lightning flickering on the horizon, far to the south. As he climbed the steps to the main entrance, Bob Nussbaum caught up with him.

'Some freaky weather, Jim! Did you feel those tremors this morning?'

Jim pushed his way in through the door. 'It's the end of the world, Bob. Didn't you know it?'

'Well, I hope it doesn't end before Saturday afternoon. I've been invited to play golf at the Wilshire Country Club.'

'Why don't you ask Father Simmons to have a quiet word with God for you? I'm sure that the Almighty won't mind postponing Armageddon for something as important as a round of golf. Stop the world, I want to tee off!'

'You're a cynic, Jim. It's important to *me*. It's social. Senator Mulligan's daughter Jacquie is going to be there.'

'And you have a chance with her? I don't think so, Bob.'

Jim went into his classroom and walked across to his desk. Special Class Two were uncharacteristically subdued this morning. Teddy was still scribbling but the rest of the class were sitting around as if they were waiting for somebody to tell them what to do. Some of them had laid flowers across Maria's desk – red roses and white lilies and perfumed purple stocks. They had left cards, too, with pictures of rabbits on them, and little children, and messages written on torn scraps of paper. *Maria, Miss U Girl. So sorry, Maria, XXX. CU in heaven.*

The windows at the back of the classroom were so dark that Jim could see his own reflection in them, and sparkling droplets of rain began to creep down the glass.

'Sad day,' he announced. 'We're all going to miss Maria. But I want to tell you this. None of you should ever think that your life isn't worth living, even when you're feeling really frightened, or depressed. At this age, you think you can see what the future has in store for you, but you can't. It's an old cliché, but life is full of surprises.'

'I agree with that, Mr Rook,' said Kim.

'You do? I thought *you* thought that life held no surprises at all.'

'But of course it does, Mr Rook. Life is full of surprises for those people who don't know what's coming. Mostly unpleasant, I have to say.'

'But what if you *do* know what's coming? What then?'

'Then you have a choice. You can go on, or you can decide to do the same as Maria.'

'Let me tell you this, Kim. No matter how bad you think things are going to turn out, walking into a lawnmower is never an option.'

Kim shrugged. 'There are other ways of ending your life, Mr Rook. There are *always* other ways. There is a Korean proverb which says that the same fate can be found behind many different doors.'

Jim sat down and took the register out of his drawer. Even before he opened it, however, he realized that Patsy-Jean was missing.

'Anybody seen Patsy-Jean this morning?'

Tamara put up her hand. 'Me, sir. I saw her looking at the notice board in the corridor. But she hasn't come into class yet. The last time I saw her, she was going into the little girls' room.'

'What was she going in there for?' asked Arthur. 'Patsy-Jean is a *big* girl!'

Nobody laughed, and Jim said, 'That's enough size-ism for one day, thank you.' He looked up at the clock on the wall and said, 'What time was that, Tamara?'

'I'm not too sure, sir. I guess about a half-hour ago.'

Jim stood up and said, 'Today, we're going to talk about the past, the present and the future. If time-travel were possible, and you were ever given the choice, I want each of you to think what period you would prefer to live in – whether it's some time in history, or now, or some time that hasn't yet happened.'

There was no response. Kim gave him a knowing look that – for some reason – he found deeply unsettling, as if Kim were aware that something had gone badly wrong but wasn't going to tell him about it.

'Have a think about it, anyhow,' Jim told them. 'I'll be back in a couple of minutes.'

He left the classroom and walked along the hallway to the students' restrooms. Through the main doors at the end of the corridor he could see that the sky was still black, and that lightning was still stalking across the horizon. As he reached the door of the girls' restroom, he felt the floor move under his feet. It was only a slight tremor, but it was enough to make him feel that the ground was no longer trustworthy.

He knocked on the door and called, 'Patsy-Jean? Patsy-Jean Waller? Are you in there?'

There was no reply, so he knocked again. Eventually he pushed open the door and went inside. 'Anybody in here?'

Nobody answered. He went along the row of cubicles, opening each door in turn, in case Patsy-Jean was sitting unconscious on one of the toilets, but there was nobody there. He was just about to leave when one of the girls from Sheila Colefax's class came bursting in.

'Mr Rook!'

'I'm sorry, Nadine. It *is* Nadine, isn't it?'

'Nadia.'

'Oh, yes. That's right. Nadia. I was looking for Patsy-Jean Waller. You haven't seen her by any chance?'

'Sure I have. I was just coming out of the gym after my morning workout when she was going in.'

'Patsy-Jean was going into the *gym*? When was that?'

'About ten minutes ago, I guess. I was surprised because I didn't never see her in the gym before, like *never*. I asked her what she was doing there, and she said she was going to get rid of all of her excess weight, like right now, and forever.'

'"Right now and forever?" You're sure that's what she said?'

'That's exactly what she said, because I said, "Good for you, girl, but it's going to take you a whole lot longer than that."'

Jim said, 'Excuse me, Nadia,' and dodged his way past her.

'Mr Rook?' she said. 'What's going on?'

'Call Nurse Okeke! Do it now! Have her meet me at the gym!'

'Nurse Okeke? What for?'

'Do it *now*, Nadia!'

Jim pelted along the hallway, his loafers squeaking on the polished floor. There were a dozen steps at the end of the corridor and he leaped up them four at a time. He took a sharp right, pushed open the double doors, and ran along the arcade that led to the college gymnasium. The left side of the arcade was open, and rain was slanting across the concrete paving slabs. As he reached the doors to the gymnasium, Jim saw more crackles of lightning over the Hollywood Hills, and heard the stentorian bellowing of thunder.

The gymnasium was gloomy inside, because Dunstan hadn't come around to switch on the lights. It smelled of leather and coconut matting and stale teenage sweat. Every now and then, lightning flickered through the windows, and Jim could see the headless vaulting horse standing in the corner, and the basketball hoops, and the climbing ropes that were looped up and tied on to the parallel bars on either side, like the legs of a giant spider dangling from the ceiling.

But one rope wasn't looped up. Somebody had untied it so that it was hanging straight downward, as taut as a plumb line. On the end of it, slowly rotating, was Patsy-Jean. One yellow Croc lay on the floor beneath her.

'Patsy-Jean!' Jim yelled at her. 'Patsy-Jean, hold on there!'

Jim ran across the gymnasium. He wrapped his arms around Patsy-Jean's knees and tried to heave her up a few inches, to take the strangulating pressure off her neck. He managed it for almost half a minute, but she weighed so much and she was so inert that he had to lower her down again, gasping with effort.

He looked up at her. She was staring at him with her piggy little eyes open. Her double chins bulged over the rope, and the tip of her tongue was protruding from one side of her mouth. She looked more like a greedy little girl who was just about to lick an ice-cream cone than an overweight young woman who had hanged herself out of despair.

He hurried to the far end of the gymnasium and dragged the vaulting horse across the floor, its feet scraping and bumping on the parquet blocks. He climbed up on it, and took hold of the rope. Patsy-Jean had tied it in a large simple knot. She hadn't been able to fashion it into a proper hangman's slipknot because it was much too thick and inflexible, but it had been enough to strangle her, even if it had taken five or ten minutes.

Jim was still desperately trying to tug the knot free when the gymnasium doors opened and Nurse Okeke came running in, followed by Nadia.

'Oh, my God!' said Nurse Okeke. She came loping across the gymnasium and took hold of Patsy-Jean's legs in one swoop, lifting her upward. She was strong as well as tall, Nurse Okeke, and she supported enough of Patsy-Jean's weight for Jim to tug the end of the rope free, and unfasten the knot. Immediately, he caught Patsy-Jean under her armpits, almost losing his balance and toppling off the vaulting horse, but between them, he and Nurse Okeke managed to lower her on to the floor.

Jim jumped down. He took out his cellphone and punched out 911, while Nurse Okeke tried to feel Patsy-Jean's pulse. The lightning flashed again, and Jim could see that Patsy-Jean's lips were blue, and that the pupils of her eyes were speckled with red. He had watched enough episodes of *CSI* to know that petechial hemorrhages were a certain sign of strangulation.

'Is she dead?' asked Nadia, standing twenty feet away and hugging herself as if she felt cold.

'She may have a chance,' said Nurse Okeke. 'Can you run to Dr Ehrlichman's office and tell him what's happened? Mr Rook has called for the paramedics so they should be here soon. And can you switch on the lights, please?'

Nadia ran over to the gymnasium doors. She flicked all of the light switches but nothing happened. 'They don't work! Maybe it's the storm!'

'OK, then, just go find Dr Ehrlichman. And make sure the paramedics know that we're here in the gym!'

Nurse Okeke rolled Patsy-Jean on to her back, knelt close beside her and started to give her CPR. Every now and then she pinched Patsy-Jean's nostrils and breathed into her mouth, filling up Patsy-Jean's lungs with air, but Patsy-Jean didn't respond.

'She's gone, hasn't she?' asked Jim.

Nurse Okeke kept on compressing Patsy-Jean's chest. 'Nobody has gone until their spirit has gone. And this young woman's spirit is still with her.'

Jim looked at her. Then he looked at Patsy-Jean and realized that Patsy-Jean was smiling at him.

'Patsy-Jean?' he asked her, hunkering down next to her. 'Can you see me, Patsy-Jean?'

Patsy-Jean nodded. 'I can see you. I can see both of you. I can hear you, too.'

Nurse Okeke stopped giving her CPR and sat back on her heels. 'I'm wasting my time doing this, aren't I, Patsy-Jean? You're just about to leave us.'

Jim said, '*You* can hear her, too?'

'Yes, Mr Rook, I can hear her,' said Nurse Okeke. 'I have always had that gift, the same as you. Ever since I was eight years old, and I almost died from meningitis, I have been able to see spirits and souls and the ghosts of those who are gone.'

'But how did you know that I could do it, too? How the hell did you find that out?'

'Because two years ago my grandfather came to see me here at the college and I was talking to him in the corridor and you passed us by and complimented my grandfather on his necktie. But nobody else could see him, let alone his necktie, because he died in 1973, and he was buried in that necktie in the Victoria Court Cemetery in Lagos. Only you could see him, apart from me.'

Jim turned back to Patsy-Jean. Her eyes were still open and she was still smiling.

'What are you smiling for, Patsy-Jean?' he demanded. 'You've made me really angry now, hanging yourself like that. I *told* you that I would take care of you, didn't I? You shouldn't have done it. That's your whole life, wasted. And how do you think your mom and dad and your sisters are going to feel?'

Patsy-Jean gave him a resigned shrug. 'You didn't see what I saw, Mr Rook. I saw myself when I was forty. I saw myself ending up so fat that I had to stay in bed twenty-four-seven, with a bag for going to the toilet. I was covered all over in bedsores and half of my hair had fallen out. I stank all greasy because nobody could get in between all of those folds of fat to keep me clean. I saw myself like a whale, Mr Rook, stranded on a beach.'

She took two wheezy breaths, and then she said, 'I didn't want to be like that, Mr Rook. I'd rather be dead. I *am* dead.'

Jim took hold of her podgy little hand. It felt damp and cold, and he knew for sure that there was no hope of saving her.

'You should have told me,' he said. 'When you saw yourself all fat like that, that was only one future, out of *thousands* of possible futures. Maybe there is a really fat you, somewhere in the universe. But I believe that there's a medium-sized you, too, and maybe even a very *thin* you, and you can choose whichever of those yous you want to turn into. Well, you could have done, before you hanged yourself.'

'Kim said that was my fate and I couldn't escape it.'

'Kim wanted you to think that. But Kim was telling you only half the truth. Like I say, there could well be a fat and miserable forty-year-old Patsy-Jean somewhere in the future, but all the chances are there's a happy, regular-sized Patsy-Jean, too.'

Patsy-Jean frowned. 'Kim was lying to me? Why would he do that?'

'Because he wanted you to take your own life,' said Nurse Okeke, very gently. 'When people take their own lives, their spirits are like abandoned children, because the gods they believe in will not accept them. Our gods granted us life, and only our gods have the right to take it away from us. If we take it ourselves, our gods will turn their backs on us.'

Patsy-Jean looked frightened now. There was another deafening burst of thunder, right over the gymnasium roof, and the floor was shaken by another earth tremor. 'So where am I going?' she asked. 'Who's going to take care of me now?'

Almost on cue, the gymnasium's double doors slammed wide open. A lightning flash lit up the arcade outside, and

Jim saw the silhouette of a woman standing there, with the
rain glittering behind her. It was the fox-woman, in her
conical black hat, and her veil, and her shiny gray robes.
She stayed where she was, unmoving, her arms by her sides.

'*Kwisin*,' whispered Patsy-Jean. 'Kwisin has come to take
me away.'

'No, Patsy-Jean,' Jim told her. 'You don't have to go with
her if you don't want to. I'm sure that we can find some
other spirit to take you in.'

He gripped her shoulder tight but he could hold on only
to her physical body, and her physical body was floppy and
cold. Her spirit rose to her feet, as slippery and insubstan-
tial as oil shimmering on the surface of a puddle, and glided
away across the gymnasium toward the open doors. As Patsy-
Jean approached, the fox-woman raised her arms as if to
embrace her, and Jim was sure that the fox-woman began
to grow taller, and to lean forward in the way that she had
done when she had appeared in his bedroom, like a four-
legged animal standing up on its hind legs.

'*No!*' Jim shouted. 'Patsy-Jean! Don't go with her! Don't!'

He stood up, but as he did so the fox-woman stretched
upward until she almost reached the top of the arcade. Her
arms grew longer and longer, and as Patsy-Jean came through
the doorway she folded them around her and drew her in
close. Patsy-Jean screamed, a terrible despairing scream, and
then Jim heard a sound like a dog crunching a chicken's
carcass between its jaws.

He lunged forward, although he had no idea how he was
going to rescue a spirit that had no physical substance. But
he had stumbled only two or three paces across the gymnasium floor before Nurse Okeke caught at his sleeve and
stopped him. He twisted around and stared at her. Her eyes
were wide and she looked terrified.

'Don't try to save her! She is dead already! If you try to
save her, the demon will kill you, too!'

Jim turned back to the doorway. The doors were already
closing again, but he was just in time to see the fox-woman
turn around and hurry away, and in spite of the thunder and
the clattering rain, he was sure that he could hear claws
rattling on the paving slabs.

Nurse Okeke said, 'Mr Rook – Jim – really, there is nothing that you can do.'

Jim said, 'I let her down. I knew she was feeling bad about herself.'

'It is too late. She is gone. There is a demon in my religion called Mama Chola who takes spirits in the same way. As far as she is concerned, the spirit of every person who commits suicide belongs to her, and she will kill anybody who tries to take them away from her.'

'It's Kim,' said Jim. 'That Korean kid. *He's* responsible. Somehow he can make people see how they're going to turn out in the future, and he takes away their will to live. I saw myself when I was eighty-something, and I was almost tempted to end it all.'

Nurse Okeke nodded. 'Mama Chola also has her helpers, who whisper in people's ears when they are asleep, and give them nightmares, so that they believe that they are going to be sick, or lame, or lose their sight. They become so depressed and exhausted that they stop eating, or drown themselves, and then Mama Chola takes their spirits.'

'Well, this can't go on,' Jim told her. 'I'm going to have to get rid of him somehow.' He checked his watch. 'Where the hell are those paramedics?'

'Why don't you go find out?' Nurse Okeke suggested. 'I'll stay here with Patsy-Jean.'

'I just hope that Kwisin doesn't show up again.'

Nurse Okeke shook her head. 'I doubt if she will. She is probably satisfied by now. Besides, she is not looking for people like me, who know what kind of trickery demons can play. There is no better way to protect yourself against demons than to acknowledge that they are real.'

'Thanks,' said Jim. 'And thanks for trying to save Patsy-Jean. If we'd been a couple of minutes earlier . . .' He looked down at Patsy-Jean's body. Although she was dead, Patsy-Jean was frowning, as if she had forgotten something and was trying to remember what it was.

FIFTEEN

As Jim opened the gymnasium doors, Dr Ehrlichman came bustling in, accompanied by his lanky vice-principal, John Pannequin, and one of the college security staff, a thickset Mexican with a huge gray moustache.

'What's going on, Jim? Nadia Feinstein just told me that one of your students has *hanged* herself.'

Jim nodded toward Patsy-Jean's body. 'True, I'm sorry to say. Patsy-Jean Waller. Nurse Okeke gave her CPR but we were too late.'

'This is *awful*! This is such a tragedy! First Maria Lopez and now this poor girl. Do you have any idea why she did it?'

'She told me that she was very depressed about her weight. Other than that, I don't really know.'

Dr Ehrlichman walked across to the body and took off his spectacles. 'You poor young girl. What a terrible, terrible thing to do. I've called the paramedics, by the way, and the police. I don't know what kind of press we're going to get. Did you see the *Times* this morning? They called us the "College of Carnage." Doesn't do much for our reputation in the community, does it?'

Jim said, 'I have to get back to my class, tell them what's happened.'

'Yes, OK. Very well. But when you've done that, I need you back here to talk to the police.'

Jim left the gymnasium and walked back along the empty corridors. Through the windows he could see lightning crackling almost continuously behind the trees, and before he reached Special Class Two there were three loud collisions of thunder, so close to the college that he heard some of the girls in Sheila Colefax's class screaming in fright.

When he reached the door of Special Class Two he was puzzled to see that the blue blind had been drawn down over the porthole window. He turned the handle to find that the door was locked.

He knocked, and shouted out, 'Open the door!'

There was no answer, so he knocked again, louder. 'Open this goddamned door, will you?'

Still no answer. He tried rapping on the window with his ring finger. 'This is Mr Rook and if you don't open this door right now I am going to make your life hell! Do you hear me?'

He was still waiting there when another member of the college security staff came hurrying past him, followed by two paramedics.

'Having some trouble, Mr Rook?' asked the security man.

'Door's stuck,' Jim told him. 'Show these guys to the gym first. Then come back. I think my students are just playing me up.'

'OK, Mr Rook. No problem.'

Jim waited for a while longer, leaning on the door with both hands pressed against it. He couldn't imagine why his students would want to lock him out of his own classroom, especially since Maria's suicide had left them all feeling so distraught.

He knocked yet again. 'Will somebody unlock this door, please? This is pointless and unfunny and I have some very serious and important news to tell you.'

Another few seconds went by, and then Jim heard a soft, complicated click. The door opened, although only by a half-inch. He wasn't entirely sure why, but he hesitated for a moment before he pushed it open any further. There was another peal of thunder, and the fluorescent lights in the corridor flickered off for a moment, and then flickered on again.

He opened the door and stepped into the classroom. At first he couldn't understand what he was looking at. Special Class Two were all standing up behind their desks, facing him, but all of them had their heads wrapped up in clear plastic cling film, so that Jim could barely make out their features. They were all breathing laboriously, and the film was sucked in and out of their mouths as they struggled for air.

'What the hell are you guys *doing*?' he demanded. He was so shocked by their appearance that it took him a few more seconds to realize that not only did they have their heads wrapped up in layers of film, but all of them had their right elbows crooked up, and all of them were holding box-cutters against their throats.

All of them, that is, except for Kim Dong Wook, who was standing by the chalkboard. He had written on it, in large capital letters: ETERNAL PEACE AWAITS THE CHILDREN OF KWISIN.

Jim stalked up to Janice Sticky and tried to snatch her arm, but Janice immediately shied away from him. He tried again, but then he saw that there was blood welling up between her fingers, and that she had cut herself on the side of her throat. Her green eyes stared at him through the cling film like a drowning fish trapped beneath the surface of a frozen pond.

'Janice,' said Jim, 'you really don't want to do this. Listen up, all of you! None of you want to do this! Kim here has made you all believe that your lives are going to turn out to be crappy. He did it to me, too, and I felt like killing myself. But he's misleading you. All he ever shows you is the worst-case scenario.'

Kim came forward with a smile on his face. 'You won't be able to persuade them, Mr Rook. They have seen their future for themselves and they have decided what they want to do. Better to find peace in the land of death than suffer pain and sickness and poverty in the land of life.'

Jim seized the front of Kim's white shirt and twisted it around, pulling Kim right up to him so that their noses were almost touching.

'Whoever you are, Kim, or *whatever* you are, you are a cruel and sadistic bastard, and I'm going to make sure that you get what you deserve.'

He turned back to the class and announced, 'Patsy-Jean is dead! She hung herself from a rope in the gym! Kim made her believe that she was going to stay fat for the rest of her life and she couldn't face it. But what Kim told her, it wasn't true!'

'Of course it was true, Mr Rook,' said Kim, still smiling, although there was no humor in his smile at all. 'How could I have shown her what her future was going to be like, if it did not happen that way?'

Jim twisted his shirt even tighter. 'Oh, it *did* happen that way, for sure. She *did* get fatter and fatter. She got so goddamned fat she had to stay in bed for the rest of her life. But what you failed to tell her was that this was only *one* of her futures. She had another future waiting for her, too – and in *that* future she got her weight under control and she was healthy and she was happy. And there was yet another future, in which she got so skinny that she was a model and she appeared on the cover of magazines.'

'This is not true, Mr Rook. Each of us has only one future and that one future cannot be avoided, except by death.'

Underneath the cling film on her face, Tamara started to squeak for breath. When Jim looked around the classroom, he could see that all of his students were having serious difficulty in breathing – Georgia, Teddy, Ella and Arthur. In the back row, Grant was leaning forward over his desk, coughing, and even through the cling film, Jim could see that his mouth was turning blue. But all of them kept their box-cutters held up to their throats, and Jim didn't dare to try and rush at any of them, in case they cut themselves like Janice, or worse.

A devastating rumble of thunder shook the whole room, and three polystyrene tiles dropped off the ceiling and see-sawed down to the floor.

'Who the hell are you?' Jim shouted into Kim's face. 'What gives you the right to take these young people's lives?'

'Me? I do not take them,' Kim retorted. 'They take their own lives, themselves, with own hand. It is Kwisin who is taking their souls. That is why Kwisin was so grateful to you, and brought your cat back to life. But what did you do? You showed no gratitude in return, so the cat died for a second time.'

At that moment, Judii collapsed sideways on to the floor, and lay underneath her desk, whining for air, her sneakers kicking spasmodically against her shoulder bag.

'Do not even think of helping her, Mr Rook,' Kim warned him. 'One move from you and they will all immediately cut throat.'

'It seems to me like they're determined to die anyhow. What difference will it make?'

'Yes, they are all determined to die. But if you try to stop them, then you will have encouraged them to do it.'

Jim pulled Kim even closer. 'Tell them to throw down those box-cutters, you little bastard. Tell them to take that Saran wrap off of their faces.'

'I cannot do that, Mr Rook. Kwisin wants their souls, and I do whatever Kwisin asks me to do.'

Jim wrenched Kim's shirt so violently that he tore off the top two buttons. It was then that he saw that Kim was wearing what appeared to be two necklaces. One was made of brown and yellow tiger's eye beads, but the other was a plain metal chain with two rectangular ID tags hanging on it. They looked like the aluminum tags worn by the US military, in the days when they were called 'dog-tags.'

Jim grabbed at the dog-tags and held them up in his fist, so that the chain cut into Kim's neck. 'Is this you? Let's take a look, shall we, and see who the hell you are!'

Kim tried to twist away, but the chain broke.

'*Give me those!*' he screamed, and his face was contorted with rage, like a Korean demon-mask.

Jim dangled the dog-tags up in front of him, but he was at least four inches taller than Kim, and when Kim tried to snatch them back, he lifted them out of his reach.

'You do not understand! You do not understand! Give me those back!'

Jim pushed Kim hard so that he stumbled backward, and collided with Jim's desk. He threw himself at Jim again, but Jim dodged to one side and tripped him up. He tumbled on to the floor, and when he tried to get up, Jim kicked him hard in the hip and said, 'Stay down! You got me?'

Kim desperately reached up for his dog-tags, his fingers clenching and unclenching. 'You do not understand!'

Jim kicked him in the shin, harder this time. 'I said stay the expletive-deleted down!'

He squinted at the dog-tags. The classroom lights went out for a few seconds, so that he was unable to read them at first. But then the lights jumped on again, even brighter than before, and he could see them clearly. Embossed in both rectangles of aluminum was the name *Rook, Roland G., Blood type O, Episcopalian*.

He felt as if another earth-tremor had run through the floor beneath his feet. He said, 'These are my grandfather's dog-tags, from the Korean War. What the hell are you doing with my grandfather's dog-tags?'

'You do not understand.'

'You bet your ass I don't understand! Do you want to explain it to me?'

'Your grandfather, Mr Rook.' Suddenly, Kim sounded quite humble. 'Your grandfather. *My* great-grandfather. You and I, we have same blood in veins. Same inheritance.'

'What? What are you trying to tell me? We're *related*?'

'Your grandfather, Mr Rook, he marry Korean girl in Pusan.'

'Are you *kidding* me?'

'I promise it is true. Your grandfather marry Korean girl in Pusan and together they make boy-child. But at the end of the war, he go back to United States and leave them behind.'

'And that boy-child, he was *your* grandfather? Is that what you're saying?'

Kim nodded, and wiped his eyes with the back of his hand. 'What your grandfather did not know, he married Kwisin. Unmarried dead girl.'

'So what happened to the baby?'

'Kwisin's family took the boy-child to the Sŏn masters in the monastery at Songgwang-sa, so that they could raise him to follow the Great Way that has no gate, and see the future as well as the past. Also to learn the language of Hwadu, which cannot be understood by ordinary men and women. And even though the Sŏn masters forbid it, he learned also to speak with demons.'

The lights dimmed again and another detonation of thunder shook the whole college right down to the depths of its foundations. Smoke alarms were *meep-meep-meeping* in every classroom, a high-pitched chorus of hopeless panic, and plaster dust was dredging down from the ceiling. The windows at the back of the classroom cracked from one side to the other like pistol-shots, and two of them fell out completely and shattered on the floor. In the dust and gloom, the students of Special Class Two looked like a gathering of aliens, their film-wrapped heads glistening, their eyes bulging as they slowly suffocated. Four of them had now collapsed on to the floor, shuddering, but all the same they kept their box-cutters held against their throats.

Jim reached down, gripped Kim's arm, and hauled him on to his feet. 'You can forget about the past! It doesn't matter a damn if you and me are related, even if we really are! You have to tell these kids not to hurt themselves! *Tell* them, Kim, or I'll break your goddamned arm! Do it now!'

'I cannot,' Kim gasped. 'I have to give Kwisin what she wants. It is a promise that I cannot break.'

'What promise? Who promises anything to demons?'

Kim coughed, and coughed again, and then he said, 'My grandfather, Eui-kon Wook. When he came of age his mother Kwisin visited the monastery and they spoke together. She made him promise that he would take revenge on my great-grandfather for leaving her. She made him promise that he and his sons and his sons' sons would look for the sons and the sons' sons of Roland Rook, and bring her the souls of all the people they cared for the most.

'My grandfather could never find any of your family, and neither could my father. They were both poor men, and could not travel to America to search for you. But then came internet, and I look for Facebook, and there you were. I found you.'

'So you came here, and you started to take the souls of the people I care about?'

Kim was sobbing now. 'I have to keep promise. I cannot defy Kwisin.'

'For Christ's sake, Kim! How many souls exactly were you planning on taking? Or is there no limit?'

'One for every year since Roland Rook married her. Sixty-one. Then Kwisin will be satisfied. Then Kwisin will be able to find peace.' He looked at Jim in utter distress. 'Please, forgive me.'

'Forgive you? You want to encourage sixty-one young people to kill themselves, and I'm supposed to *forgive* you?'

Jim let go of Kim's arm and Kim sank to his knees on the floor, still coughing, with tears running down his cheeks. Jim turned back to Second Class Two, feeling angry and helpless.

At the top of his voice, he shouted out, 'If I ask you drop your box-cutters on to the floor, would you do that for me?'

He negotiated his way between the desks, stepping over Tamara, who was still gasping for breath on the floor. He went right up to Billy and said, 'If I ask you to pull that stuff off of your face, Billy, would you do that for me?'

Billy stared at him through the cling film, his chest rising and falling underneath his cheap washed-out sweatshirt, half-asphyxiated by his own hopelessness.

'Would you do that for me, Billy?' he asked, as quietly as he could.

Billy turned his head toward the classroom door, and then he shook his head.

'You don't want to die, Billy, believe me. Dying is no fun at all. Especially if your soul gets taken for all eternity by some vicious Korean demon.'

But Billy wasn't looking at him any more, and neither were any of his other students, and when Jim turned around, he saw why.

Framed in the doorway was the fox-woman, Kwisin, in her hat and her veil and her shiny gray robes. She hesitated for a moment, and then she made her way into the room, with a curiously stilted gait, and even from the back of the room Jim could hear the sound of claws on the floor.

Every member of Special Class Two stood up straighter as she approached. Leon reached down with his free hand and helped Tamara to climb back on to her feet. The cling film around their faces crackled as they sucked as much air into their lungs as they could.

Kwisin swelled larger and larger, as she had in Jim's bedroom. Her hat tumbled back, and the veil that covered her face began to rise, as her jaws grew long and pointed, like the fox-demon she was. Her gray silk robe opened up and slithered to the floor, and within only a few seconds she was standing in front of them as a black hairy beast, with poisonous yellow eyes and curved horns and incisors that were dripping with saliva.

The classroom was filled with the reek of smoke and incense and rotting blood, and Jim felt that he was choking.

'Get the hell out of here!' he shouted. 'Get the hell out of here, Kwisin, and leave my kids alone!'

Kwisin stared at him, as if she found it impossible to

believe that anybody would dare to defy her. She snarled,
and tilted forward, challenging him to come closer. Jim knew
that it was madness. She would bite his head off and rip him
open, the way that the crows had ripped Tibbles open, and
then she would crunch up his soul like Patsy-Jean's. But all
the same he pushed his way between Tamara and Arthur and
Janice to the front of the class, until he was facing Kwisin
from only three or four feet away.

Kim was still on his knees on the floor, behind Jim's desk.
He was crying out, 'No, Mr Rook, you cannot defy her!'

Jim seized Kwisin's front leg. It was viciously prickly,
like the thick stem of a thorn bush, and he shouted out,
'Shit!' Kwisin immediately knocked him away, and he staggered back against the stationery cupboard with a loud
metallic bang, jarring his shoulder. He looked down at the
palm of his hand and it was bleeding where Kwisin's bristles had torn his skin.

Now Kwisin let out a high, ululating scream. Jim had
never heard anything like it in his life. It was the sound of
human beings in agony, human beings who know that they
have been crushed so badly that they cannot possibly survive.
It was the sound of people throwing themselves out of build-
ings, or trapped in burning automobiles. It was the sound of
hopelessness, of utter despair. It was the sound of no future.

Without hesitation, as if they had rehearsed it, Special
Class Two simultaneously drew their right hands across the
left side of their throats, slicing open their carotid arteries.
Blood spurted out everywhere, splattering across the papers
on their desks, flooding down the fronts of their T-shirts and
their sweaters and their dresses, spraying in hieroglyphic
patterns on the walls. In twos and threes, the students
collapsed, and lay quivering under their desks while their
hearts pumped out the last few liters of their lives.

Kwisin, the fox-demon, let out another screech, harsh and
triumphant. She threw back her head and raised both of her
forelegs, as if she was preparing to welcome the souls of
Special Class Two into her dark, bristling embrace.

Jim was stunned. He shouted out, '*Yaaaaaahhhhh!*' and
threw himself at Kwisin again, but again Kwisin knocked
him aside with her bristly forepaw, so violently that he

rolled right over the top of his desk and fell heavily against his chair. He lay back, winded, but he was just about to climb on to his feet and attack Kwisin yet again when he thought: *She could easily have killed me. She could easily have bitten off my head like Charlie the Boston terrier*.

He thought of the first time that Kwisin had appeared in his bedroom, too. She had swelled up into this same black bristling beast, with horns and fangs, and she had scared him shitless, but she hadn't touched him. Maybe there was a good reason for that. Maybe she hadn't hurt him because he was Roland's grandson. Roland had deserted Kwisin, just like Lieutenant Pinkerton had deserted Madam Butterfly, but maybe there was still some dark particle in her demonic brain that still loved him – and Jim, of course, carried Roland's genes.

He gripped the edge of his desk and heaved himself on to his feet. Kwisin was still standing with her head thrown back and her forelegs wide apart, and when he looked around the gloomy, blood-glistening classroom, Jim could see that the souls of Special Class Two were beginning to rise from their fallen bodies. Tamara's first, semi-transparent and shimmering in rainbow colors, closely followed by Teddy's and Judii's. As they glided toward Kwisin's bristling embrace, all three of them turned toward Jim and gave him sad, regretful smiles.

'You're not having them!' Jim shouted. 'Do you hear me, you bitch? You're not having them!'

This time, he didn't try to launch himself at Kwisin again. This time, he went for Kim, who was still kneeling close beside her. Kim gasped, and tried to struggle, but Jim grabbed him around the neck with both hands and threw him backward on to the floor. He pressed both thumbs into Kim's throat and banged his head again and again, as hard as he could.

'You started this!' he shouted at him. He was so angry now that the spit flew out of his mouth. 'You started this, just to save yourself! Sixty-one people killing themselves, just to save you! You miserable, cowardly bastard!'

Kim started to turn purple, and let out a thin, guttural whine, but Jim dug his thumbs into his throat even deeper, and banged his head so many times that his eyes rolled up into his head.

Kwisin twisted her head around and snarled at him, but now the souls of Special Class Two were clustered all around her, their arms held out wide, trying to embrace her, and to her they were just as substantial as real, living people.

Jim squeezed Kim's throat relentlessly. 'This is finished, you got it? This is over. No more kids are going to die. Not for the sake of your worthless skin.'

At that moment, however, he heard a voice shout, 'Let him go! Let the kid go!'

He turned around and saw Detective Wong and Detective Madison pushing their way into the classroom, with Nurse Okeke and Dr Ehrlichman close behind them. Detective Wong tugged his gun out of his holster and pointed it directly at Jim's head.

'Let the kid go, or I'll shoot!'

At the same time, Detective Wong saw the bloody bodies of Special Class Two lying underneath their desks. 'Jesus Christ, what's happened here? Madison – call for some back-up! Tell the lieutenant! You! Mr Rook-like-the-bird! Let the kid go!'

But Jim kept up his relentless grip on Kim's throat. He couldn't hear him breathing any more and he thought that he was probably dead, but he wanted to make absolutely sure.

'Let the kid go, Mr Rook! This is your last warning!'

Detective Wong came across the classroom, his automatic held steady in both hands. What he didn't realize was that he was walking through a crowd of invisible souls, and that a hideous demon was only two feet away from him. He stepped forward until the muzzle of his gun was pressed right up against Jim's right ear.

'Let him go,' he repeated.

'I can't. He has to die. There's no other way.'

'Detective!' called out Nurse Okeke. 'Whatever you do, don't shoot! There are things in this room that you don't understand!'

Detective Wong cocked his gun. 'I understand that Mr Rook is trying to strangle this kid to death and that I'm going to shoot him if he doesn't desist.'

'Detective!' shrilled Nurse Okeke. 'There is a demon in this room! There are human spirits! You cannot shoot!'

Now Kwisin had gathered all the souls of Special Class Two together in a restless mingling of light and color and shadows and sliding images. Jim could see glimpses of their faces and their expressions as she pulled them into the darkness of her embrace. She snarled again, and let out another of her warbling, high-pitched screeches. Then she lowered her head and Jim could hear the crunching of souls as she started to devour the very substance that had made up each of his students' lives – their character, their memories, the love that they had been given as they grew up, sunny days, tears, and then hopelessness. This was what Kwisin fed on.

Nurse Okeke hurled herself across the classroom. She seized Detective Wong's wrist and tried to twist the gun out of his hand. There was a deafening bang and she fell sideways on to the floor, right next to Kim, with a bloodstain spreading across her white nurse's coat. She stared up at Detective Wong, her eyes wide, and then at Jim.

Detective Wong shouted, 'Paramedics! Get me a bus, now!'

Jim let go of Kim. As he did so, Kim let out one long breath, the last air that had been trapped in his lungs as Jim throttled him. Nurse Okeke turned her head and whispered, 'Is he dead, Mr Rook? Have you killed him?'

Jim laid a hand on her shoulder. 'It's OK. Just stay with me, OK? You're going to be fine. It's only a gunshot wound.'

'Only?'

Just then, Kim opened his eyes. He looked up at Jim and whispered, 'Forgive me, Mr Rook. What you did, I deserved it. I was a coward, you were right.'

'Can you put things back the way they were?' Jim asked him.

'Who the hell are you talking to?' Detective Wong demanded. 'Come on, stand up, put your hands behind your back.'

'Doors close, Mr Rook. But doors open, too. There are so many doors, and all we have to do is choose which one.'

Kim's soul rose from his body, fluid and iridescent. He pressed his hands with their palms together and bowed his head. 'Goodbye, Mr Rook. Remember me.'

He walked across to Kwisin and pushed his way in between all of the souls that were gathered around her. He held his arms out wide, and held her close. Kwisin lifted up her head and gave one last screech. Jim didn't know if it was pain, or joy, or despair. All he knew was that Kwisin would now have the eternal peace for which she had been waiting so many years.

Kwisin began to shudder, and fade. Quite suddenly, she seemed to twist around, like black smoke caught in a gust of wind, and then she vanished. She left behind her the souls of Special Class Two, standing together in bewilderment. Some of them had been scratched and bitten, and some of them were glowing with that dazzling essence that courses inside a soul instead of blood, but most of them appeared to be uninjured.

Jim stood up. Detective Wong pointed his gun at him and said, 'Hold it. Just hold it right there. You're under arrest for homicide. Madison? Where's that back-up? Jesus!'

Jim went over to the souls of Special Class Two, and said, 'Listen to me. Listen. I know you're in shock. But what you have to do is go back to your bodies, and lie down, and close your eyes, and pretend that you're asleep.'

'We're dead,' said Arthur. 'We cut our own throats.'

'For once, Arthur, just do what I tell you. Please.'

'But we're *dead*.'

Jim said, 'We'll see about that.'

SIXTEEN

He was woken up the next morning by Tibbles licking his face. He didn't like Tibbles licking his face at the best of times, but Tibbles had obviously just finished a bowl of Instinctive Choice shrimp dinner.

He sat up in bed and pushed Tibbles away. 'Jesus,' he said, wiping his face on the sheet. 'Your *breath*, dude.'

He climbed out of bed and pulled up the blinds. It was a sunny, clear morning, with only a few small puffy clouds in the sky. He went to the bathroom for a pee, and while he stood there he looked at his face in the medicine cabinet mirror, as if he were looking at a portrait of himself.

He flushed the toilet and washed his hands. He was trying hard not to think about anything at all. He didn't want to ask himself how he had gone to sleep in the West Hollywood police headquarters and woken up here, in his own bed. He didn't want to ask himself if any of his students had killed themselves, or if Nurse Okeke had been shot dead. He just wanted to go through today as if it was a normal, boring day.

He put three heaped spoonfuls of Arabica coffee on to brew, and then poured himself a large glass of grapefruit juice. He hesitated for a long time before he switched on the TV, but when he did, the main stories were an unexpected drop in share prices and an air crash in Juneau, Alaska, in which four people had been killed.

It was 7:09 a.m. on September 7, the first day of the fall semester.

He slammed the front door really quickly to make sure that Tibbles couldn't escape. He double-locked it, just to make sure that Tibbles couldn't get out and that nothing else could get in.

On his way along the landing below, he hesitated outside Summer's front door, wondering if he ought to ring the bell

and ask her how she was. But then this was another
September 7, and he had stepped through another door.
Maybe he and Summer would get together, but then again
maybe they wouldn't.

Mrs LaFarge's apartment was pristine; no smoke stains
and no windows broken. As he passed he could see Mrs
LaFarge on her balcony, feeding her pet canaries.

He climbed into his car and fastened his seat-belt. He
pulled down the sun vizor and flipped open the vanity mirror.
To his genuine surprise, he saw that he was crying.